BACK
IN
TIME

BACK
IN
TIME

D E McLean

Library of Congress Control Number:		2019904969
ISBN:	Hardcover	978-1-5434-9544-7
	Softcover	978-1-5434-9543-0
	eBook	978-1-5434-9542-3

Print information available on the last page.

Rev. date: 04/26/2019

To order additional copies of this book, contact:
Xlibris
0-800-443-678
www.Xlibris.co.nz
Orders@Xlibris.co.nz
777123

AUTHOR'S NOTE

If you visit the town of Thames at the base of New Zealand's Coromandel Peninsula and walk up Pollen Street to its northern end, you will find yourself in historic Grahamstown. Thames was once a booming gold-mining town, evidence of which is still apparent in many of the buildings still standing today. The township itself was once two settlements – Grahamstown and Shortland – which eventually combined to form the modern town of Thames.

This story, however, is not historical. It is science fiction/fantasy. I have in no way tried to recreate or document anything that may have happened here in our reality. In fact, if anything factual occurs, it is entirely coincidental. I have merely borrowed the name and used a loose historical connection to weave my own story. I liked the idea of setting my story in this location because of the way the past feels very close to the present in parts of the town. It's no huge stretch to imagine another reality running alongside ours. Nor is it too hard to imagine the odd time traveller washing up by accident on these shores from another reality.

PROLOGUE

Prof Archibald Popkiss turned his back on the group of people gathered around his time machine and strode off without looking back.

He felt disappointed in his dear friend Lady Elspeth Lovelace. He thought she would agree with him regarding the importance of what they had achieved here. The fact that she didn't support his plan to keep the time machine operational and to report his research to the Academy of Time Travel felt like a knife wound, but he also understood her stance.

She was correct in assuming that keeping the machine they had built to transport her friend Kev back to his own world and publishing what they had done would cause trouble. Lots of trouble. And while the professor didn't mind bringing that trouble down on himself – he was old, after all, and had little else to live for – he didn't really want to bring that trouble down on Lady Elspeth or, for that matter, Millicent Darlington, captain of the airship *Elizabeth Anne*, whom he had developed a very high regard for.

The professor wasn't a silly man. He knew that Millicent didn't think of him as anything more than a friend of Lady Elspeth's, and in fact, he would have been disappointed if she did.

He was a man of huge intellect who harboured a surprisingly romantic soul. However, the professor had discovered over the years that his penchant for romance was much more enjoyable if it remained in the realm of fantasy and unrequited longing.

On the odd occasions when he had ventured to form an attachment with one of his romantic interests, he found himself to be entirely disappointed with the experience, the objects of his affections proving to be merely flawed human beings and not the angelic ones he had imagined them to be.

So he was happy to continue admiring Millicent from afar rather than risk a closer friendship and discover she did something appalling, like fart in bed. Besides, he knew she was totally enamoured with her long-time beau Phineas Leviticus Kidd.

The professor got the feeling Phineas Kidd did not like him overly much. But as the professor did not like Phineas all that much either, the thought did not bother him.

It did annoy him, however, that Phineas seemed inclined to push his way into the professor's own business, namely, the time machine he had so painstakingly built. Even though it had not been the professor's money that had paid for it, it had been his expertise and years of research that had gone into its success.

He knew that even if Lady Elspeth had agreed with him and tried to keep the time machine viable, Phineas would have stepped in and destroyed it as they were doing now and that nothing he, the professor, could say or do would have stopped him.

He had decided it would do no good to go head-to-head with Phineas over the time machine. Reluctantly, he had realised he would have to let it go. It gave him a little pang of regret to do so, but he was unable to stand up to Phineas or even Lady Elspeth.

He had to come up with another plan entirely. His time machine was lost to him, but that didn't mean that Walter was – at least not yet. Lady Elspeth thought all he cared about was the fame and the chance to prove to the Academy of Time Travel he had been right all along when he and Walter had wanted to find out if it was possible to travel not just through time but to other dimensions as well.

And although that was a part of it, it wasn't the real reason he so desperately wanted to keep his machine. As much as he would love to rub the academy's noses in his success, the real reason was and always would be Walter.

The professor had never recovered from the night Walter had gone through the portal opened by their new and untested time machine – to see if it was possible to travel between different worlds – and never come back.

The academy had ordered the destruction of the machine before he had been able to rectify the faults and attempt to get Walter back home again, and he had never been able to forgive himself.

He knew somewhere in the back of his mind that he wasn't to blame, but it always felt as if he was. He often tortured himself by thinking he should have persisted in trying to convince the academy to let him keep trying, even though their minds were set against him and nothing he could have done or said would have changed their views.

The grief he felt at losing Walter, a very dear friend and colleague, was undiminished by the passing of time. Walter had been a highly trained and seasoned time traveller who knew the risks involved with time travel and took them, knowing that one day it might mean he didn't return home. But not even knowing this and the fact that Walter himself would not want him to carry this grief for so long could stop the professor from feeling he should be doing more to get Walter home.

The time machine he had built with the help of Lady Elspeth and her friend Lenore Ravenwood was the result of all he had learned since the night of Walter's disappearance, and he had pinned his hopes on using it to get Walter back.

Once he realised Lady Elspeth would not support him in keeping the time machine operational, he had turned his mind to devising another means of trying to get Walter home again, and so he was able to walk away from the machine now without a backward glance.

Once he was sure the others were absorbed in the destruction of the machine and no one was paying attention to him anymore, he veered off into the bush and made his way to where he had hidden a small canvas bag in the leaf mould.

The professor opened the bag and drew out a small brass box and two coiled antennae. Deftly, he attached the antennae to the box before creeping his way back towards the campsite.

Hidden on the edge of the clearing in the bush made to accommodate the time machine, the professor waited until the dismantling of the machine was over before pressing the switch and activating his box. Quickly, he found the hiding place he had settled on earlier and, kneeling down, pushed the box into it. He adjusted the antennae until he was satisfied with the signal.

Standing up, he looked down at the box's hiding place. It was virtually undetectable, not that anyone would be looking for such a thing in the bush, but the professor didn't want any accidental interference with his box either.

He was satisfied that the box was safe and working properly. He was extremely pleased with himself. It wasn't a time machine which could open a portal, but he felt it was the next best thing.

The box emitted a signal that energised the shadow of the portal opened up by the time machine, which Kev had passed through on his return to his own world.

The professor knew that once a time portal had been opened, the fabric of time became slightly thinner or weakened in that spot. This made travelling through that particular portal easier each time it was done. Much like the treading of many feet eventually wore down a permanent pathway, repeated time travel through a particular point created a 'path' down which other travellers could venture.

Although this particular portal had only been used once, the professor was hoping that by keeping it activated with his little brass box, it would mean Walter could get home easier. He was, in fact, hoping the energy generated by the portal would act as a homing beacon and guide him back.

It had never occurred to him that after all this time, Walter may well have made a new life for himself and not be trying to return or that he may not have access to the technology he needed to build a time machine.

The professor needed to believe in his brass box, and he needed to believe in Walter's return. For the first time since Walter's disappearance, his aching heart was a little bit eased, knowing he had done all he could do under the circumstances to get his friend home again.

Feeling much lighter in spirits than he had felt for many a year, the professor turned and made his way back to camp to help with packing up. Behind him in its hiding place, his brass box pinged out its signal into the aether, and if anyone had been watching, they would have noticed the portal flicker and shimmer as the signal passed over it.

CHAPTER 1

'I say, Kev. Pay attention, old chap,' admonished Walter. Kev shook his head and brought his attention back to the task in hand. He had been lost in his own thoughts, daydreaming of Persephone. Walter was giving him a disapproving look, and Kev looked down at the workbench, where his hand was supposed to be holding a metal spike steady. The spike had drifted off to one side as Kev had been lost in his own thoughts. He gave Walter a sheepish grin and brought it back into its proper position.

'Ah, that's more like it,' said Walter with satisfaction as he brandished a sturdy-looking hammer. 'I need you to hold it really still, Kev, while I give it a good whack.'

Kev fingered his forehead where his eyebrows had yet to grow back from the last time he had acted as Walter's assistant and tried to anticipate the accuracy of the strike. Walter's own splendidly intact eyebrows contracted as he took aim and gave the spike a blow that sent shock waves up Kev's arm. Kev let go of the spike with a curse and stood shaking his hand. Walter was oblivious to his discomfort as he bent over, squinting critically at the spike where he had driven it through a thick metal plate.

As much as he liked Walter and enjoyed their developing friendship, there were times when Kev wondered why he let himself in for these kinds of things. Walter never had much success with the many wild ideas he was continually experimenting with, so it wasn't as if the sacrifice of his own personal safety was going towards anything worthwhile.

'Just what is this supposed to be?' he queried, still nursing his tingling hand.

Walter straightened up and gave Kev his devil-may-care grin. 'It's a discombobulator, old boy. Or it will be if I can get it to work.'

Kev sighed and shook his head. 'Is that likely to happen, do you think?'

Walter just laughed. 'Probably not, old man, but I like trying. Not many things I used in the old world work well in this one, but I do enjoy finding out which ones might.'

Kev knew Walter had invented some kind of revolutionary widget based on technology from his old world that had created enormous wealth for him, so he supposed it wasn't such a ridiculous idea to keep pursuing this line of thought.

Walter couldn't explain why things from his world wouldn't work here in Kev's, but it fascinated him, and he spent a lot of time trying out the different forms of technology in the hopes of finding something that would.

Kev watched his friend as he fiddled with the discombobulator and thought back to the day he and Walter had met on the side of the road when Walter had stopped to help him fix his broken-down car.

He had quickly come to the conclusion that this Walter and the Walter Lady Elspeth knew were one and the same but hadn't known how to broach the subject of his own time travel, feeling a little worried his new friend would think him crazy if his hunch was wrong.

Eventually, he had hit upon the idea of showing Walter the sepia print of the *Elizabeth Anne*'s crew, given to him by Millicent Darlington as a gift when he had left their world. He reasoned that if Walter didn't recognise Lady Elspeth, he would merely think it a curious old photograph, and no harm would be done.

Walter's reaction, however, was everything Kev could have hoped for. Kev hadn't really thought it through very well, and it wasn't until he handed over the photograph to Walter that he realised even though he had a hunch about Walter, his friend was unprepared for the revelation Kev was handing him in the form of an innocent-looking photo.

Kev might have found it funny to watch Walter's expression turn from friendly curiosity to shock and disbelief had he not been overwhelmed with remorse at his thoughtlessness in not trying to warn Walter or soften the blow in some way.

Walter had gone very pale and had held onto the photo with a hand that had begun to tremble. He looked at Kev with disbelieving eyes, his mouth opening and closing but unable to make a sound.

'Where did you get this?' he croaked out when he eventually regained his power of speech. 'How do you know Elspeth?'

After apologising for the shock he had caused, Kev quickly filled Walter in on his story. Walter had listened without interrupting, studying the photograph intently as he did so.

When Kev had finished, Walter had handed him back the photo and sat staring into space for a long time. Eventually, he had turned to Kev and tried to grin, but it looked more like a grimace.

'I haven't thought of my old life or Elspeth for a long, long time, Kev,' he had said. 'This has come as quite a shock, old boy. When I first arrived here, I felt for sure Archie would be able to get me back. It was weeks before it dawned on me he wasn't going to rescue me. I try hard not to think of my old life because if I do, I remember those early days in this world, and they're something I do my best to forget. I've been lucky, Kev. Luckier than I probably deserve to be, and I've managed to do well for myself here, but I've only managed because I made myself forget I had another life before I ended up in this world.'

Now as he watched his friend busy himself with his strange invention, Kev wondered for the first time if Walter secretly wished to return to his old life and if the incessant inventing wasn't, in fact, a way to return – at least mentally – to the days he had loved.

'Ever wish you could go back?' he asked.

Walter looked at Kev. He didn't pretend not to know what he was talking about. Ever since the day Kev had revealed his own experiences with inter-dimensional time travel, he had found his thoughts drifting back more and more to the old world he had left so many years ago.

As he was not one to think past the moment or reflect on the consequences of his actions, it had been a rude awakening to find himself stranded here without hope of return to his old life, knowing it was his own recklessness that had brought him here.

At first, it had been very hard, and he couldn't remember those early days without remembering the wave of grief and desolation that had threatened to swamp him when he had realised he was on his own.

Suddenly coming face-to-face with himself through his own thoughtlessness was sobering and had forced him to grow up in ways he hadn't realised he needed to. He had worked hard to make a life for himself here, with the help of many others who had befriended him and extended a helping hand when it was required.

Even so, it had taken a lot of hard work to get where he was now. Slowly, the sadness of being cut off from his friends and family receded, and he had been able to embrace his new life wholeheartedly. However, he had been always been careful not to allow thoughts of the old world to overshadow the new.

Now as he considered Kev's question, a long-dormant part of his mind began to stir and, along with it, the remembered thrill of time travel, the satisfaction of helping Archie with his calculations, and the stimulating conversations they'd had as they debated their various theories.

'At first, it was all I thought about,' he confessed, 'but as I got more settled here and had the means to really become a part of this world, I started to think about it less. One day it occurred to me I was really rather happy here, and the desire to return home had left me. Not even the thought of Elspeth was enough to make me want to go back, and we were very close at one time, you know. She's a bricky girl, no doubt about that, but as time went on, I discovered I had begun to think of her with a more brotherly kind of affection. Besides, I love my cars too much to want to leave now.' Walter laughed, finding the thought amusing.

Kev didn't laugh with him. As Walter had been speaking, his mind had started to race, and he was beginning to pull thoughts together that, to this point, had only been scattered desires and half-hearted wishes. 'Do you think it's possible to get back if we wanted to?' he asked urgently.

Walter gave him a funny look. 'I guess so, Kev,' he replied, 'but why would we want to . . .' He broke off as he looked at the expression on Kev's face, and it suddenly dawned on him that Kev wasn't as happy in this world as he had assumed him to be. 'You want to go back, Kev?' he asked, although it sounded more like a statement.

Kev nodded slowly. 'Yeah, mate,' he said. 'Matter of fact, I think I do.'

Walter said nothing at first, merely giving Kev a long considering look. Eventually, he said, 'If you're serious about this, then I'm happy to try making a time machine, but there's no guarantees it will work here, you realise.'

Kev shrugged. 'I know, but something in me wants to give it a go. If we try and fail, at least I'll know we gave it our best shot.'

Walter inclined his head. 'All right, old chap,' he replied. 'I'll start drawing up some plans, and we'll see how we get on. No promises, but I must admit I'm intrigued to find out if this will work or not.'

CHAPTER 2

K ev tipped his chair back, rested his feet on the top of the veranda rail, and took a sip of tea as he squinted out over the roofs of the township of Thames spread out below him. He often did this as by half-closing his eyes in this way and looking out towards the horizon, he found he could imagine the huge airships he had once seen anchored above the Firth of Thames were really there, hanging in the sky, and he wasn't, in fact, sitting on the front veranda of his tiny cottage perched on the hillside but back once more in Grahamstown with the crew of the *Elizabeth Anne*.

He wasn't really any more settled now than he had been on first arriving back in his own reality. Moving into his tiny two-bedroomed cottage had been a way to try and feel close to the time he had spent in the other world. It had originally been a miner's cottage, and even though a previous owner had updated the kitchen and bathroom sometime in the 1970s, Kev found he could look past the orange bath and geometric wallpaper to the 1800s charm still evident in other rooms and feel the move had been partially successful and helped to ease the sense he had of being caught not just between times but between worlds as well.

Finishing his tea, he let his chair fall back with a thud and, placing his mug on the rail, stretched his arms over his head to ease the kinks out of his back before getting up and going inside.

Depositing the mug in the kitchen sink, he meandered through into his bedroom, where the photograph of the crew of the *Elizabeth*

Anne caught his eye, propped up on his tallboy, next to an antique music box.

Going over, he wound the music box and lifted its lid to let it play. He had discovered it in the antique shop in town and had thought at once of Persephone. Unable to resist the romantic notion of buying it, even though he couldn't give it to her, he had brought it home and given it pride of place beside his treasured photograph.

Some of the notes were missing, but Kev liked that. It fit in with how he felt, as if parts of him were missing too, lost somewhere in the fabric of time. As the music box slowly wound itself down and the notes came slower and slower, Kev picked up the photograph of the crew and studied it, as he often did, trying to imagine what they were all up to and if they missed him as much as he missed them.

Kev drove along the winding Thames Coast Highway on his way back to Walter's, glad to be leaving Thames behind him and the thoughts that dogged him there.

Climbing the steep driveway to where Walter's house stood in splendid isolation, overlooking the Hauraki Gulf, he pulled to a stop in front of the house. Kev knew not to bother looking for Walter inside and so wandered around the back to where he knew he would be – in one of his many sheds or workshops.

Kev found him with his head under the bonnet of one of his cars. Although Walter had several sleek, fast cars he loved to drive, he always had a couple like this one that needed a bit of doing up.

Once, on a night out on the town, Walter had drunkenly declared to Kev that in his opinion, the internal combustion engine was the greatest invention of mankind. Even in his own befuddled state, Kev had felt there must be inventions more worthy of the title, but as he couldn't think of many at that point, he hadn't tried to correct him.

It was Walter's love of cars and all things modern that had at first confused Kev about Walter and made him wonder if he had truly come from the same world he himself had travelled to. He had assumed without really thinking about it that Walter would be as homesick for his old world as he was.

Hearing Kev approach, Walter withdrew his head from under the bonnet of the car and wiped his hands on his overalls. 'Hello, my good chap,' he greeted him. 'Come and see how far I've got already.'

Kev followed Walter around behind the sheds to where another shed sat, half concealed by overgrown shrubs and harakeke. Walter drew a bunch of keys from his pocket and unlocked the door. Pulling it open, he led the way inside the dim interior.

In the middle of the shed sat an unmistakable shape. Although it was a frame only at this stage, Kev drew in a breath as he recognised its unmistakable outline. Admittedly, he had only ever seen the one constructed by Professor Popkiss with the help of Lenore and Lady Elspeth, but even so, that was enough to assure him that this was indeed a time machine.

Walter smirked smugly at Kev's reaction. 'You are right, Kev,' he said. 'This is the beginning of our time machine.'

'How . . . Where . . . What . . . How?' stammered Kev, almost unable to take in how quickly Walter was moving.

Walter laughed at his confounded expression. 'Never fear, old boy. I know what I'm doing, and I don't let the grass grow under me once an idea hits me.'

Kev walked around the time machine, inspecting it more closely. 'Do you think it will work here?' he asked.

Walter shrugged. 'We won't really know that until we start it up,' he admitted.

'Can you get parts here?' asked Kev, beginning to wonder how practical Walter's idea of building a machine really was.

'Ah yes, not as such,' replied Walter. 'I can make the components we need or adapt things from here as substitutes though,' he continued with a dismissive wave of his hand. 'I'm more concerned with how to power it, to be honest. That will take a bit of thought, but I'm sure I can come up with something when the time comes.'

Kev scratched his head, wondering again just how realistic they were being, but a large part of him was eager for this to succeed, so he pushed the doubts to the back of his mind and listened as Walter tried to explain the finer points of time machine construction.

He was soon lost in the details as Walter rambled on, enthused by the idea of what he was attempting and oblivious to Kev's lack of understanding. Kev allowed the drone of Walter's talking to drift over him as his thoughts followed their own path, absentmindedly handing Walter the various tools he indicated he needed as required.

Now that they were actually beginning the project, small half-formed thoughts began struggling through his subconscious to the surface, and he realised leaving would be impossible, even if Walter managed to get the machine working.

'I can't go through with it,' he blurted out, cutting across Walter's conversation like a bucket of icy water.

'Eh? What?' queried Walter, justifiably confused at the sudden twist in conversation. 'What are you on about, Kev?'

'I can't leave,' explained Kev miserably. 'I came home because I was worried about my mum. I can't just disappear into thin air again. It wouldn't be fair.'

Walter stopped his tinkering. 'I take it you've never told her what happened to you.'

Kev shook his head. 'No, never,' he replied. 'How could I?'

The topic of time travel was an alien concept to his mother, and Kev had always felt at a loss as to how to try and explain to her what he had gone through. So he had resolutely avoided the topic, afraid to risk the possibility that his mother might think he had lost his mind.

Just because he was unwilling to talk about the subject, however, didn't mean his mother was unaware that he was holding something back. The unspoken topic sat heavy in the air between them whenever they were together. Kev knew he was to blame as he wasn't the same man he had been before the kidnapping, and even his best efforts to appear as such fell way too short to convince anyone, let alone his mother, who knew him so well.

'Maybe you should try explaining all of it to your mother, old man,' said Walter kindly. 'You might be surprised at how much she does understand if you give her the chance to think it over. I think maybe you owe it to her and yourself to give it a try.'

Kev watched his mother as she went back to the kitchen for something else she had forgotten. Any task took his mum far longer than most people to complete as she constantly forgot where she was up to and sometimes, Kev suspected, what she was actually doing.

His grandmother had once told him when he had been an impatient teenager that the death of her beloved husband and childhood sweetheart when Kev was still an infant had affected his mother deeply and that she deserved his understanding and not his censure, and so he had adjusted his expectations and managed to find a way to get on with things, letting his mother find her way through life on her own terms.

It seemed to Kev as though his mother lived her life listening to voices coming from somewhere else, audible only to her. Even so, she was an affectionate and kindly parent, and Kev was very fond of her and more than a little protective, able, as the years went on, to see past the absentmindedness to the young woman she must once have been.

Now seeing his mother gazing at the table in a puzzled manner before returning to the kitchen for yet another forgotten item, Kev resigned himself to waiting a bit longer for dinner. Eventually, everything was in order, and his mother took her seat, giving Kev a beatific smile as she did so.

'It's lovely to have you drop in, Kev,' she said, reaching out and giving his hand a little squeeze.

Kev squeezed her hand in return before picking up his fork and moving the food about his plate, his mind racing, searching for ways to begin the conversation he was here for.

'Mum,' he began nervously, 'I wanted to talk to you about some things I think you should know about.'

'Did you, dear?' asked his mum as she searched the table vaguely, looking for a serving spoon with which to add another helping of mashed potatoes onto Kev's plate. Not finding it, she rose and went back to the kitchen. Sitting down again, she dolloped a hearty serving of potatoes onto Kev's already laden plate, her satisfaction at being able to feed up her boy evident in her expression. 'Is it a girl, Kev?' she asked out of the blue.

'Well, yeah, kind of,' Kev admitted, taken aback. 'How did you guess?'

His mum smiled. 'I'm not silly, Kev,' she told him. 'I can see something is up with you. I know things were difficult for you when you came home, but that was almost a year ago, and you're still not settled. I figured there had to be a reason for it. I wasn't sure, but I had a feeling it was something to do with affairs of the heart. They're always a little disruptive – well, the good ones are anyway.'

The unexpected way his mother had steered the conversation down the exact path he had been struggling to find meant Kev was having a little trouble keeping up. Floundering a little and trying to gather his thoughts and herd them down the path after his mother, he replied, 'It's a bit complicated.'

'Isn't it always?' queried his mum - a tinge smug at having hit on the right reason for Kev's visit. 'I didn't imagine it would be straightforward because you've never brought her home to meet us.'

'Well, I can't,' explained Kev, and he proceeded to tell his story, starting from the appearance of the pirate slavers' airship and waking up not just in another time but in another reality altogether. He told her about being rescued by the crew of the *Elizabeth Anne* and how he had fallen in love with the ship's medic, Persephone Mockett, before relating how the crew had managed to send him back home with the help of Professor Popkiss.

'Well,' said his mother once he had finished, 'when you said it was complicated, I imagined it was because she was married to someone else or some such thing. This isn't quite what I was expecting.'

'So you believe me?' Kev asked anxiously.

His mother didn't reply for a while as she thought over everything Kev had told her. 'I don't *not* believe you,' she told him eventually.

'It's a very odd story, but I raised you to be honest, so unless you've completely lost your mind, I have to accept it as true.'

Kev felt relieved. 'Thanks, Mum,' he said.

'It certainly explains why you've been so out of sorts since you've been back,' she continued. 'I'm glad you told me, dear. It's been such a long time since you returned, and I felt you should have been getting on with your life better by now, but you've been so detached, almost as if you'd put your life on hold. I didn't know what to say or do to jolt you out of it. It's been very hard to watch.'

'Sorry, Mum,' Kev said. 'I just didn't know how to explain what had happened. I was afraid you'd think I was crazy.'

His mother smiled. 'I could never think that, dear,' she said fondly. 'But what are you going to do to get yourself back into the swing of life here?'

Kev took a deep breath. 'Well, it's like this, Mum,' he began. 'When I was in that other world, I heard about a time traveller by the name of Walter. It was his adventures that made it possible for me to come home, really, and the thing is . . . well, I've met him here, in our world. We met by chance, and I had a hunch he might be the same Walter I'd heard of. Turns out he is, and he's been living here in our world for a long time. It was his idea that I should talk to you and explain what had happened.'

His mother just nodded, and Kev continued.

'He thinks it's possible for me to go back if I want to.'

'And do you?' his mother asked, a tiny tremble detectable in her voice as she began to realise just where Kev was leading this conversation.

'The thing is, Mum, I think I do,' Kev answered her.

His mother didn't reply at once but sat quietly, pushing her own food around her plate. Kev couldn't see her face, but he could tell by the tenseness in the set of her shoulders that she was struggling with his admission.

Eventually, she lifted her gaze and looked Kev in the eye. 'I won't pretend this isn't a shock, Kev,' she said, 'but I can see you must love your Persephone very much.'

'I do, Mum,' Kev admitted. 'I think if it hadn't been for her, I could've adjusted to being back here easier. But it's not just that. I also miss the others and the whole way of life there. I never expected to miss it so much, to be honest. If you're not happy with the idea, I'll stay here and try to adjust to how my life is now, but I'd like to try and get back if I can.'

Kev's mum nodded. 'I understand, love,' she said, reaching over to pat him on the hand. 'It's how I was with your father.' She paused, and a wistful, dreamy look crept across her face. 'There was never any one for me before I met him, and there's been no one since.'

She sat lost in her thoughts for a moment, and Kev found himself regretting not knowing the shadowy figure who was his father. For the first time, he thought he must have been a remarkable man to inspire such devotion in another.

His mum shook herself and appeared to come back to the present as she took Kev's hand properly in hers before saying, 'sometimes love only comes once in our lifetime, Kev, and while there are no guarantees of a happy ending, we shouldn't let the chance slip through our fingers when it comes along. If you want to return to your Persephone, you have my blessing, love. OK?'

Kev nodded, unable to speak just at that moment, and he squeezed his mother's hand in his.

She smiled at him, with the merest hint of sadness evident. 'All I want is for you to be happy, Kev, and if that means you have to leave me and go back to Persephone and live in her world, then that's what it means.'

'I don't want to go if it's going to make you unhappy, Mum,' Kev told her. 'I don't think I could be happy if I thought you were sad or worried about me.'

His mum shook her head. 'It's all right, love, truly. One day I won't be here anymore, and you'll be on your own anyway. It wouldn't be right for me to stand in the way of your chance to be happy and experience the kind of love I had with your father. We didn't get as long together as either of us wanted, but that only makes me more certain you shouldn't throw away this chance.'

Kev nodded. 'OK, Mum,' he said. 'Thanks for your blessing. I want to really think it through a bit more and talk to Walter about how he's going to go about it before I finally decide. If I do go back, what will we tell Deb?'

'Leave your sister to me,' his mother answered.

⧖

Kev sat on his veranda, waiting for Walter. He had wasted no time in organising a get-together with Walter and his family to discuss his return to Persephone, and a few minutes ago, his family had arrived en masse.

His mum had greeted him calmly, but his sister had shouldered her way past him, her lips pursed in disapproval, pointedly saying as little as possible to make sure he understood her stance on his situation, which his mother had filled her in on prior to their get-together. Shane, Deb's husband, gave Kev a sheepishly sympathetic look but had shooed the children, Lily Ann and Zac, in before him without commenting.

Kev decided the best course of action was to keep out of Deborah's way for a bit and had retreated outside to allow her some space to get into a better frame of mind. This did not appear to be working as he could hear a lot of loud banging and exclaiming coming from his kitchen, where his sister was busily venting her disapproval. Shane had taken refuge out the back, where he was perched on the tiny strip of land between the cottage and the hillside, manning the BBQ, while Kev's mum entertained the children.

He saw Walter's car approaching and exhaled a loud sigh of thankfulness, grateful he would have a smidgen of moral support in the face of Deborah's opprobrium.

Climbing the steps to the house, Walter joined Kev on the veranda. For the first time since he had met him, Walter seemed a little unsure of himself, much to Kev's surprise. Seeing this new, nervous version of his friend and thinking of his sister and her cat's-bottom mouth, Kev was glad he hadn't left him to walk in on them all unaccompanied.

'Ready for this, Walter?' Kev asked him.

Walter nodded. 'As ready as I'll ever be, I guess. This feels a bit like sitting for an exam. The first time I meet your family, and I'm going to be explaining how I can whisk you away from them forever. Not a surefire way to make them like me.'

Kev just laughed. 'I don't need them to like you,' he pointed out. 'I just need them to believe you.'

Walter sighed. 'Ah, but there's the problem, old boy. They'll be more inclined to believe me if they like me.'

'Yeah, you may have a point, actually,' admitted Kev. 'Maybe it wouldn't hurt for you to try to win them over if you can.'

'Just watch me.' Walter laughed and, squaring his shoulders, followed Kev inside.

Kev quickly made the round of introductions, and Walter rose to the occasion, switching his charisma onto high beam, proceeding to disarm them all with his wit and charm. Deborah, who had at first indicated she had every intention of refusing to be won over, was hanging on Walter's every word by the time lunch was ready, as flustered and giggly as an awestruck fan. As the afternoon wore on, Kev was beginning to feel superfluous to requirements as his entire family was drawn into the warmth of Walter's regard and retired somewhat grumpily to the kitchen to tidy up.

'What a lovely young man,' his mother announced from behind him. 'I admit I had serious doubts about you entrusting yourself to someone whom you hadn't known all that long, but now that I've met him, I realise you couldn't be in safer hands.'

Kev gave her a little pat on the shoulder. 'That's good, Mum. I'm pleased you've come to that conclusion because he's the one with all the know-how.'

'Yes, about that, I think perhaps we'll make a pot of tea, and then your lovely friend can explain all about this time travel business.'

Once they were all seated and the children were happily colouring in on the floor, Walter explained how he had come here from the same world Kev had been transported to. He told them of his early struggles and his subsequent success and how he was certain he could get Kev back to the other dimension.

'That's all very well,' Deb began once Walter finished, with shades of her earlier disapproval shadowing her face. 'I don't think it's a question of whether you can send Kev back there. I don't think he should go back, even if he can. How can you even think of it, Kev?' she queried, turning to him. 'How can you even consider it? I know you think you're in love,' she continued as Kev opened his mouth in a vain attempt to speak, 'but everyone gets their heart broken. We all get over it. What's so special about this girl that you'd leave your entire family for her?'

Kev opened his mouth to try and explain, but before he could, Deb was off again.

'You imagine she's the love of your life, but that's just romantic nonsense. Look at me and Shane. If anything happened to him, I'd move on.'

'I say steady on,' protested Shane.

Deb rounded on him. 'Shut up, Shane,' she told him, the bit firmly between her teeth now. 'Keep out of it. He's not your brother.'

'That's quite enough, Deborah,' her mother told her in the tone of voice neither she nor Kev had heard since they were kids. 'You need to calm down right now. You're getting out of hand.'

Shane stood up. 'I think I'll take the kids and go out for a bit. I don't really need to be here, and little pigs have big ears and all that,' he said with a nod, indicating the children busy colouring in with apparent absorption.

'Yes, and they have big noses too,' remarked Lily Ann without looking up from her picture.

Shane gave Deb a significant look at the eavesdropping abilities of their offspring before quickly escorting them out with the promise of ice cream.

Once they'd gone, Deb, who had merely been biding her time, launched back on the attack. 'You'll get over her, Kev. Believe me. She's not worth leaving your family forever for.'

It took quite a lot of provocation for Kev to lose his temper, but he could feel Deb pushing him inexorably towards the brink of no return. 'How would you know, Miss Prissy Pants?' he countered crossly, falling back on his childhood taunt, feeling goaded by her much the way he had as a boy.

Much to both his and Deb's surprise, their mother burst out laughing. They looked at her as though she had lost her mind, but it stopped them both in their tracks, and they had the grace to grin at each other sheepishly.

'I never thought I'd be treated to a reprise of your childhood squabbles at your age,' their mother told them, still chuckling. 'If you've both calmed down, maybe we can begin to discuss this in a sensible, adult fashion. What on earth must you think of us, Walter?'

Walter grinned. 'I was enjoying it immensely,' he said. 'It's been a while since I've been so entertained.'

Kev's mother smiled at him before turning to her children. 'Very well. Let's get a few things straight. First, it's none of your business whether Kev feels he must go back to his young lady or not, Deb. None of this has anything to do with what you want or what I want, for that matter.'

Deb opened her mouth to protest, but her mother held up a hand to stop her from speaking.

'I think we all know how you feel about the matter, Deb. Let's hear what Kev has to say, shall we?'

Kev gave his mum a grateful glance before turning to his sister. 'You're wrong, Deb, about Persephone not being the love of my life. She is. You might be able to imagine a life without Shane, but I'm facing a life without Persephone, and I know it's a life that doesn't feel right or complete without her. I had a hunch it would be like this before I came back, and now that I'm here, I know for sure there won't be anyone else for me. But it's not just that. Perhaps I could manage to make a life for myself without my life's love. Plenty of others have had to, but I can't settle back into life here either. I don't feel a part of this world anymore.'

'Why not?' demanded Deb. 'Why can't you be a part of us again? Walter's done it, and he wasn't even from here to begin with.'

'I don't know, Deb,' Kev replied. 'I never thought it would turn out like this, honestly. I thought I'd be sweet once I was home again, but it's not turning out like that. I want to go back because somehow that world has become more like home than this one.'

'So you're going back,' Deb stated flatly.

Kev nodded. 'Yeah, I think I am. Ever since Walter told me about the possibility, I've felt a lifting inside, a feeling of, I don't know . . .'

'Hope,' his mum said softly. 'You feel hope.'

Kev nodded. 'Yeah, that's it, Mum. I'm beginning to feel hopeful I can be happy again.' He held out his hand to his sister, who took it in hers. 'Please try and understand, Deb,' he asked her.

Deb nodded, blinking away the sudden rush of tears that came to her eyes. 'I'll try, Kev,' she promised. 'I can't say I'll like it, but I'll do my best, OK?'

Kev smiled and nodded, grateful tears standing in his own eyes. 'Thanks, Deb,' he told her, 'and it's not as if I'm leaving right this minute. We have time to make some memories for all of us before I go and for the kids to remember me by.'

'The kids!' exclaimed Deb. 'What are we going to tell the kids?'

'The truth,' her mother told her, 'when they're old enough to understand, but for now, we just tell them Uncle Kev has to go away for a bit and they won't be seeing him much.'

Deb sighed and nodded. 'It seems a sorry explanation for what's really going to happen, but you know what Lily Ann's like. Perhaps it's best if she doesn't know too much until she's old enough for us to rely on her discretion.'

Her mother nodded. 'This is hard for all of us to process. We really don't need any further complications brought down on us by the children inadvertently letting something slip out.'

CHAPTER 3

Walter hung upside down from his knees where they were hooked over the top frame of the time machine taking shape in his shed, his head buried in the machine's bowels.

He was talking volubly, but Kev couldn't understand a word he was saying. Not only was his voice muffled by the machine, but also, Walter was banging so loudly on something, that conversation was pointless. Not letting either of those facts hold him back, Walter was explaining his every move, convinced if he just talked long enough, Kev would begin to understand the intricacies of time travel.

Swinging himself back up and leaping down to where Kev was standing, Walter tucked his hammer away in his tool belt. 'So what do you think, old boy?' he asked expectantly, his face returning to its natural shade as his blood flowed back to where it was supposed to be.

'About what?' Kev asked in return.

'Have you been listening to a word I've been saying?' demanded Walter, slightly affronted.

'It's been a bit difficult to hear you over all the hammering,' pointed out Kev.

'Oh. Right,' said Walter, laughing. 'I was saying how I thought there must be some kind of anomaly in the space–time fabric here, which is why we managed to break through into each other's worlds.'

Kev shook his head. 'I've never thought about it at all.'

'How can you not think about it after all that's happened to you?'

'Time travel isn't a topic most people in this world have any reason to think about too closely,' pointed out Kev.

'True enough, old chap,' admitted Walter. 'I suppose so. I've always been fascinated with time travel and all it entails. I forgot for a moment that this is a different world.'

'Did you always want to be a time traveller?' asked Kev as Walter went over to the workbench in search of something he wanted.

'Ever since I was a nipper,' said Walter over his shoulder. 'As soon as I was old enough, I enrolled in the Academy of Time Travel. I was a bit of a hotshot back in those days,' he continued with a grin as he turned back to Kev, 'keen as mustard and a bit of a know-it-all, if I'm honest.'

'Do you miss it?' asked Kev.

Walter sat down on an upturned crate, lost in thought. 'Sometimes I do,' he admitted eventually. 'I miss the thrill of exploring a new time. I really miss the evenings with Archie when we were building our machine and the conversations we had about it.' Walter sighed. 'I used to believe those were the best days of my life.'

'Don't you ever wish you were coming back with me then?' Kev asked.

Walter just grinned and shook his head. 'No. As I've said before, I like it here. And it's not as if Archie and I can go back to exploring travel between worlds. We'll just get shut down again, and I've changed since those days.

'The academy have strict rules governing time travel for good reason. I didn't always appreciate those reasons when I was younger. I was always pushing the limits of what was permissible – just little things, really, like bringing items back with me from other times or travelling to times on the restricted list.

'Each time I got away with it, it just reinforced the idea that the academy were being overly cautious, and I began to believe the rules couldn't possibly apply to me. The night I went through the portal in Archie's lab, I really believed I was bulletproof.

'I'm not going back, Kev. Time travel's lost its appeal for me, in a way. Besides, I have so much here in this world now. I'll be satisfied with sending you back, Kev. That will be enough for me.'

⧗

Kev awoke to a grey day. He lay still for a while, staring at the ceiling of Walter's spare room, and tried to bring his thoughts and emotions into some kind of order.

In the passing months, he had been in a frenzy of activity, tying up all the loose ends of his life here in this reality.

He had been so busy, it hadn't really sunk in that he was actually preparing to leave the world he had been born into and make a life for himself somewhere else in the fabric of time and space. Up until this point, it hadn't seemed quite real, but this morning, now that the distractions of preparing to leave were done with, the enormity of it hit him.

As he lay in bed, allowing the thoughts and emotions to flow through him, he could feel the excitement of returning begin to take hold, and the thought of seeing Persephone again filled him with sentimental happiness. His thoughts continued to drift as he folded his arms behind his head, gazing at the ceiling and thinking back over everything that had happened over the last few months.

Walter had had a great many ideas on how to prepare Kev for his return journey. Kev had listened to all his friend's suggestions and had been happy to follow most of them. He had sold his little cottage and invested most of the profit, creating a trust for his mum and sister. The rest of the money, Walter had converted into gold for Kev to take back with him so he wouldn't be penniless on arrival. This was something Walter felt quite strongly about, naturally enough, and Kev had seen no reason not to go along with it, feeling he would like to be able to return to the *Elizabeth Anne* without empty pockets.

He had told Walter about his propensity for time sickness, and even though this was something Walter himself had never suffered from, he remembered enough of his early training to be able to coach Kev through some exercises and breathing techniques to help alleviate the symptoms. These, Kev had practised diligently.

One day he came home to discover Walter erecting some kind of contraption faintly resembling a rotary clothesline with a harness attached, which he proposed to hang Kev from and spin him around to mimic the effects of time travel. At that point, Kev put his foot down and adamantly refused to take part, telling Walter to concentrate on the time machine, preferring to rely on the efficacy of the exercises.

Walter's time machine had slowly but surely taken shape, and he was now putting the finishing touches to it. Kev had moved in with Walter as they counted down to the time Kev would leave.

Having arrived at this point in their preparations, Kev wondered if he hadn't been a bit hasty at shunning Walter's training machine and if, in fact, he was adequately prepared for his return through the portal. The thought made him leap out of bed, in a hurry to practise his exercises.

Kev had just finished his breakfast and was finishing a second cup of coffee in the lounge when the outside door opened and Walter wandered in. He came through to join Kev in the lounge, carefully unloading the items from the pockets of his cargo pants onto the coffee table.

Walter was the only person Kev knew who actually used the deep pockets of his cargo pants for carrying his possessions around in. Remembering how his friends aboard the *Elizabeth Anne* had all tended to decorate their person with the things they deemed necessary and useful, Kev assumed this was a habit Walter had found hard to break.

As the pile of objects continued to grow, Kev wondered how Walter had managed to walk, but he watched without comment until his friend had finished and sat down. Rubbing his hands together, Walter looked at Kev with a pleased grin.

'Well, old boy,' he said, 'the machine is all ready to go. All I need now is a way to power it, and you'll be on your way.'

Kev drew a deep breath, not quite sure how he felt. 'That's great news, of course, but this is the first time it's begun to feel real. I'm going to have to adjust my thinking a bit, I reckon.'

Walter nodded. 'There's no pretending this isn't a big deal, old boy,' he told him soberly. 'What you're doing is a huge step outside your comfort zone. As long as you still feel you're doing the right thing, you'll come to terms with it.'

Kev thought for a while before answering. 'Yeah, I know I'm doing the right thing. Even though sometimes I admit I have doubts. If I think about not going, that's when I start to feel really unhappy again, so I know even though this is a hard thing to do, it's the right thing for me. The only thing I still worry about is how Mum will cope with me gone again. I know it's not quite the same, but I came back mostly for her, and it seems a bit rough to be leaving her when I've not long been back, you know?'

Walter nodded. 'I understand that,' he said. 'If it's any help, I'll look after her for you. Don't forget, I have no family of my own here, so I'd be happy to look after yours as if they were my own. They won't want for anything, if I have any say in it, old man.'

Kev reached out his hand to his friend, and the two men shook on it. 'Thanks,' said Kev. 'That's a weight off my mind, to be honest. I know Mum has always told me to go, but I couldn't help feeling sometimes I shouldn't abandon her. Deb will be all right. She has Shane and the kids. Knowing you'll be there for Mum makes all the difference.'

The two men fell into a contemplative silence, which was only broken by Walter standing and saying, 'Wait here, Kev. I've got something for you,' before leaving the room.

When Walter returned, he was carrying several items of clothing and a leather satchel. He handed Kev the satchel and spread the clothes out over the coffee table.

'This is my traveller's gear,' he told Kev, who had opened the satchel to look inside.

It had multiple compartments and a long strap, so it could be slung across the body, leaving the user's hands free. Kev could see an emblem stamped into the leather that he assumed was that of the Academy of Time Travel.

Kev turned his attention to the clothing. There was a dark brown shirt and long brown trousers, a leather waistcoat that had pockets and rings for attaching tools to, a pair of leather gauntlets, and a wide-brimmed hat that looked a little like a drover's hat – although it had a slightly higher crown – with a pair of brass goggles still resting on the brim.

Walter held up a calf-length coat made of worsted material. It too was dark brown and had a shoulder cape with a collar that could be turned up against the elements. A row of three buckles fastened the deep cuffs, and it could be done up in front by three columns of brass buttons that ran down the front.

'What are these?' asked Kev, picking up a pair of knee-length leather items that fastened up by means of a row of brass buttons along the outside length.

'Gaiters,' replied Walter. 'The strap goes under the sole of your boot. They'll protect your legs. These should all fit fairly well,' he continued. 'We're much the same size.'

Kev nodded. Although he was thinner than Walter, the two men were almost the same height. The clothes would be a bit loose on him, but that was preferable to being too tight.

'Thanks, Walt,' he said. 'This is very kind of you.'

Walter waved away his thanks. 'Don't mention it, Kev. I really have no use for them anymore. I'm glad you'll get some use out of them and figured you may as well look like a traveller seeing as how you seem to be making a habit of it.'

Kev continued to prepare as best he could, both physically and mentally. He was much more at peace with his decision since he knew Walter was going to look after his mum, and his main emotion was one of longing to be reunited with Persephone.

He had spent many bittersweet hours with his mother and the rest of the family, and although none of them were overjoyed at his imminent departure, they too were at peace with it.

While he knew he would miss his family, Kev also knew that none of them could take the place of Persephone. He wished sometimes that he hadn't fallen for someone who necessitated him leaving his family and indeed his entire world for. He mentioned this to his mother one day and wondered how it was that he was prepared to leave everything familiar in the pursuit of love and a different life than the one he had. His mother had smiled and pointed out that New Zealand was a country pioneered by those willing to leave their homelands in search of a better life, beginning with the very first migration from Hawaiki thousands of years ago.

Walter continued to finalise the preparations of the time machine. The problem of how to power it had given him many hours of anxious thought. He was aware of the difference of energy sources between the two worlds and wasn't sure how to adapt the resources available to him in Kev's world. Electricity seemed his best option, but he knew the amount of energy required was more than the national grid could deal with in one hit. Having come so far, he hated the thought of having to abandon the project for want of a means of getting the machine up and running.

Eventually, he hit upon the idea of harnessing the power of nature in the form of lightning and had cobbled together a lightning rod. He calculated that one strike should provide enough energy to power the machine for a single trip – not much of a margin but hopefully enough to get Kev back through the portal.

On the odd occasions when his natural sense of competence wavered and he began to doubt his ability to send Kev back, he managed to think his way back into a more optimistic frame of mind quickly by focusing on the things he knew well and discarding the worries about the things he was less sure of. He very carefully selected the information he wanted Kev to know, not out of a real intent to deceive but more because his own confidence in his abilities was such that he felt it would be counterproductive to fill Kev's mind with doubts.

Kev remained blissfully unaware of the dangers in trusting his trip back through the portal to Walter and believed him when he had said that everything was bound to go exactly as planned.

Bit by bit, the time machine began to look like something that could work as Walter tweaked the design here and there. All that remained was for Mother Nature to provide the power. Walter began to get restless and anxious as each day passed, with no storm systems on the weather radar.

Walter's edginess was beginning to rub off on Kev too. He had tied up all his loose ends, said his final farewells, and now found he could do nothing other than wait around and watch as Walter polished the time machine until it almost glowed. The waiting gave him too much time to think, and for the first time, the thoughts of *What if something goes wrong?* began to bother him. He took courage from Walter's confidence and endeavoured to push the worrying thoughts aside, preferring to concentrate on imagining his reunion with Persephone.

Finally, as late autumn gradually melted into early winter, the day came when Walter informed Kev that thunderstorms were forecast for the Coromandel Peninsula. The energy level in the house rose dramatically as the men hastened to finish all the last-minute preparations that they hadn't realised they'd neglected until now.

Kev was standing in his room, sifting through his few remaining possessions. He could only take what would fit into Walter's satchel and his pockets. He decided he was taking the music box, even though it was an awkward shape, mostly because he intended to give it to Persephone but also because he couldn't bear to leave it behind.

Walter knocked briefly on the open door to alert Kev of his presence. He held out two letters.

'I've written to Elspeth and Archie,' he explained. 'I thought you might be able to deliver them for me.'

'I'd be glad to,' Kev replied, taking the letters and tucking them into the satchel next to the sepia print of the crew of the *Elizabeth Anne*.

Walter disappeared, reappearing moments later with several small items in hand. There was a leather belt with a holster to hold the pocket knife and compass that Walter handed over amongst other things, along with a small brass telescope and a strange flat device that had small buttons and knobs with a crystal lens that lifted up on a hinge.

Kev had no idea what it was or what it did and gave a Walter a puzzled look. 'What does this do?' he asked.

'It's a scanner, Kev,' Walter replied. 'It won't work in this dimension, but once you get back, you can use it if the visibility is poor or the light is low, and it will help you find your way.'

Kev didn't know when he would need to use something like that. He had given Walter the coordinates from the gold disc Persephone had given him before he had left her world with her space–time coordinates on it, and he expected to be transported directly into Grahamstown itself. But he took the items from Walter gratefully, realising they may be useful in the future, even if, at this point, he wasn't aware of how.

'The weather's closing in,' Walter remarked. 'We need to set up the lightning collector.'

Kev nodded and, placing the things Walter had given him on his bed, joined him by the back door.

The rain had begun to fall, and the night was closing in. The wind had picked up too, and it promised to be a stormy night. Donning wet-weather gear and picking up torches, the men made their way behind the sheds to the hidden workshop, behind which Walter had constructed a tall tower topped with the copper rod from his junk pile. Walter had insulated the tower and connected strong cables that ran into a transformer, which would then send the electricity from the lightning through more cables into the machine inside the shed.

The men grappled with the equipment in the rising storm and checked over all the connections one more time. Satisfied, they went back to the house, where Kev quickly donned his traveller's gear and double-checked everything he wanted to take before they made their way back to the shed to wait.

Outside the shed, the storm built in intensity, and the lightning began to flash. The thunder echoed around the ranges, and the rain fell even more heavily. They could hear the storm getting nearer, and Walter got up and began to pace restlessly back and forth between his chair and the time machine and its cables. He kept checking the monitors he had attached to it and making minute adjustments before changing them back again.

The night wore on, and the storm continued to rage – flash after flash of lightning, followed by the booming, echoing thunder – and yet their lightning rod stood untouched.

Kev began to feel his eyelids growing heavy, and the effort of trying to stay awake was beginning to feel like a battle he wasn't winning. Walter, however, was humming with a nervous energy that kept him pacing restlessly when he wasn't checking his gauges.

Kev realised he must have dozed off the moment the sky was lit by a bright flash of lightning that occurred simultaneously with a reverberating boom of thunder directly overhead. Kev was on his feet in seconds, heart racing. He looked for Walter, who was hunched over the monitors of the time machine, flicking switches and turning knobs as the energy from the lightning strike powered it up.

The moment had arrived, the one they had both been working towards all these months. It was a surreal feeling to be standing on the cusp of such an adventure that, even though anticipated so strongly, had tended to take on the quality of a dream.

Kev realised a part of him had not believed he would really be leaving everything in this world behind, and a sudden fear of the unknown gripped him. He took a deep breath and, slinging the satchel across his body, took a resolute step towards the time machine before he could change his mind.

CHAPTER 4

Walter took a steadying breath. This was the moment of truth. As the machine began to vibrate and the lights on the control panel flickered and then glowed steadily, he let out another breath he hadn't realised he'd been holding. It worked!

In his more honest moments, he hadn't been totally sure it would. But now the doubts faded from his mind, and the sense of satisfaction that flooded through him created an expansive euphoria he hadn't experienced since arriving in this world all those years ago.

Had he been a more introspective man, he may have been alerted to the fact that this was the same illusion of invincibility that had led him here in the first place. As it was, he basked in the glow of his own cleverness and failed to listen to the small quiet voice in the back of his mind that was trying to warn him to take care.

He looked over at Kev, who was standing anxiously, watching, and gave him a thumbs up. 'It's all working as it should, Kev,' he told him.

Kev nodded and adjusted the satchel strap over his shoulder.

Walter handed Kev a plain brown envelope. 'It pays to be careful transferring items between times,' he explained, 'but I think this will be OK.'

Kev took the envelope and drew out a photo of his family. Walter had had it printed out in sepia tones so that it resembled the photograph of the crew of the *Elizabeth Anne*. Kev was touched.

'It shouldn't stand out as obviously coming from another time,' Walter pointed out, 'and I thought you would like a keepsake to take with you.'

Kev nodded, resolutely keeping his emotions in check. 'Thanks,' he said as he slipped the photo into his satchel along with the other things he was taking back. These were very few in number and mostly small and compact, apart from the music box and the gold, which, although it fit into a fairly small pouch, was reasonably weighty.

Walter turned back to the time machine and continued with his preparations, and Kev began the breathing exercises Walter had shown him, schooling his body for the trip back through the portal. Eventually, Walter turned and nodded at Kev. 'It's all ready to go, Kev,' he said.

Kev nodded and shook himself out, rotating his neck and shaking his arms in much the same way a boxer loosens up before a fight.

Walter programmed in the coordinates and slowly pulled the lever that opened up the portal. It shimmered and flickered, sparking now and then. Walter frowned and adjusted the knobs. The portal stopped sparking and began to shimmer in a steady fashion.

Satisfied, Walter turned again to Kev. 'This is it,' he said.

The two men shook hands.

'Thanks for everything,' Kev said.

Walter nodded. 'You're welcome, old man,' he said. 'Good luck.'

Kev stood hesitantly before the open portal and reflected that this moment just before leaving didn't get any easier.

'I don't want to rush you, Kev,' Walter pointed out as Kev hovered nervously, 'but we only have a limited energy supply. If you're going, you need to go now.'

Kev nodded, took a final steadying breath, pulled the goggles over his eyes, and stepped through the portal.

At first, the now familiar sensations of the portal's energy pulling on his body created a claustrophobic sensation of panic, but then the months of practising Walter's techniques kicked in, and Kev began to breathe automatically as he'd been shown. The panic subsided, and Kev surrendered himself to the tug of the void and allowed it to pull him in.

Back at the control panel of his machine, Walter was making minute adjustments, aware that the energy was draining from it. Behind him, the portal sparked and fizzed, and the needle on one of the gauges began to flicker unsteadily. Walter frowned, uncertain of what was going wrong.

Behind him, the portal wavered and blinked, and the machine itself began to shake, its gauges and meters spinning wildly. Walter turned knobs and adjusted levers feverishly, trying to regain control.

The portal was flickering erratically, and the whole machine was beginning to shudder as if it would lift off from the ground. Walter was beginning to feel the panic rise up inside, threatening to choke him, and he feared what may be happening to Kev inside the portal. Desperately, he worked to steady the machine, trying to read from the gauges what was going wrong.

After what seemed like minutes but in reality was only a few seconds, Walter managed to bring the machine back under control, and all appeared to be working as it should once more. Turning, he watched as the portal closed, telling him Kev had arrived at the other end. The power gave out at that moment, and the machine went abruptly still and dark.

Feeling relieved and more than a little pleased with himself, Walter disconnected cables from the machine and threw a tarpaulin over it, certain that Kev had arrived at his final destination safely.

He locked the shed and returned to his house to ring Kev's mum and let her know that Kev had left and that he would be, even as they spoke, striding the streets of Grahamstown on his way to the *Elizabeth Anne* and Persephone.

Inside the portal, the blackness of unconsciousness was threatening to overwhelm Kev's mind. He managed to keep it at bay by concentrating on the breathing techniques Walter had taught him. The months of training were paying off, and even though Kev wouldn't go so far as to say he was enjoying it, he found it tolerable.

He seemed to be moving very fast, and the fabric of time and space around him bulged and receded in a manner that made him feel dizzy if he watched it for too long.

He wondered if he was travelling upright or if, in fact, he was tumbling through space like an astronaut cut free from a spacewalk. It was hard for him to tell as he felt as though he was completely still while the void rushed past him and yet, at the same time, as if he was the one moving, falling from a great height through a static world.

The sensation of speed was increasing, and as it did so, the strange visual effects of the portal were beginning to induce a faint sense of nausea. Closing his eyes to concentrate on his breathing, Kev became aware of a faint tugging sensation. It felt as though someone was pulling gently on his sleeve.

Opening his eyes, he saw the walls of the portal begin to separate, and two tunnels opened up before him. He was confused. Did he need to choose which path to take? And if so, which one was the right one? As he neared the openings of the tunnels, he felt panic grip him. There was no way of telling, just by looking at them, which of the tunnels he should aim for.

The nagging doubts he had experienced intermittently coelesced into something more solid. He wondered if it had been wise to entrust himself and his safe arrival to Walter's untested time machine, and if he would end up where he was supposed to be or somewhere else completely - or, worse still, swirling through the fabric of time with no way to anchor himself into a reality.

As he neared them, one of the tunnels began to pulse in a rhythmic manner, and Kev could feel it pull him towards it with each beat, almost as if it were beckoning him. He found he was powerless to direct himself and could do nothing except allow the portal to pull him towards it.

As he entered the tunnel, the walls appeared to become a little more solid, as though he were actually travelling through a pipe of some sort, and far away in the distance, he could detect a faint glow of light.

Kev felt himself slowing. Feeling relieved that his time in the portal was coming to an end, he burst through the time membrane with a pop and enough residual momentum to send him tumbling head over heels along the ground before coming to an abrupt but soft landing.

CHAPTER 5

K ev found himself on his hands and knees, his hands buried deep in leaf mould. He shook his head to clear it as the earthy smell of the disturbed leaf litter filled his nostrils. He blinked and raised his head, feeling only a very slight sense of uneasiness in his stomach. Walter's exercises and breathing techniques had indeed worked, for which he was extremely grateful. Lying sick and dazed on the streets of Grahamstown hadn't been a scenario he had looked forward to, not knowing what could've happened to him while he was out of it.

As he pushed himself back onto his heels and removed his goggles, he took stock of his surroundings properly, and he realised that things hadn't gone exactly to plan. Instead of finding himself in Grahamstown, he was, in fact, sitting in some kind of clearing in the bush. It had been here for some time as he could see evidence of the bush regenerating to fill the gap, and he wondered where he was.

He looked around him for some sign that he may have landed on the steep bush-clad slopes of the ranges that loomed over the town, but it was hard to get his bearings. Apart from the clearing he found himself in, the trees grew so tall and thick around about that it was impossible to see past them. Not knowing what might have gone wrong with Walter's machine that meant he wasn't where he was supposed to be, Kev decided to get on with it and find a way to Grahamstown.

As he walked around, he stumbled across the remains of what looked to him to be a firepit, and it suddenly dawned on him where he was. He looked around him, and sure enough, he saw the kauri tree Rosalind Porter, youngest crew member of the *Elizabeth Anne*, had launched herself from in Persephone's parachute jacket the day he had returned to his own world, and he knew he was in the campsite the crew of the *Elizabeth Anne* had made to accommodate the time machine to transport him home.

This was good news because he now knew exactly where he was. It was also bad news because he was on the wrong side of the Firth of Thames. Grahamstown was on the other side of the wide expanse of water he knew lay beyond the trees. He had no idea how he was going to get across. The only thing he could think to do was make his way south and hope that somehow, somewhere there was a way across the rivers he knew stood in his way.

He looked around him to see if he could gauge the time of day, which was when he noticed that where he had landed, the air was flickering and shimmering periodically. Going closer, wondering if another portal was opening up, he heard a faint pinging sound. Intrigued, he followed it. He came to a spot in the bush where the pinging sound was definitely louder.

Following the sound, he was led to a spot where it sounded as though whatever was making the noise was buried in the leaf mould. Rummaging around, he unearthed a brass box, showing signs that it had been buried there for some time. The sound was definitely coming from it, and as he looked back to where the portal might be, he noticed that the flickers coincided with the pings.

He looked down at the brass box and wondered how it had gotten there. He figured it could only have been put there by Professor Popkiss or maybe Lady Elspeth, but to what purpose, he couldn't begin to guess. As the box was quite heavy and Kev wasn't keen to carry it with him, he decided to rebury it and leave it where he'd found it, reasoning that whoever had left it there had done so for a purpose he wasn't aware of and feeling reluctant to interfere with that.

Once he had reburied the box and returned to the old campsite, he judged the day to be too far advanced towards sunset for him to realistically set out, so he searched for a suitable spot to shelter for the night.

Eschewing the clearing, he pushed into the bush at the perimeter, looking around until he found the half-rotted remains of a tree trunk. Pulling the dead fronds off the ponga trees and other dry dead foliage from the various ferns near the edge of the clearing, he took them back and began to construct himself a thick bed of criss-crossing fronds in the lee of the trunk.

Once he thought it was thick enough, he began to gather more fronds to cover himself with. These, he heaped in a pile next to his bed, ready for when he would need them.

As he had been gathering the fronds, he had taken note of the amount of dried plant material about and estimated there was enough to start a fire – if he only had the means to do so. Rummaging through Walter's satchel in the hopes of finding something of a fire-starting nature amongst the various small items gifted to him by his friend, he found a flint and a steel.

Part of his mind had been hoping for a box of matches, and his spirits fell fractionally before his natural optimism buoyed him up again. At least attempting to build a fire would give him something to do. Setting to it, he gathered up as much dry wood and dead foliage as he could and scraped out a hollow to begin his fire.

Knowing he had to start small, he made a tangled nest of dried plant matter and began to strike the steel on the flint. This was not easy, and he tried repeatedly to strike a spark – to no avail. Maybe the steel was too worn or he just didn't have the knack because no matter how hard he tried, he couldn't get a spark.

Eventually, he knew he was going to have to admit defeat and retire to his shelter before the sun went down to try and keep as warm as he could for the night. Abandoning his fire-lighting attempts, he lay down on the bedding and pulled the remaining fronds over him, building them up into a thick covering.

Satisfied there were no gaps in his roof, he lay down, thankful for the worsted coat and knowing he was in for a long cold night. His stomach grumbled, reminding him he would need to eat soon, and a new appreciation for Walter's plight in his own world bloomed in his mind.

He must have dozed off at some stage through sheer exhaustion, but eventually, in the wee hours of the morning, the cold woke him, and he lay shivering in his shelter until the sun had managed to shine into the clearing.

Gratefully, he emerged and went to bask in the weak rays of the wintery sun. He sat with his back to it and let the warmth begin to seep through his coat and the icy chill to leave his bones.

As he sat waiting to warm up again, he sorted through the items in the satchel. Always believing he would be going straight into Grahamstown, he hadn't really taken much notice of all the small items Walter had carried with him on his travels, but now it seemed like a good idea to take an inventory.

His rummaging hand unearthed a small paper bag that had been sitting right in the bottom, wedged into a corner, trapped there by the weight of the music box he had carried from his own world. Drawing it out and looking inside, he was overwhelmed to discover it contained scroggin. Walter must have put it there. It wasn't a very large amount as Walter hadn't expected Kev to be so far off course either, but his training and experience had obviously prompted him to include it.

The scroggin didn't really go very far in satisfying Kev's hunger, but it was better than nothing, and by the time he had finished it, he was warm enough to begin walking. Keeping the morning sun on his left, he began to make his way through the bush. It was hard going, and he wondered if he wouldn't be better to try for the flatter land closer to the firth, so he headed towards the coast.

As he got lower, he noticed the bush changing, and the kahikatea forest slowly took over the landscape. Where the ground was particularly boggy, the huge trees and the harakeke had made islands with their interlocking roots and the silt they captured in them, and he made his way laboriously from island to island.

He lost track of how long he'd been walking, but his stomach informed him that it had been too long since the scroggin and asked what he was going to do about it. Catching sight of some supplejack that, thankfully, had some berries still on it, he plucked a meagre, unappetising snack and resumed his journey, aware that he needed to find civilisation quickly.

Struggling through a swampy patch of ground, he burst through into a long straight cutting through the bush, down the middle of which ran a road. It was raised well above the surrounding land, and as Kev scrambled up the embankment, he discovered it was little more than a rutted cart track.

Nevertheless, it was still a road, running roughly east to west across the plains. Kev stood in the middle and, for the first time, got a really good look at the surrounding countryside. In his world, the plains had been drained and turned into fertile farmland, criss-crossed by a network of paved roads.

Finding himself in this very different landscape was a little disorientating, but he could see the Coromandel Ranges in the distance and knew he was heading in the right direction. He surmised that if someone had gone to the trouble of constructing the road, they had probably made a way across the rivers too. Feeling much heartened, Kev set out along the road, avoiding the ruts, staying on the grassy rise in the middle.

Eventually, Kev found himself standing at the end of the road, looking across what he guessed to be the Piako River. The road led down to a wooden landing and a ferry in the form of a wide flat-bottomed barge big enough to accommodate a horse and cart.

Unfortunately, the barge was on the other side of the river, its hull resting on the thick mud of the opposite bank. Kev inspected the pulley system that allowed the barge to be pulled from one side of the river to the other. It looked simple enough, and he gave it an experimental tug.

Trying with a bit more strength to shift the barge off the mud, Kev realised he would have to wait for the high tide to flood back up the river as the barge proved too heavy for him to drag through the mud. Despondently, he sat down on the landing to wait for the tide to turn. The hours dragged by, and Kev could do nothing other than sit and watch the day pass. Little by little, the water level rose, and eventually, there was enough water for the barge to lift off the sucking mud and float.

Kev leaped into action, pulling the barge back across the river. Jumping on board, he began to pull on the rope to haul himself across the water. Clambering up onto the landing on the other side, he realised that the day had faded away on him while he was waiting for the tide and the dusk was beginning to deepen.

Kev knew he could be in for a cold night if he didn't find somewhere to shelter soon, so he decided to press on, thinking he would be better to keep moving. The night deepened, and there was no moon to light the way. Kev's eyes adjusted to the blackness, but he was overly cautious and unsure of the way ahead, so his progress was slow.

Near the river, the land had been open wetland, where the river was in the habit of flooding its banks, but gradually, the farther away from it he moved, the more the kahikatea forest began to dominate the landscape once more, and Kev found himself in the deeper gloom of the bush.

Remembering Walter's scanner, he removed it from his belt and lifted the crystal lens, peering through it. It did indeed make it easier to see, but as the effect was only through the lens – and that was quite small – Kev wasn't sure he would be able to make much faster progress with it.

As he was scanning the road ahead, he noticed flickering light half hidden in the bush ahead and off to one side of the road. Making his way towards it, Kev could hear voices, a little muffled by the bush but still carrying on the night air as sounds do.

As he approached, Kev saw that the flickering light was a campfire, and he could see the shapes of people sitting around it. Nothing in Kev's life experiences to this point had caused him to be wary of approaching a group of strangers, so with an overwhelming sense of relief, he stepped into the circle of light cast by the fire.

The three men seated around it stopped talking and looked at him. It dawned on Kev that they didn't look overjoyed to see him.

They didn't look friendly at all, in fact, and Kev was beginning to think he might be better off back on the road.

The smallest of the three slowly stood up and looked Kev up and down. He was scrawny and dirty, and although Kev didn't feel immediately afraid, he projected a sense of cunning cruelty that made Kev feel distinctly uneasy. He grinned to reveal a set of metal teeth, all sharply filed into points like shark's teeth.

'Well, well, what have we here, chaps? A traveller, no less. What are you doing in these parts, eh?'

Kev took an involuntary step backward as Shark Teeth sniffed loudly and drew a mittened hand under his nose. The fact that his metal teeth caused him to lisp slightly in no way detracted from his menace, and Kev realised he was out of his depth.

Glancing around at his companions, Shark Teeth gave a nod in Kev's direction. 'Let's see what he's got, eh, lads?'

At this, the other two men stood up and moved towards Kev, and he could see they both wore metal body armour. The largest of them was wearing a heavy padded jacket with a boiler strapped to his back. His right arm was completely encased in metal, ending in an oversized fist. His other arm was also clothed in metal, the fingers ending in sharp blades.

His counterpart circled around to block Kev's retreat. He was wearing leather gauntlets, the knuckles of which were covered in sharp metal spikes. He wore a face mask over the lower half of his face, and his breath hissed out through twin respirators, his eyes protected by goggles. As he moved into position, he drew a gas gun from his holster.

Kev was cornered. If he tried to make a break for it, Gas Man would no doubt shoot at him with whatever toxic gas he had in his gun. Desperately, he turned in a vain attempt to reason his way out of the situation. The big fellow drew back his fist with a hiss of steam from the boiler on his back.

This is going to hurt, Kev thought moments before the steam-powered punch hit home, and he crumbled to a heap.

Chapter 6

Kev awoke to a massive throbbing in his jaw and a burning ache in his shoulders. As his senses returned, he realised he was lying on his side at the edge of the firelight, his hands tied behind his back. The cold damp was rising up from the ground on which he lay, chilling him to the core.

Gingerly, he tried moving his jaw, and although it was painful, he didn't think it was broken. The pain in his jaw was rivalled by the pain in his shoulder joints, where his arms had been pinned behind him. Rough cords bit into his wrists, but his captors hadn't bothered to tie his feet.

Kev was grateful for this as it enabled him to wriggle around, using his legs and feet for purchase, and so slightly ease the discomfort of being in one position for too long. He shifted around until he could see the men seated around the fire. They had his satchel and looked as though they were about to empty it out. The only thing of real value he had was the small bag of gold, and Kev felt they were welcome to it if they would let him go. The fact that he was still alive seemed to him to be a good sign, but he had no idea what they intended to do with him.

The men were muttering in low voices, and it looked to Kev as though they were in disagreement over something. Kev thought that Shark Teeth wanted to do something the other two weren't keen on doing, and he was trying to convince them to do as he said.

Kev caught the odd word that drifted towards him on the night air, and he figured out that Gas Man and Steam Fist were all for dispatching him forthwith. Shark Teeth, however, was keen to keep him alive in the hopes of being able to get some money for him.

Kev was trying vainly to eavesdrop more closely on this conversation, having a vested interest in the outcome. It proved to be impossible to hear much more than the odd word, however, and so he slumped back against the ground.

As he lay there, he felt what seemed like a breeze or a shifting in the air. Looking up, he noticed several dark shapes swooping down between the trees.

He watched as a group of men landed in a circle around his captors, all pointing weapons. They had mechanical wings strapped to their backs, and it was the disturbance of the air created by their passing that Kev had felt.

The wings were constructed from some kind of hide stretched over metal frames, much like a bat's wings, and they folded up to rest down the men's backs as they landed.

As the armed men held Shark Teeth and his companions at weapon point, a small dark aircraft manoeuvred its way down through the bush canopy and landed softly. A man clambered out. He was slight and wiry and dressed in a dark collarless shirt, his pants tucked into high boots. He wore a wide belt secured by four buckles from which a variety of different knives protruded. He had on leather arm guards and a brown top hat over his dreadlocks, which hung down his back.

He also had a leather shoulder holster, to which what looked like a speaking device was attached, and as Kev watched, he turned his head. 'Tell the captain we have them,' he said into it.

Casually strolling over to Shark Teeth and company, the newcomer plucked a knife from his belt and, whistling softly to himself, began to clean his fingernails with the tip.

Kev could see that his captors were afraid. Steam Fist was virtually shaking. It was impossible to read Gas Man's expression, but Kev could tell by the set of his body that he wasn't at ease. Shark

Teeth was trying to project an air of nonchalance, but it wasn't quite working.

At that moment, a magnificent mechanical flying horse swooped down through the trees. Its metal body gleamed, and it pawed the air as it descended, snorting steam through its nostrils. It landed delicately on the ground and stood snorting and tossing its head, eyes glowing red.

From its back, a woman descended. She was tall and strong. Her black hair was drawn up and secured to the top of her head by an intricately carved bone heru. Her lips and chin were tattooed with the traditional moko kauae. She was wearing trousers and a white shirt, over which she wore a velvet frock coat of deep purple. She wore a holster belt, and her chest was criss-crossed with bandoliers. A sword was strapped in its scabbard to her back.

She strode up to Shark Teeth, who was on his knees, bobbing his head and baring his fangs in the same ingratiating manner Kev had seen dogs do to show their submission.

'Huia,' he began, 'I can explain—'

He got no further as, barely pausing to get her balance, Huia lifted her leg and kicked him squarely in the chest with the flat of her foot. Shark Teeth went sprawling backward, winded, and Huia turned to the other two, her hands on her hips. They lowered their gaze and cowered abjectly. Huia snorted in derision.

Turning to Knife Man, she issued a command Kev couldn't quite catch. Turning, she noticed him for the first time. She strode over towards him, and Kev struggled to get himself to his knees, feeling at a distinct disadvantage. He managed to half-get his legs under him before Huia, reaching down and gripping the front of his clothes, hauled him to his feet.

He stood before her, feeling slightly shaky as she perused him from head to toe. Kev wasn't sure if he should speak or not and so just waited for Huia to speak first. She remained silent, however, and turned on her heel.

'Bring him,' she commanded Knife Man as she walked back past him with a nod towards Kev.

Striding back to her flying horse, she mounted it, and it unfurled its metallic wings. It began to paw the ground as its wings beat against the air, and – steam hissing from its nostrils – it rose into the air and carried Huia into the night.

Kev found himself being bundled towards the aircraft and pushed aboard. It was very similar to the Hummingbird used by the crew of the *Elizabeth Anne*. Knife Man got in beside him, and the craft began to lift into the sky. Looking down, Kev could see his former captors being bound and led away by the remaining men, and he wondered what was going to happen to them.

The fact that his hands remained tied behind him meant although Huia and her men had rescued him, he was still considered a prisoner, and he began to question what his fate was to be.

Up ahead, Kev spotted the familiar shape of an airship, and Knife Man began the descent towards it. It was much larger than the *Elizabeth Anne*, and to one side, it had an outrigger platform, on which Knife Man landed the aircraft. Looking around him, Kev could see the swooping shapes of men in their bat wings as they came in to land on the deck.

Knife Man hauled Kev out of the cockpit and deftly cut the ropes around his wrists. The rush of blood back into his arms was painful, and Kev tried to shake and rub the sensation back into them.

He was prodded at knife point below decks to the brig and locked away in a cage-like cell. It was bare of any form of comfort, and Kev hunkered down in a far corner, trying to ignore his encroaching hunger and nagging thirst.

He lost track of how long he'd been sitting there when Huia's men brought in Steam Fist and Gas Man, both now stripped of their weapons and armour. They were no longer in any way intimidating, and Kev watched with interest as they huddled together in the back of their cage.

Kev wondered what had happened to Shark Teeth when a horrendous wailing was heard from above deck. The shudders that ran through his cell neighbours gave him enough of a clue to wonder no more.

The sound set Kev's teeth on edge, and he wondered if he hadn't just exchanged one danger for another. Whoever Huia and her crew were, they were obviously not people to be messed with, and Kev began to have serious doubts about his own safety.

CHAPTER 7

H uia stood on deck, her anger burning in her like a white flame. An icy rage that left her calm and self-possessed, her thoughts as honed and sharp as a beam of sunlight through a magnifying glass. Anger always affected her this way. Over the years, she had seen too many other captains make errors in judgement in the heat of anger, and so she had learned to focus hers until it had become an asset and not a hindrance, clarifying her thoughts and instincts.

She'd been simmering on the brink since the night she'd discovered three of her crew had disappeared along with her personal property – a treasure with deep personal significance as well as value cut from around her neck while she lay asleep, drugged, as had been the rest of her crew.

At first, she had been stunned by disbelief at its theft, not believing anyone on board could possibly be so foolhardy as to steal from her. The subsequent discovery of the missing crew members had jolted her quickly from this disbelief, and she had swiftly sent out men to track them and bring them back to face justice.

She hadn't been surprised to discover one of the missing crew had been that weasel Mako, a relatively new recruit she had had doubts about hiring – her intuition warning her he was unreliable and, she suspected, a coward as well – but she had been desperately short of crew and felt at the time, she had little choice but to take him on.

It was a decision she now bitterly regretted as not only had he managed to turn two other crew members against her, but also, he had escaped with her most valued possession. Now they would be three men down as the other two would suffer the same fate as their former ringleader and walk the plank into oblivion.

She glanced over to where her second in command, Cobb Milburn, was leaning against the ship's rail, nonchalantly twirling one of his knives between his fingers with a careless ease that gave a lie to the amount of skill required. Huia knew his disinterest was feigned. It was a front in the same way her serenity masked her anger, and Cobb was intensely aware of every shift and nuance in the aether, ready to unleash his lightning reflexes at any moment.

She had left Cobb in charge of extracting information from Mako, and her men were going about it with an enthusiasm that told her how deeply they too felt the betrayal by their crew mates.

Mako's front was saturated with blood where the blows had caused his ridiculous teeth to cut his mouth to shreds. Huia sneered inwardly; he thought they made him look dangerous, and she had heard him boasting that he had once ripped a man's throat out with them, something she doubted given the nature of the man.

Huia lifted a hand, and Cobb immediately stepped forward and halted the punishment. Coolly, he pressed the tip of his knife to Mako's throat and began his questioning. Huia folded her arms across her chest and listened as Mako tried to blame his companions before the insistent pressure of Cobb's knife persuaded him he wasn't believed.

With a cunning gleam in his eyes, Mako attempted to bargain for his life, whining and carrying on as if he had a leg to stand on. Huia had had enough and called a halt, ordering the other two to be brought up on deck. It wasn't long before they were kneeling in chains before her.

'Where's the captain's taonga?' demanded Cobb.

Without hesitation, the men began to stammer out their confession. 'Mako said Silas hired him to steal the taonga and that she was finished once Silas had it. He said if we wanted to live, we should throw in our lot with him.'

Huia drew in a sharp breath as a chill ran through her, and Cobb shot her a meaningful glance. It was much worse than she had thought. Silas obviously meant to wage war on her, and he had arranged for the theft of her taonga, knowing its significance. He thought to unnerve her and make her crew believe she could be defeated by its theft.

Silas Elmstone was a notorious crime lord. Sneaky and treacherous, he had spread his tentacles out over this side of the Waihou River from his fortress, deep in the swampy wetlands. Huia hadn't believed him to be much more than a nuisance until now, but the theft of her taonga meant he was growing stronger and bolder and becoming more of a threat than bargained for. But Huia wasn't known as the Queen of the Skies for nothing. If Silas was after war, war would be what he would get.

The fact that Silas had planted a spy on her ship told her he meant business, and from now on, she was going to have to watch her back. For now, she would enact her revenge on Silas by taking it out on Mako's hide – literally. He would walk the plank – but not before he had suffered for his treachery.

'Where is it now?' she asked, hoping it hadn't already been delivered to Silas.

The two men shook their heads; they didn't know. Not wanting to appear worried in front of her crew, she gave orders for Mako's punishment. The three thieves would walk the plank tomorrow, but she intended for Mako to suffer first.

Going back to her cabin, she sat behind her desk and looked around, trying not to let the men's revelations rattle her. Her cabin was more of a stateroom, luxuriously appointed as befitting a pirate captain of her standing, but the comfort she normally gained from the visual evidence of her success and prosperity was absent. The truth was she was disturbed by Silas's plans to topple her from her throne. He obviously had ambitions to extend his kingdom across the river and felt she stood in his way.

A knock on the door announced the arrival of Cobb, who only paused briefly before entering. He was holding the traveller's satchel.

'We need to decide what to do about the traveller,' he said as he closed the door behind him.

'Press-gang him,' suggested Huia. 'We're three men down.'

Cobb handed the satchel to Huia, who took it and tipped out the contents onto her desk. Gazing at the jumble of items on her desk, Huia spread them out with her hand. Amongst them lay a beautifully carved pounamu pendant in the form of a manaia, its cord cut. Picking up her taonga, she looked at Cobb, who was staring back at her intently.

'Well, well, well,' she said, her voice hardening. 'Perhaps it's time we had a word with our traveller.'

CHAPTER 8

Kev had watched as the men in the opposite cell had been taken away. When they returned, they had been subdued and nervous but not looking any the worse for wear. As the two men had settled back into their cell, bloodcurdling screams from the deck above had set Kev's teeth on edge. The other prisoners reacted by huddling down even lower as if in an attempt to make themselves less visible. Kev wondered if they were expecting to suffer the same fate as their former companion, and anxious thoughts about his own safety began to chase themselves through his mind.

No one had thought to feed them, and Kev's stomach was growling and gurgling in a disconcerting manner, but it was his thirst that was causing him the most discomfort. He had never been so thirsty in all his life, and he was desperate to alleviate it.

Two men appeared in front of his cell and unlocked the door. He was disappointed to see that neither of them held any form of sustenance. The men grabbed him roughly and hauled him out of his cell, and Kev was aware his status of prisoner had not changed. Hoping he wasn't being led off to suffer a similar fate to Shark Teeth, he could do nothing other than go along with his captors and hope for the best, his insides twisting with an uneasy sense of trepidation.

One of his guards opened a door to a cabin, and Kev stepped through into a large, spacious stateroom. Huia stood behind a large desk, and the man with the knives was standing by the window, leaning against the frame with his arms folded. On the desk lay his satchel, with all the contents spread out over the surface. Kev stood in front of the desk as Huia nodded to his guards, and they turned and left, closing the door behind them.

Huia said nothing for some time, only regarding him in a thoughtful fashion. Kev was beginning to feel restless under her scrutiny when eventually, with a small gesture to the items on the desk, she asked, 'These are your possessions, traveller?'

Kev nodded and stepped closer, wondering if anything was missing. 'Yeah,' he answered, looking down. 'All except that.' He pointed to where a greenstone pendant lay amongst all the other paraphernalia on the desk. 'I've never seen that before. I don't know how it got in my bag.'

Huia exchanged glances with the man by the window. 'Why should I believe you?' she queried. 'How did you know Mako?'

Kev was feeling confused. 'I don't know anyone by that name,' he insisted. 'I was making my way to Grahamstown when I came across those guys in the bush. I was silly enough to think I could share their fire for the night.'

Kev wasn't sure what exactly he was being accused of, but the fact that both Huia and her companion seemed to think he had somehow done something to them was making him nervous. Desperately, he tried to explain he was innocent of any wrongdoing against them.

'Look, I don't know what's going on, but those blokes knocked me out and tied me up. You saw that for yourself.'

Huia shrugged. 'For all I know, you had a falling out. But I'm inclined to believe you,' she said while picking up the photograph of the *Elizabeth Anne*'s crew, 'if you can explain to me how you know Millicent Darlington.'

Bewildered by this twist in the conversation, it took Kev a moment to adjust his thinking. Stammering a little, he filled Huia in on his adventures, starting with his abduction by the time slavers.

Huia nodded once he had finished. 'You're lucky, traveller,' she told Kev, 'that you have this in your possession. Otherwise, I might not be so inclined to believe your story.'

'How do you know Millicent?' Kev asked, feeling a little relieved the conversation appeared to be taking a more positive turn.

Huia looked at the photo for some time before answering. 'I have known Millicent for many years. We aren't exactly friends, but we understand each other. I respect her as a wahine toa, a strong woman. I had thought to press-gang you into my crew, but I will release you and help you get to Grahamstown for her sake.'

Kev was overwhelmed with relief not only by Huia's offer to help him get to Grahamstown but also by the fact that the conversation was taking an altogether friendlier turn.

'You will dine with me and Cobb tonight,' Huia informed him, 'and tomorrow we will take you as close as we dare to Grahamstown.' Huia gathered up Kev's scattered belongings and returned them to the satchel except for the pounamu pendant and the bag of gold. 'The gold is forfeit to me,' she explained, tossing it to the man by the window. 'The rest of these things, I have no use for.'

Kev didn't mind about the gold too much, figuring things could have worked out much worse, and he was grateful the items of sentimental value were being returned to him.

'Cobb will show you to a cabin where you can freshen up before dinner. He will come and fetch you when it's time to eat.'

Kev nodded, and while not feeling entirely at ease, he at least felt his adventures were beginning to take a happier turn.

Cobb indicated for Kev to follow him with a nod. As the cabin door closed behind them, Kev got a glimpse of Huia sitting at her desk, a meditative look on her face as she turned the pounamu pendant over and over in her hands. Cobb led Kev to a small but adequate cabin. It was sparsely furnished, but Kev was overjoyed to spy a pitcher of clean water on a stand in the corner.

Once Cobb had left him to his ablutions, he quickly sculled a large portion of the water in the jug, relieved to be able to slake his thirst. Although he had spent the better part of his time back in this world struggling through a watery landscape, he had been too mistrustful to risk drinking any of it.

Reluctantly leaving enough to wash his face and hands, he smoothed his hair with his damp hands and vainly tried to clean off the mud that clung to his boots and gaiters. Giving up on that as a bad job, he perched on the edge of the narrow bunk bed and waited for someone to come and fetch him for dinner, beginning to feel his adventures were taking a more positive turn.

CHAPTER 9

The next morning, Kev breakfasted with Huia and Cobb before following them on deck, where they found Huia's entire crew assembled. The men stood in rows, silent and sombre, a mood of heavy anticipation filling the air. Kev found it eerie and unsettling, and the back of his neck prickled uneasily.

Huia walked over to a box set before her men and stood on it, while Cobb went and stood before her, slightly to her right. Kev wasn't sure where he should stand, and as it seemed as though everyone had forgotten his presence, he settled for standing a little behind Huia, hoping he would be out of the way.

He had no idea what was going on, but he had decided it was not going to be anything good when his captors of the previous night were brought up on deck and dragged in front of Huia. Steam Fist and Gas Man were unscathed but obviously frightened. Mako, however, was unrecognisable. His face was swollen and purple from his beating and his mouth badly cut up. Dried blackened blood covered his face and clothing, and he could barely walk. When his guards let go of him, he collapsed to the deck, and Kev caught sight of his back, where his shirt was sticking to the dried blood. He had been flogged – almost to an inch of his life, from the looks of it.

Kev had no idea what he had done to deserve this punishment, but it made him grateful to be on the right side of Huia. Huia raised her hand, in which she held a black handkerchief, and at a nod from

Cobb, two men stepped forward and began to manoeuvre a long plank of wood over the rail of the airship and lash it tight.

Kev felt his neck prickle again as he realised what was happening. Huia was going to make the prisoners walk the plank. He had no idea how high up they were, but he knew no one could survive a fall from such a height. Mako was almost beyond noticing or caring, but his two companions were well aware of what was in store for them.

Huia let her hand fall, and the first man was led to the plank. As he was hoisted up onto it, his knees buckled, and he was unable to stand. Not only that, but also, a dark stain spread between his legs, and Kev realised he had pissed himself in terror. No one laughed or so much as sniggered, and his guards prodded him along the plank on his hands and knees until he reached the end.

The plank was bouncing up and down under his weight by then, and even though he gripped onto it with desperate fingers, the guards had only to press down on it from their end, and the momentum toppled him off the side. Kev could see his fingers, white from the effort of gripping on for a few seconds, before he lost his grip and fell.

The second man was made of sterner stuff, and although he was white and tense, he climbed up onto the plank without assistance when his turn came and shuffled his way to the end. Kev could see him taking several deep breaths before he stepped off the edge and disappeared from sight.

Kev was feeling shaky by this time, and his knees had a strange jelly-like feel in them as though his legs would collapse under him like a demolished tower block. Even though the prisoners had been intent on killing him and he was certain they would have shown him no mercy, he was not enjoying this at all.

The entire process had been carried out in complete silence, which only added to the intensity, and Kev knew it was going to haunt him for a long time to come.

Now it was the turn of Mako. He had to be dragged bodily to the plank. When he realised where he was, he began to whimper and struggle feebly, all to no avail as his guards merely hoisted him up onto the plank and prodded him along. He didn't even make it to the end before he lost his grip and slipped over the edge, too weak to even attempt to hold on.

Once he had disappeared from sight, the plank was hauled back in, and at a nod from Cobb, the crew dispersed. Kev was left standing on deck with only Huia and Cobb.

'It's a bad business, Cobb,' Huia said wearily.

Cobb nodded. 'Aye, Captain,' he replied. 'This is likely only the beginning.'

Kev had no idea what they were talking about, but he doubted they were having regrets about the execution of the prisoners and surmised there was more to this story than was first apparent. Not being an expert on pirate politics, he decided it was probably best not to get too involved.

'Full steam ahead, Mr Milburn,' Huia said. 'We sail for Grahamstown.'

⧗

Huia had taken her airship, the *Taniwha*, back across the Waihou River and sailed up close to the ranges, eventually taking refuge in one of the deep valleys between the mountains.

'This is as close to Grahamstown as I will sail,' Huia informed Kev. Turning to Cobb, she ordered, 'Ready Stormsong.'

Cobb went off to oversee the preparations of Huia's Pegasus, and Huia handed Kev a small bag. Weighing it in his hand, he realised it was his gold, much lightened. He nodded and slipped it into his satchel. He had no idea why Huia was returning some of his gold, but he guessed it had more to do with Millicent than it did with him.

He followed Huia over to where her huge mechanical horse stood. It was already snorting steam and pawing the deck. Effortlessly, Huia swung herself up onto its back and held out her hand to Kev. He could see small metal footholds on its side and so, grasping Huia's hand and boosting himself on one of them, swung up behind her.

Huia held on to the horse's neck by metal handgrips that helped her to control the horse, but Kev had no option but to wrap his arms around Huia's waist. The back of the horse was slippery, and Kev marvelled at the ease with which Huia sat. He felt as though he was in danger of sliding off at any moment, so he held on as tight as he dared and closed his eyes.

He heard the beating of the horse's mighty wings and felt it lift off the deck. The Pegasus banked and swooped off in the direction of Grahamstown. Eventually, Kev found the courage to open his eyes and look down. The momentum was surprisingly smooth, and once he got used to it, Kev found he could hold on quite well, steadying himself by using the footholds. It was an exhilarating experience, riding through the air on the back of a mechanical horse, and Kev was really beginning to enjoy the trip when Huia turned the horse towards the ranges and began the descent to the ground.

'This is as far as it is safe for me to go,' she told Kev as she steadied him for his descent.

He swung himself to the ground and took Huia's outstretched hand in his. She held on for a moment and fixed him with a stare.

'When you see Millicent,' she said, 'tell her the debt is paid. We're even.'

Before Kev could question her further, she let go of his hand. Her horse began pawing the ground, its wings unfurling once more, taking her skywards.

Kev stood and watched her disappearing into the distance before turning and heading on his way. Huia had set him down close to a meandering cart track, and Kev followed it. The winter's sun was weak, but even so, he was getting warm and decided to stop and rest for a while. He removed his coat and sat on it to stop the damp from seeping into the seat of his pants and allowed the peace and warmth to melt away the residual feelings from the execution.

He must have dozed off because the next thing he was aware of was the sound of music and a sweet high soprano floating to him over the air. The sound of the singing was coming from behind him along the road he had already travelled, and he wondered if he should hide off the road, his experiences in the kahikatea forest still fresh in his mind. Deciding that anyone who could sing so sweetly was unlikely to be dangerous to his safety, he merely stood up and donned his coat once more. He stood and waited for the singer to make it around the bend in the road.

The music and singing gradually got louder, and eventually, Kev could see a woman approaching. She was riding astride the back of a shaggy Highland cow, one leg hooked casually over the beast's neck and swaying effortlessly with the its movements. She was accompanying herself with some kind of clockwork instrument. It resembled an accordion, but the clockwork mechanism operated the bellows and played the notes, much like a music box.

Following docilely behind were two more Highland cows, their backs and wide horns bearing all kinds of items that clinked and tinged together musically as they swayed along. Seeing Kev, the woman tapped her cow on the neck with her foot, and it slowed to a halt beside him. The other two ambled to a stop behind.

Kev couldn't tell from looking at her how old she was. Her hair was grey and tied up on top of her head, wispy strands escaping in every direction, but her face was smooth and unblemished. Twinkling blue eyes regarded him with amusement. She was dressed in a hodgepodge of different garments, none of them seeming to relate to one another in any respect. Some of them were held together with lengths of twine and strips of cloth.

'Hail, traveller,' she greeted him. 'Nellie Sprocket at your service.'

Kev introduced himself and accepted her offer to walk alongside her to Grahamstown.

'You'll have to walk,' she informed him. 'You're too big a fellow for my girls.' She went on to introduce him to her cows. 'This is Flora,' she said, indicating the one she sat astride, 'and this is Pansy and Milkweed.'

Kev said hello to the cows with a rub on their noses. Then with a nudge to Flora's side, the little herd moved off, Kev easily keeping pace with the cows' plodding gait.

After his experiences with Mako and his gang and Huia's double-edged hospitality, Kev found Nellie and her cows' gentle company a balm to his agitated spirits. They soothed him and restored his faith in the goodness of his fellow man. He listened as Nellie continued to sing, filling him with tranquillity and a strange euphoric optimism.

That night, surrounded by the warm, sweet bulk of Nellie's cows, Kev drifted off to sleep, listening to the haunting call of the ruru from the bush, feeling the most hopeful since his arrival.

The next morning, Kev awoke against Pansy's shaggy, comforting side and stuck his head out from under the blanket Nellie had given him. The ground and his blanket were covered in dew, but the cows had kept him warm. Nellie was already up, and as Kev stood up and stretched, she roused her cows and sent them off to graze.

After they had eaten and reloaded the cows with Nellie's paraphernalia, they set off once more. Nellie appeared disinclined to sing today, and instead, they fell to talking.

'I'm a tinker, I suppose,' Nellie told Kev when he asked her what she was doing on the road, 'a travelling clockmaker, to be precise. Anything that uses cogs and gears, I can make or mend. I earn enough for me and my girls, and I can move on when the whim takes me. What about you, traveller? What brings you on this road? It's not usual to see a time traveller in these parts – and certainly not on foot.'

Kev quickly filled her in on the details of his story. Nellie was very intrigued and questioned him avidly about his old world. She became sentimental and misty-eyed on learning about Persephone and told him to invite her to the wedding.

'Leave a message for me at the Clockwork Owl,' she told Kev. 'I always stop in there on my travels, and that's how most people get word to me.'

Nellie proved to be an entertaining companion, and the time passed pleasantly, filled with stories and Nellie's songs. They stopped for lunch and to allow the cows to graze. The winter sun was warm in the sheltered spot they had chosen to rest in, and as the cows sat contentedly, chewing their cud, Kev found himself dozing off.

When he awoke, he lay there not quite knowing where he was for a moment or two. As his awareness of his surroundings returned, his memory rushed back, and he felt a momentary dislocation of time and place. Shaking his head, he looked up and noticed Nellie some distance off, talking to a shadowy figure in the bush on the side of the road. Kev didn't move but lay watching as Nellie concluded the conversation and accepted a small package from the other person, which she slipped inside her clothing before returning to their campsite.

She sat down next to Kev without speaking. She appeared to be in an introspective mood, and Kev thought she looked troubled, but he didn't know how to broach the subject of the mysterious visitor, feeling he wasn't supposed to know about that, so he remained silent, and the rest of the journey was spent in not-so-comfortable silence.

As they neared Grahamstown, Kev could feel the excitement begin to build within him. He had been gone for over a year, and it had become almost a mythical place in his mind. But now he was able to see the airships in port and spot the odd roof through the trees.

They ambled across a wooden bridge spanning the Kauaeranga River and made their way into town. Nellie halted her cows and held out her hand to Kev, her eyes twinkling with her restored good nature, the gloominess of the last miles forgotten.

Kev shook her hand warmly, feeling he had made a friend, and wished her well on her travels. Nellie laughed a tinkling laugh as musical as her singing voice and reminded him to invite her to the wedding before nudging Flora gently and moving off.

CHAPTER 10

Kev stood and absorbed the atmosphere of Grahamstown. He did indeed feel as though he had returned home, and he spent a few pleasurable minutes looking out for all the landmarks he remembered. He wondered if he would be lucky enough to find the *Elizabeth Anne* in port or if he would have to wait for her to return from one of her trips.

Feeling strangely apprehensive now that he was here, he decided nothing could be achieved by waiting and set off for the port. As he approached, he scanned the airships in dock, hoping to see the familiar shape of the *Elizabeth Anne*. She wasn't a large ship, and he knew some of the bigger vessels could be masking her presence.

He had walked the entire length of the dock before he spotted the *Elizabeth Anne*, tethered in the last available berth. His heart began pounding in his chest, and the excitement created a weird buzzing in his ears as though he would pass out at any moment.

Joyfully, he raced to the lifting platform and, after operating the controls to raise it, stood bouncing on his heels with impatience until it reached the top. He hadn't realised until this moment how uncertain he had felt on his journey of ever reaching Grahamstown and Persephone; now he had the feeling of a lost traveller seeing the welcoming lights of home, and he stepped aboard, filled with happy anticipation.

There was no one on deck, and Kev felt ridiculously disappointed. Even though he wasn't expected and none of the crew would have any idea he was coming back to them, he had entertained visions of joyful reunions as he came aboard like a conquering hero.

Smiling at himself, he decided to head for the galley, knowing if anyone was at home, that was where they would most likely gather. As he approached, he could hear voices, and he pushed open the door, expecting cries of delight and surprise.

Mina Myra McGill and Rosalind Porter were sitting at the galley table, books and slates in front of them. Mina Myra was talking, and Rosalind was listening with a glazed look in her eyes as though the conversation had been very one-sided and had been going on for a very long time.

As Kev burst in, Mina Myra glanced up at him. 'Oh, hi, Kev,' she said, barely pausing to take a breath. 'You're back.'

This felt a trifle anti-climactic to Kev, who had envisioned a much more rapturous response.

If he was disappointed in Mina Myra's welcome, Rosalind's was everything he could have hoped for. Leaping up from the table, she launched herself at Kev and nearly toppled them both to the floor.

Kev laughed, and Rosalind was giggling too in an almost hysterical manner. She clung on to him, with her arms so tight around his neck, he began to see spots before his eyes.

Prising her arms from around his throat with difficulty, Kev managed to calm her by saying, 'It's OK, Sprat. I'm not leaving again. I'm here to stay.'

Setting her down, Kev got a good look at her for the first time. She had changed, grown. In his mind, the only image Kev had was of the little girl she had been a year ago. She was much taller, of course, and her hair had grown. It hung down her back in ringlets and was pulled back off her face with a big blue bow. But there was more to it than a change in physical appearance. She seemed more settled. There was an air of confidence and assertiveness in the way she held herself, and Kev had a feeling she would grow into a force to be reckoned with.

If Kev was surprised at the changes he observed in Rosalind, then he was flabbergasted in those he saw in Mina Myra. Gone was the tangle of bird's-nest hair she had always favoured when he had known her before, and instead, her hair was smoothly brushed and tied back in a sleek French braid. Her clothing too was no longer the mismatch of garments she used to wear, although Kev could see the beginnings of a distinctive flair. She had on a rather splendid red tailcoat decorated with enormous brass buttons and gold braiding over tight-fitting black trousers and beautifully soft leather boots.

'You look very smart,' Kev told her.

Mina Myra smoothed down the lapel of her coat smugly. 'Thank you, Kev,' she replied serenely. 'I have enough money to buy my own clothes now – from a real shop. It's important to dress properly, you know, especially when you're famous.'

Kev agreed and sat down at the table across from Mina Myra, with Rosalind pressing herself firmly into his side. He reached out and picked up one of the books on the table. 'School lessons, eh?' he asked, flicking through the pages.

Mina Myra huffed and looked woefully at him. 'Yes,' she sighed. 'Millicent said we had to start doing them. Lenore teaches us. It's not fair. Orson said he knows enough to be able to fly an airship, and Sherlock just refuses. They're too big for Millicent to make them,' she continued with knowing world weariness, 'but me and Rosalind *have* to do them.' She sighed again at the injustices of life.

'Where is everyone?' asked Kev.

'Well, Lenore's gone to fetch more nibs because the last one broke,' explained Mina Myra, holding up her pen for him to see. 'Lenore says I'm old enough to start to write using a pen,' she continued with smug superiority. 'Ros still has to practice on the slate, but I get to use paper.' So saying, she lifted her page, covered with shaky cursive script and liberal blots, to show him. Mina Myra allowed him a few moments to admire her work before continuing, 'And everyone else has gone to the church.'

'To the church?' queried Kev. 'Why?'

'For the wedding, of course, silly. It needs to be made beautiful for the wedding tomorrow. We're all allowed to go because we're all just like family, and I have a new dress especially for it.'

Kev began to get a bad feeling. Just who was getting married? Was it Persephone? Was he too late? Had she forgotten him already? It was difficult to interrupt the flow of Mina Myra's conversation once she got going, but he was trying vainly to do so when Lenore walked in.

Kev was so upset by the thought that he might have missed his chance with Persephone, he forgot that Lenore wasn't expecting to see him sitting at the galley table. He missed her stunned expression and intake of breath and sprang up to grab her by the arms.

'Where's Persephone, Lenore?' he demanded.

Lenore opened and shut her mouth a few times like a stranded goldfish. 'At the church, of course, Kev,' she managed to squeak out.

Kev sat heavily in his chair and buried his face in his hands. 'Who's she marrying?' he mumbled through his fingers.

Lenore sat down at the table, her hand on her chest, still shocked at seeing Kev but beginning to see where his mind was leading him. She took a steadying breath and put Kev out of his misery. 'No one, Kev,' she told him. 'It's not Persephone getting married. It's Edgar.'

Kev sat up. 'Edgar?' he queried in disbelief. 'Edgar's getting married? That was unexpected.'

Lenore managed a smile. 'Yes, it's taken us all by surprise, not least of all Edgar himself. He's marrying Morag. He'll be leaving the *Elizabeth Anne* and going to help Rabbie in the mine.'

Kev nodded and rubbed his hands over his face. He was feeling a little light-headed from the relief. He looked up to find Lenore looking at him, her face still showing the shock of finding him sitting in the galley.

'Hello, Lenore,' he said with a grin. 'I've come home.'

Jonas Enoch Emerson put down the load he was carrying in the vestry of the church. Millicent had definite ideas about how this wedding was going to go, and all of them seemed to involve heavy lifting. He adjusted his signature dark glasses, which had slipped slightly while lugging the boxes. He glanced through the door to where Persephone, Morag, and Lady Elspeth were busy arranging the flowers.

He thought briefly about going in and trying to speak to Elspeth, but the set of her face persuaded him not to bother. He sighed. She had been out of sorts for weeks ever since the wedding plans had really taken off.

They had been together for over a year, and now Edgar and Morag were going to beat them to the altar. Jonas couldn't blame her for being upset with him. She had tried on several occasions to steer the conversation towards their future, but he had steadfastly refused to be drawn. It wasn't that he didn't like the idea of marrying her, but he didn't feel it was fair to marry her while he was a secret assassin for the Ministry of Dark Affairs. It didn't seem right to marry her with such a large secret between them.

Not only that, but also, he knew there was every chance of leaving her a widow should one of his missions go awry – not that he was accepting many these days, not since meeting Lady Elspeth, but neither could he resign. Once an assassin, always an assassin.

He felt caught between what he wanted for his future and the decision he had made so many years ago when he had been too young to fully understand the consequences. At this point, he couldn't see a way out of his dilemma and could only watch as Lady Elspeth became more upset by the day, helpless to make the step she was expecting.

Phineas came in behind him with another load and put it down next to Jonas's. As he straightened up, he froze and appeared to be watching his own thoughts. Jonas knew that look; it meant something was disturbing the aether and Phineas was about to follow the clues.

'We need to go back to the ship,' he said.

There was no need to explain further, and Jonas followed him out of the church without question.

Stepping aboard from the lifting platform, they found Lenore pacing about the deck as if she had been waiting for them.

'Thank God you're back,' she said fervently.

Phineas reached out a comforting arm. 'What's up, Lenore?' he asked, shooting a worried frown at Jonas, who instinctively placed his hand on his holster.

'You'll never guess,' continued Lenore, 'but Kev's come back. He's here in the galley.'

Phineas and Jonas exchanged stunned glances.

'Really?' queried Phineas. 'Not quite what I was expecting, to be honest.'

Lenore nodded. 'Yes, really. I was so shocked. I mean, it's great but so unexpected. The thing is I think someone should go and warn Persephone – you know, prepare her. My heart nearly stopped when I saw him sitting there as large as life.'

Phineas nodded. 'You may be right, Lenore. I'll go and tell Millicent, and she can break the news gently.'

Lenore visibly relaxed. 'Thanks, Phineas. I'd feel so much better about it if she's a little bit prepared for Kev being back.'

Dr Persephone Mockett tied the last of the ribbons to the end of the last pew and then turned around to look at the decorations. The church looked very pretty. In spite of the lack of flowers available in winter, they had managed to create a festive and celebratory atmosphere, and Persephone felt sure Millicent would approve.

Absently, she raised her hand to her throat where the small gold disc with Kev's time coordinates rested and touched it gently. Just this morning, she had removed the gold ring Kev had given her before leaving to return to his own world. She had been reluctant to do so, but Morag had reminded her she needed to put the past behind her.

'I felt as ye do when ma Jamie died,' she had said. 'I thought ma heart should break, and I never thought to love again, but here I am, in love wi' a wonderful man and a bride agin.'

She had developed a very close friendship with Morag and her brother, Rabbie, since coming back into their lives to ask Rabbie to help the crew of the *Elizabeth Anne* cash in the pirate treasure they had salvaged to fund the scheme to get Kev home to his own world.

She knew Morag only had her best interests at heart, and so she had put the little ring away in her handkerchief box, but she was unable to bring herself to remove the gold disc. It was still a comfort to be able to feel a connection with him through it. She could touch it and think of him somewhere out there in the fabric of time.

She wondered if Morag was right or if the fact that Kev was still alive and well made it harder for her to accept that he wouldn't be coming back to her. As hard as it had been for Morag to lose her husband in a mining accident, it was very final. Persephone felt that under those circumstances, one could only move on as best as one could. There were times when Persephone felt Kev was only gone for a short time, and no matter how hard she tried, she couldn't shake the feeling that one day he would return.

Lately, the feeling had been even stronger, and nothing she did seemed to shake it. She lay awake each night yearning and praying for something her mind told her was impossible, but the small, secret part of her told her to keep hoping for.

Turning around, she noticed Phineas and Millicent engaged in what appeared to be a very intense conversation. Millicent turned her head and looked at her, and something in Persephone broke open, and she knew – she just knew – what they were discussing. She watched calmly as Millicent walked down the aisle towards her, a strange look on her face.

As Millicent took her hand and told her to sit down, Persephone smiled at her and said, 'It's Kev, isn't it? He's come back.'

The noise in the galley had not abated from the moment everyone had rushed back from the church on hearing the news of Kev's return. Pot after pot of tea had been consumed and Kev's story listened to and news shared. Kev had finally received the welcome he had been imagining and was gratified at how enthusiastically he had been welcomed back by the entire crew.

Orson and Sherlock had grown in the year of his absence, especially Orson, who was showing the signs of the young man he was growing into. Kev teased him about the dark hair sprouting on his top lip. Orson had only laughed along, not quite able to hide his pride in his burgeoning manhood.

Sherlock too was taller and his hair even longer so that now he had to wear it tied back to keep it out of the way. Still a few years away from adolescence, he retained the fine features of boyhood and looked to Kev like an elven prince.

Although, unlike the children, the adults of the *Elizabeth Anne* hadn't changed much in appearance, Kev was aware that all of them were different in small but significant ways. The most noticeable were Jonas and Lady Elspeth. It was clear to Kev, who wasn't always the quickest to pick up on such things, that something was wrong between them. The closeness he had witnessed between them when he had been with them before was strained, and he felt as though they were making an effort to keep things as they had been, but it wasn't working. He felt sad for them and hoped he and Persephone wouldn't fall into the same state.

Edgar was delightfully bemused at his own happiness, and Kev felt he was still a little stunned at the turn his life had taken. He had filled Kev in on the wonders of falling in love with Morag and her children, telling Kev he believed himself to be the luckiest man on earth, and although he felt a little sad to be leaving the *Elizabeth Anne*, he was looking forward to going to work with Rabbie in the mine as the two men had developed a good friendship.

Lenore was now a published author of gothic thrillers and was working on her second novel. Her first book had proven very successful, and she had become something of a minor celebrity. She told Kev all this modestly, almost shy about her own success, but Kev could tell she was thrilled and very proud of her achievements.

Although both Millicent and Phineas had appeared to Kev at first to be just as he had known them before, he soon began to notice they seemed to be distracted, as though there were things weighing heavy on their minds. They joined in the festivities and had welcomed him wholeheartedly, but it was as if they were both listening out for something. There was a slight edginess to them that hadn't been there when he had left.

Persephone, Kev was surprised to discover, was the only person he was having trouble figuring out. She was pleased to see him, obviously, but he felt as though somehow he wasn't really reaching her. She had smiled serenely and let him kiss her, but it had felt to Kev as though he was meeting a replica and not the real Persephone he had known and dreamed about all these months. Even when he had presented her with the music box, so lovingly bought and transported through time, she had merely expressed mild interest and set it aside without winding it or asking him any questions. He had imagined they would share a little joke about him bringing something so old back from the future and felt hurt by her reaction.

He was uncertain of how to proceed. He was feeling a little unsure of himself and beginning to wonder if she still loved him or if she had experienced the same fading of emotion as Walter with Lady Elspeth and now viewed him more with fondness than passion. He felt disappointed and apprehensive and wanted to take her away somewhere quiet so they could have a good talk, but as that wasn't possible just yet, he tried to put it out of his mind and enjoy the reunion with the rest of the crew.

Of course, the crew wanted to know how Kev had managed to get back, and Kev told them about bumping into Walter in his own world, which had shocked and surprised everyone, especially Lady Elspeth, who had questioned him avidly about Walter and how he was. Kev filled her in on Walter's success and how he had built a time machine and managed to send him back to them all.

Lady Elspeth became a little misty-eyed and sighed over Walter, to Jonas's obvious discomfort. Kev had passed on the letters Walter had written to her and Professor Popkiss, and she had slipped them into her pocket with a tearful sniff and another deep sigh.

Once every detail of Kev's return journey had been fully dissected and discussed, everyone settled and began to disperse to go about their various tasks until only Millicent and Phineas remained at the galley table with Kev and Persephone.

'So you're really back for good then, Kev?' Millicent queried.

Kev nodded and took hold of Persephone's hand under the table. 'Yeah, I'm back for good. I hope you'll have a place for me aboard the *Elizabeth Anne.*'

Millicent glanced at Phineas. 'Well, we will be one crew member short after tomorrow,' she replied. 'Being a full-time part of the crew is a little different to childminding though, Kev. Your duties would be much different this time around.'

Kev nodded. 'I gathered they would be, but I'm sure I can learn. Will you give me a chance to prove myself?'

Millicent shook her head. 'You don't need to prove yourself, Kev,' she told him. 'You've more than done that already. It's more that you'll need different skills if you're really going to be able to pull your weight. We're adventurers, Kev. That means that even though we stay mostly within the law, there are times when we don't. Mainly a bit of smuggling here and there, nothing too extreme. There may be times when you'll have to fight if the need arises. Do you think you can do that?'

Kev nodded. 'Yeah. Since bumping into Huia and her lot, I figured this world is a bit more dangerous than I reckoned on. I can shoot a bit, but I've never had to fight anyone in my life before.'

Phineas and Millicent exchanged glances again.

'We can help you get your fighting skills up to scratch,' Phineas said. 'Jonas trains the girls every afternoon. He'll be willing to include you as well, I'm sure.'

'Sweet,' declared Kev. 'After my run-in with those blokes in the bush, I want to be sure I can take care of myself.'

Millicent nodded. 'Good, Kev. If you're happy to train and defend this ship if needed, then you'll be a big help. You're welcome aboard always, for your own sake and Persephone's, but it's good to have you as a crew member.'

So saying, she reached out her hand and shook Kev's heartily. Phineas too extended his hand, and the two men shook hands warmly, Phineas slapping Kev on the shoulder.

'Good to have you aboard,' he said.

Kev grinned. 'Thanks. It's great to be back,' he told them as they refreshed their teacups once again. Kev turned to Millicent. 'How did you meet Huia?' he asked her. 'I've been wondering about it ever since she mentioned she knew you.'

Millicent didn't reply at once, but when she did, her voice was sober. 'Huia and I have a bit of history, I guess. We had a difference of opinion over a cargo we both wanted many years ago. She's a fierce warrior and not a woman to back down easily. We managed to sort it out in a way but only because I can be just as stubborn as she is if the need arises. I wouldn't back down either.' Millicent gave a little laugh. 'We fought it out, and even though I lost the cargo to Huia, I earned her respect by being willing to take her on.'

'There's no one as fierce as Millie when she thinks she's been unjustly treated,' interjected Phineas fondly.

Kev was touched by the evident pride in Phineas's voice as he raised Millicent's hand to his lips and kissed it. Millicent turned and smiled at him, giving him a pat on the knee.

'Don't praise me up too much, Phin,' she warned. 'I may have been better off retreating discreetly in that instance.'

Phineas shook his head, not convinced.

'Mind you, we met you, Persephone, remember?' continued Millicent, caught up in her reminiscing and giving Persephone a fond look.

'As if I could forget,' answered Persephone. Turning to Kev, she explained, 'Phineas brought Millicent to me to get patched up afterwards.'

'She did such a good job, I offered her a job aboard then and there.'

'I was looking for a change,' said Persephone, taking up the story again, 'and the rest, as they say, is history. I've been aboard ever since.'

Kev nodded, enjoying hearing the memories. He suddenly remembered the message Huia had given to pass on to Millicent. 'When she let me go, she said to tell you the debt is paid and you're even.'

Millicent nodded, an unreadable expression crossing her face.

'What did she owe you?' asked Kev with interest.

Millicent smiled enigmatically and touched her left temple lightly, where the cogs that operated her eyescope were implanted. 'An eye, Kev,' she said. 'She owed me an eye.'

⧗

Kev and Persephone sat side by side in 'their' spot on the deck. It was where they had retreated to before Kev had left to return to his own world, and they needed respite from the rest of the crew, who, although trying not to make it obvious, had watched them closely in the way concerned friends often do. Kev and Persephone had both understood their worry and, in small ways, appreciated it, but there was no doubt that they had also found it oppressive, and it only added to the emotional turmoil they had found themselves in.

So it was natural for them to make their way there now, when so much remained unspoken between them. They sat close but not touching. Kev was feeling unsure of how to broach the subject of the distance he could sense between them. He wondered if maybe he was imagining it and it was all in his own mind as Persephone didn't appear unhappy, only detached. Tentatively, he took her hand in his and felt slightly encouraged when she not only allowed it but also gave his a tiny squeeze in return.

'Are you pleased to see me, Seph?' he queried.

Persephone turned her head and regarded him serenely. 'Of course I am, Kev. It's all I've dreamed of since you left.'

'It's just that you seem, I dunno, kind of remote, like I can't touch you . . . the real you.'

To his consternation, Persephone's eyes brimmed with tears, and although they didn't fall, her eyes glistened with them, and her voice trembled and caught as she replied.

'I know, Kev. I can feel it too. It's like being trapped in a bubble. I can see and hear everything, but it's as if there's an invisible barrier between me and the world. I don't know how to break out.'

Kev wrapped his arms around her and pulled her close. He sat stroking her hair soothingly while Persephone continued.

'It's the shock of actually seeing you, I'm sure,' she explained, her voice muffled from being pressed so close to Kev's side. 'Ever since you left, every day was a battle between the longing for you and living as though you had gone for good. Trying to tell myself to forget about you, to get on with my life and stop moping and wishing for something that wasn't going to happen, but underneath it all, there was this deep-seated belief you were coming back. It was like living with two minds. It was exhausting, and then when Millicent told me you had actually returned, it was as if my mind couldn't cope with the news, and it just shut down.'

Kev didn't reply. He was at a loss for words. He hadn't really understood until now how much Persephone had endured by letting him go. He had taken her bravery at face value and not noticed how much she was prepared to sacrifice her own happiness so he could leave her without feeling guilty.

'I'm so sorry, Seph,' he managed to whisper eventually. 'I'm so sorry. I'm back now, and I'll never leave you willingly again. I promise.'

Persephone wrapped her arms around Kev in return, and finally, the tears flowed, and with them, the strange inertia that had her trapped since Kev's return lost its grip over her mind. As she cried, she could finally feel the emotions of the months of Kev's absence unknot themselves and flow out along with the tears. All the grief, longing, and anger bubbled up and were washed away by the tears.

Kev continued to stroke her hair and soothe her with soft shushing sounds but didn't try to speak. Truthfully, he didn't know what to say and so, wisely, said nothing. It seemed to be the right thing to do as before long, Persephone ceased crying and sat up, rubbed her face, and sniffed heartily, appearing to be in a much better frame of mind. Relieved, Kev rubbed her back in a soothing fashion and waited for her to speak.

Persephone turned to face him. 'I'm sorry, Kev,' she explained. 'I think I might have been a little more overwrought than I thought I was.'

'That's OK, Seph,' Kev replied softly. 'I understand. I really do. It's been a hard time for both of us, but maybe now we can begin to look forward to our future, eh?'

Persephone nodded, and a soft smile crept across her face. 'Yes,' she replied almost shyly, 'we can. But we could let things rest for tonight. I'm so worn out from crying and the shock of having you come back, I think I need a good night's sleep to get back on an even keel.'

'Sure,' Kev told her, swallowing his disappointment manfully. 'We'll take as much time as you need. Now at least let me walk you back to your cabin.'

Persephone nodded, and Kev got to his feet, and taking hold of Persephone's hands, he pulled her to her feet. Hand in hand, they walked companionably towards Persephone's little cabin cum sickbay, the former feelings of closeness flowing back between them in the same way the tide swept up the mighty mouth of the Waihou River behind them.

CHAPTER 11

Lady Elspeth Lovelace sighed and closed the cabin door behind her. She leaned against it for a brief moment, closing her eyes and breathing out another deep sigh. She was thankful to be back aboard the *Elizabeth Anne* and the refuge of her cabin. At this moment, she craved solitude like a drowning man craves the air above.

She had felt completely overwhelmed by this day from the very first moment she had opened her eyes and realised she was going to have to put her best foot forward and appear to all about her as if she was enjoying Edgar and Morag's wedding wholeheartedly.

It wasn't that she wasn't pleased for them – because she was – and it wasn't as though she was jealous either. But no matter how she tried to ignore it, the fact that Jonas remained resolutely silent on their own future filled her with a melancholy longing she couldn't shake off.

It wasn't as if she cared overly much to be married, exactly. She was quite content to carry on as they were. It was more that Jonas refused to discuss the future at all. She was used to him not talking overly much; he had never been a big one for conversation, but he had always been honest with her. Now she sensed he was hiding something, and his avoidance of the topic of their future together filled her with unease. The whole topic had now taken on a significance out of all proportion in her mind, and she was unable to let the matter drop. It was putting a strain on their love for each other, she knew, but she felt powerless to let it go.

The wedding itself had been delightful; even she could appreciate that. Morag had been radiant, and Edgar had been overwhelmingly proud and so obviously besotted with his bride, it brought tears to the eyes of the guests gathered to witness their union. The church had looked beautiful and the guests joyous. It had been a simple yet moving ceremony, and the wedding party had moved on to one of the hotels to enjoy the wedding breakfast.

Lady Elspeth felt she had been composed throughout, and as she was, deep down, genuinely happy for Edgar and Morag, she had been able to wish them well. But eventually, she began to find the romantic atmosphere and the effort required to be happy a strain. She felt under siege by a love knot of misty-eyed, besotted couples, all reliving their own happiness vicariously through Edgar and Morag's wedding. Phineas and Millicent held hands throughout and sent each other little glances they thought went unnoticed, while Kev and Persephone were, naturally enough, completely absorbed in each other. So pleading a headache, she had come back to the *Elizabeth Anne* for some much-needed respite.

Sitting down at her dressing table, she picked up the letters Kev had given her from Walter. She would walk to the post office and forward Archie's on to him tomorrow. As yet, her own letter remained unopened as she had been waiting for the right time to read it. Now that she was all alone, she could feel the letter tugging at her, asking to be read.

It would probably be some time yet before the others returned from the wedding festivities, so slipping out of her wedding finery, she donned a simple day dress and, taking a shawl for warmth, headed out to the deck to find a sheltered spot to read Walter's letter.

The day was fine and still, but the winter air was crisp, so tucking herself into a sunny corner, she drew the letter out of her pocket and smoothed it down with her hand before eventually opening the envelope and drawing out a single sheet of paper.

Unfolding it, she began to read the brief missive written in Walter's familiar scrawling script. Even though she was well aware Walter had never been one for setting his thoughts or feelings down on paper, she couldn't help feeling a little disappointed he hadn't more to say to her after all this time.

> Dearest Elspeth,
>
> How very strange it was to find out we have a mutual friend who has linked us through time and space, and how influential we have both been in his story! I was happy to hear of you and Archie through Kev, whom I like immensely, by the way. You will know by now that I have helped him to return to our world, and you are probably wondering why I have not accompanied him. Well, dear girl, I am happy here in Kev's world. I am settled and wealthier than I probably deserve to be and very rarely feel homesick for my old life. I know we once had quite fond feelings for each other – more than that, dare I say it – and indeed, I do still remember you with a deep affection. I know from Kev that you have found yourself a good man to love you as you deserve, and I want you to know that I wish you all the best, my dear. Who knows if we would have stayed together had I not been so abruptly pulled from your life? But somehow I think maybe not. I hope you will continue to remember me with the fondness I feel when thinking of our days together.
>
> Walter
>
> P.S. Please forward Archie's letter on to him.

Lady Elspeth sat looking at Walter's letter, not really seeing it, and it was some time before she realised the words were getting blurry. Looking down, she discovered she was crying, and several tears had fallen on the letter, leaving soggy spots on the paper.

Giving a little cry of frustration, she scrubbed away the tears from her cheeks angrily, annoyed at herself for being all weepy. It really wasn't her style. She reflected that it was unusual for her not to have a ready solution to the impasse between her and Jonas, but she had no idea how to get him to open up and start talking about whatever was bothering him.

Discovering she really did have a headache now, she went back to her cabin to lie down. She tucked Walter's letter under her pillow and closed her eyes as a few errant tears slid out of the corner of her eyes and into her hair. Eventually, she did manage to fall asleep through sheer emotional exhaustion.

When Jonas came to check on her, she awoke feeling sticky and unrefreshed, the dry salty tracks of her tears still marking her face. Jonas was looking at her, concerned but with that closed look she was beginning to know so well. Lady Elspeth sighed and reached for his hand so he couldn't slip away and evade the topic yet again.

'Jonas, what's wrong?' she asked. 'This is not like you. I know you don't want to talk about marriage and all that entails, but I really need to know what's going on.'

Jonas looked at her miserably. 'I know, Elspeth. I understand. I really do. I'm not at liberty to discuss the reasons why I'm not free to marry you. I would if I could, but there are reasons why it's not an option right now. It's complicated.'

Lady Elspeth sighed. 'I'm tired of having this conversation, to be honest. This whole topic is changing me into someone I don't like. We can't go on like this.'

Jonas nodded. 'I know. I don't like who I am either, in more ways than one. I don't know what to say or do to help you feel better right now.'

Lady Elspeth thought for a while. 'As much as I'd like for us to get married, Jonas,' she explained, 'that's not what's really bothering me. I'm just not sure where I stand. Do you still love me? Do you see a future for us? What's going on in your head right now?'

Jonas held up a hand to stop her. 'I understand,' he said. 'If it's any help at all, I love you as much as I always have, and I want to have a future with you. I just need to work some things out. Trust me, please.'

Lady Elspeth sighed once more. 'I don't see I have much choice,' she remarked. 'Tell you what – let's get off the airship for a while, go for a walk, and get some fresh air.'

Jonas nodded. 'Good idea,' he replied.

Quickly, they readied themselves and, hand and hand, headed for the lifting platform.

They meandered along the shore front and allowed the healing balm of the winter's air and the gently lapping waves to soothe their ruffled emotions, so by the time the early dusk began to fall, they were able to make their way back to the *Elizabeth Anne* in much better spirits and more at peace with the world and each other. If they hadn't managed to settle the matter between them, exactly, they had at least managed to push it far enough away that it wasn't intruding into their lives in quite the same way.

CHAPTER 12

K ev sat and mopped his brow. In spite of the coolness of the air, he was feeling decidedly overheated. He had joined Mina Myra and Rosalind on deck for instruction on hand-to-hand combat with Jonas and was taking a much-needed breather.

Jonas took his coaching duties very seriously and worked the girls and Kev quite hard. This was a side of Jonas Kev had never seen before, and he was impressed with the elegance and skill he brought to the task. Kev watched as Jonas led the girls through a series of exercises designed to strengthen their muscles and increase their flexibility. Jonas correcting their moves, encouraging them to reach higher or lunge deeper.

Mina Myra was more interested in the performance than precision, each move accompanied by flamboyant gestures and flourishes. She had obviously been much influenced by the performers she had seen the previous day, when Kev and Persephone had taken her and Rosalind to see the circus that had set up on the edge of town. So much so that today she had dressed in a style reminiscent of her old wardrobe – in a stiff pink tutu and lacy top. She had wound a treasure trove of beads and paste jewellery around her arms and head and stuck a peacock feather in her hair.

Kev too had been impressed with the circus. Instead of real animals, it had had magnificent automaton beasts that had been so lifelike, Kev had found it hard to tell they weren't alive at first. The children had been captivated, and Mina Myra had been enthralled with the beautiful bareback riders and acrobats as they flung themselves through the air and turned somersaults on the backs of the moving automatons.

Rosalind too had enjoyed the circus, especially the clockwork elephant and lions, but she wasn't allowing that to distract her from the task in hand. Kev watched her as she followed Jonas's movements with a ferocious dedication and precision that Kev found a little unnerving in one so young. There was something about her that reminded him of Huia, and he wondered if one day she would be following a similar path.

Eventually, Jonas felt satisfied with the girls' progress and released them for the day and came to sit next to Kev. The men watched as the girls began to put their shoes back on, sitting side by side on the deck, their heads close together, whispering intently to each other, every now and then one of them looking around to check if anyone was listening.

Kev found this behaviour very suspicious and was just about to comment on it to Jonas when a cry of 'Ahoy the ship!' came up from below. Both men got up to lean over the rail to see who was trying to get the crew's attention.

Jonas obviously recognised the man standing below on the dock as he pulled the lever to send the lifting platform down to pick him up and told Mina Myra to go and find Millicent and Phineas.

The lifting platform shuddered to a stop, and the man stepped aboard. He was stocky and grey-haired, wearing a double-breasted waistcoat under a great coat with deep cuffs that concealed the numerous weapons he had armed himself with. The stranger gave Kev a piercing look, as though weighing him up. Kev felt as though he was being regarded with a certain amount of mistrust, so he refrained from introducing himself and listened with half an ear as Jonas and the visitor exchanged bland pleasantries.

As he stood, allowing the murmur of conversation to wash over him, he watched Rosalind as she waited for Mina Myra to come back. There was something distinctly furtive about the way she was looking about her, and Kev knew the two girls were up to something. He had decided it was probably a good idea to get to the bottom of it when Millicent and Phineas arrived with Mina in tow.

Mina scurried over to Rosalind, and the two girls disappeared swiftly. This was so unlike Mina Myra – who, as general rule, loved nothing better than to hang around, listening in to adult conversations – that Kev felt justified in feeling a need to investigate further. His immediate attention was drawn back to the stranger, however, as Millicent greeted him with evident pleasure tinged with enough unease to temper the delight in her welcome.

'Jeb!' she exclaimed. 'What brings you here?'

'Hello, Millicent, Phineas,' Jeb replied. 'It's not good news, I'm afraid. Is there somewhere we can talk?'

Millicent nodded and gestured for them all to follow her to the galley. When Kev made to join them, Jeb halted Millicent with a hand on her arm.

'Is this new crew member to be trusted?' he queried with a nod in Kev's direction.

'Relax, Jeb,' Millicent told him. 'This is Kev, and he may be new to you, but we have known him for a long time. He's to be trusted 100 per cent.'

Jeb gave Kev a long look. 'I hope you're right,' he replied but made no further comment.

'Kev,' continued Millicent, 'allow me to introduce Capt Jebediah Strangewayes. He's an old and trusted friend and a part of our little airship community here in Grahamstown.'

Kev reached out a hand for the captain to shake. There was an infinitesimal pause before Jebediah Strangewayes took Kev's hand in his, as if to say he did so for Millicent's sake, but he reserved his judgement on Kev's character for now.

Once everyone was seated around the galley table and tea made, Jebediah broached the subject of his visit.

'I've been pinched,' he told them. 'I've a snitch on board. Luckily, the enforcers could find no evidence, so they had to let me go, but it means I'm going to have to go legit for the foreseeable future.'

'Hard luck, Jeb,' commiserated Phineas. 'Do you know who ratted on you?'

Jebediah shook his head. 'Not yet. I've not taken on any new crew for a long time. Whoever it was has been turned somehow. I'm not the first either,' he continued. 'This has been happening too frequently lately.'

Millicent and Phineas exchanged glances.

'We know,' Millicent said. 'First Mordecai Cullen and Charles Featherstone, now you. And it's not just that. Think of how many runs have been busted by the enforcers before anyone could get to the goods.'

Jebediah nodded. 'Aye. I've counted up eight caches that were raided by the enforcers before we could pick them up. Someone is keeping a close eye on Grahamstown. I just wish we knew who and why.'

'Me too,' Phineas said. 'We're lucky. Our crew is tight, and we're not in so deep as the rest of you. We've been able to escape notice so far, but we don't know for how much longer.'

'That makes what I want to ask you much harder,' Jebediah told them. 'Believe me, if I could think of anyone else to ask, I wouldn't be here. But I'm certain the rest of us are all being watched by the enforcers at the moment. Just because they couldn't find the goods on my ship doesn't mean they've given up.'

Once more, Phineas and Millicent exchanged glances.

'No, they won't. You're going to have to keep within the law for a long time to come,' said Millicent. 'How do you want us to help?'

Jebediah leaned forward, his arms on the table. 'There's a consignment waiting to picked up. It's hidden a ways up the Kauaeranga River. As far as we know, it's not been discovered, but Cornelius is waiting on that shipment. I need you to pick it up and deliver it. He's already paid for it, and he's putting pressure on me for delivery. I'm stuck between Cornelius and the enforcers.'

Phineas watched Millicent thoughtfully. She was weighing up the pros and cons. He knew it wasn't a matter of the money, even though this would be a lucrative venture. She would be torn between helping an old friend and putting the crew of the *Elizabeth Anne* at risk.

'I don't know, Jeb,' she said now. 'We've never run guns before. We may be out of our league on this one.'

Jebediah nodded. 'I understand if you have to say no, Millicent, but I have no one else to ask.'

'I think we stand a fair chance of pulling it off,' Phineas mused, 'precisely because we've never run guns before. We've not come to the notice of the enforcers for any reason. As far as they're concerned, we're legitimate business people.'

Jebediah visibly brightened at the thought that he may have Phineas onside. Millicent was looking thoughtful, weighing it all up, when an almighty crashing was heard from the deck, accompanied by shrill, excited girls' voices.

Everyone exchanged alarmed glances and, leaping up, hurried onto the deck, where they discovered Mina Myra and Rosalind chasing a small shape around the deck. As the adults watched, both girls launched themselves through the air and wrestled with whatever they had been chasing in a tangle of limbs and stifled squeals.

Eventually, they both sat up and noticed the adults watching them. Rosalind shifted herself away from Mina Myra ever so slightly as if to say this whole escapade had nothing to do with her. Mina Myra, realising she had been rumbled, stood up, clutching a small furry creature to her chest.

Millicent raised her hand to her left temple and turned the tiny cogs implanted there to focus her eyescope. 'Is that a . . . monkey?' she asked incredulously.

Mina Myra clutched the little monkey tighter. 'He followed me home,' she explained. 'I want to keep him.'

'What do you mean, he followed you home?' queried Phineas. 'Followed you home from where?'

Mina let the monkey go, and it clambered up onto her shoulder, where it sat, glaring at them with bright black eyes.

'The circus,' explained Mina Myra. 'He likes me. Can I keep him?'

'I think you know the answer to that already, young lady,' pointed out Millicent. 'Otherwise, you wouldn't have hidden him away until now, would you?'

'Well, I thought it best not to disturb you about it,' Mina said. 'You know how annoying us children can be, always wanting this or that. I thought I'd take care of it myself to save you the bother. You have so many other things to worry about, Millicent,' she continued, giving Millicent a benevolent look.

Millicent snorted. 'Very kind of you, to be sure, but you still can't keep him.'

'Well, how about if I keep him but I keep him out of everyone's way?' insisted Mina.

'No. You can't keep him,' reiterated Millicent with the weariness of one who had entered into these kind of negotiations many times before.

'I could keep him but let the circus borrow him back when they need him.'

'No, Mina Myra, you can't keep him. We don't have the things a monkey needs.'

Kev squinted at the monkey on Mina Myra's shoulder. 'I think it's probably an automaton,' he said. 'It's hard to tell, but all the other circus animals were.'

'Well, that's even worse than a real one because you don't have his key,' Millicent declared with the satisfaction of one who had finally come up with an irrefutable argument. 'Eventually, he'll run down, and he won't work anymore. If you keep him, Mina, you'll kill him. He needs his key to survive.'

Mina Myra's shoulders slumped as she realised she'd been outgunned. 'I really wanted a monkey of my own,' she said in a small sad voice.

Kev felt his heartstrings twang at her small dejected figure, but Millicent wasn't moved.

'You'll get over it,' she told Mina Myra. Turning to Kev, she asked, 'Can you take her back to the circus and return this monkey to his rightful owners?'

Kev nodded. 'Sure,' he answered. 'Come on, Mina. Rosalind and I will go with you. Let's get it over with, eh?'

Mina Myra nodded and followed Kev and Rosalind to the lifting platform, dragging her feet as much as she dared, the little monkey clutching at her hair with its bony metal fingers and chattering to itself.

By the time Kev got back, Jebediah had left, and the rest of the crew had gathered in the galley in preparation for the evening meal. The galley was warm and steamy and smelled deliciously of cooking food. Kev had sent the girls to wash up before dinner, and he slipped quietly into his spot at the table next to Persephone and waited to get Millicent's attention.

Eventually, she turned to him. 'Did it all go well at the circus, Kev?' she asked him.

'Well, yes and no,' replied Kev.

'Don't worry, Kev,' Millicent reassured him. 'Mina needs to learn she can't take other people's property and not get into trouble. She'll bounce back.'

'It's not that exactly,' Kev began just as Rosalind and Mina Myra bounced into the galley.

Millicent did a double take as she noticed the monkey sitting on Mina's shoulder. 'I thought I told you to take that thing back where it belonged,' she began.

'Yeah, well, here's the thing,' said Kev. 'We did, but turns out they don't want it back.'

'"Take that dratted, moth-eaten thing away before I throw it at you" is what the man said,' explained Mina Myra, 'and some other words Kev thought it best I not repeat. And look. I have his key.' Mina Myra showed Millicent the key. 'The man did actually throw this at us.'

Millicent sighed. 'It looks as though you've got yourself a monkey, after all,' she said. 'It's obviously defective, so I expect you to keep it out of trouble, or I'll have something to say about it.'

Mina Myra nodded happily. 'It'll be all right, Millicent,' she said. 'He'll be good. He likes me.'

Indeed, the monkey did appear to be quite attached to Mina – almost literally, as it clung onto her possessively, winding its metal fingers through her hair and glaring at them all with its bright beady eyes.

Kev thought the monkey was a bit creepy. It was so very lifelike but not in fact alive – at least not in any way he was familiar with. He decided he didn't really take to the creature and would be happy if Mina Myra neglected to wind it. The moment the thought crossed his mind, the monkey turned its head and stared directly at him, baring its ivory fangs. Unsettled, Kev turned his attention to Mina Myra, who was tickling the thing under its chin.

'Have you got a name for it?' he asked her.

'Yes,' declared Mina Myra happily. 'His name is Norman.'

CHAPTER 13

The hubbub around the galley table was gradually dying down as everyone began to feel the effects of a warm delicious meal on a cold winter's night. The conversation gradually eased off as Millicent rose to make a pot of tea and Lenore and Persephone cleared the plates and other debris from the table.

Millicent slapped down a damp cloth on the table in front of Mina Myra where a blizzard of crumbs had fallen. During the meal, Mina had insisted on feeding Norman titbits from her plate, even though, being clockwork, he didn't eat. Norman had sat on her shoulder and, using his teeth and fingers, shredded every morsel into minute scraps that had then dropped around Mina Myra and onto the table. Meekly, Mina Myra took up the cloth and wiped away the mess without a murmur.

Once everyone was resettled with their cups of tea, Millicent broached the subject of Jebediah Strangewayes's visit and the dilemma he found himself in. From the glances exchanged among them all, Kev gathered that this kind of thing was beginning to happen frequently.

'The thing is,' Millicent said, 'I don't know how we can *not* help him, but I'm not sure we can, if you follow me.'

Phineas nodded. 'Millicent's right. We have to help a fellow adventurer, and Jeb was right to turn to us. We're the only ship flying into Grahamstown that hasn't been affected by this kind of thing. But it's also a huge step up from the cargo we normally carry, and to be honest, I'm not sure how we will manage to pull it off. Our hidden compartment isn't large enough to take a shipment of guns to begin with. Picking the guns up from the concealment site should be straightforward so long as it's not being watched by the enforcers or whoever is informing to them. Delivering them to Cornelius should be the same. It's how we conceal the guns while they're on board that bothers me.'

'Can we extend the compartment?' queried Jonas.

Phineas shook his head. 'I've already had a look at that before dinner,' he replied. 'There's no way to make it big enough for a shipment of guns without compromising the structural integrity of the ship. We have to come up with another plan.'

'No worries there,' said Kev with satisfaction. 'I've got an idea. I saw it once on TV.'

'What's tee vee?' asked Mina Myra curiously.

'Er, um, it's a screen that plays moving pictures on it, and you sit down and watch it, and it has, like, stories and stuff on it,' explained Kev somewhat lamely, his expertise on the technicalities of television limited to operating the remote control.

'Like a zoopraxiscope?' asked Sherlock. 'Me and Orson saw a moving picture show using one of those once.'

'I hope it wasn't one of those naughty ones Absalom Chickering shows out the back of the Junction Hotel,' Millicent said sharply. When Orson and Sherlock exchanged guilty glances, she sighed and turned to Phineas. 'You need to deal with that,' she told him.

Phineas nodded grimly and fixed both boys with a displeased stare, which made them both squirm.

'Er, not sure what a zoo-praxy-whatsit is,' said Kev, 'but a television is more like a receiver. Signals fly through the air and arrive in your screen, and you can watch it.'

'How does it get through the air, Kev?' asked Mina Myra. 'Does it use the aether?'

'I don't know,' replied Kev, feeling out of his depth. 'I don't think we have the aether where I come from.'

Mina Myra fixed him with a hard stare. 'You know, Kev,' she said, 'your world sounds like a really weird place.'

Kev looked at Mina tickling her clockwork pet under the chin and refrained from taking up the argument. 'Anyway,' he continued, turning back to the adults, 'what we need to do is build some crates with false bottoms. We hide the guns in the concealed compartment and place some kind of legitimate cargo on the top. Then if anyone opens the crates, all they'll see is the top part. Even if they rummage a bit, it will look like the false bottom is the bottom of the crate.'

'That's a great plan,' commented Jonas. 'Hide the guns in plain sight.'

Kev nodded. 'That's it exactly. We can make the crates so that even with the guns in them, they'll look and weigh the same as if they're filled entirely with the legit cargo.'

Phineas and Millicent exchanged glances.

'What do you think, Phin?' Millicent asked.

Phineas looked at Kev and then back at Millicent before nodding slowly. 'I think that's the edge we need, Millie,' he said. 'Tell Jeb we can take on the run for him.'

Millicent smiled. 'Good,' she declared. 'I'm so pleased we can help Jeb out. I felt bad about the idea of having to turn him down.'

'Me too, Millie,' said Phineas. 'It wouldn't have sat easily with me to do that either. So then, Millicent, you go back to Jeb and finalise the details for the drop-off to Cornelius. Jonas and I will start constructing the crates. Kev, you can scout around and find us some kind of cargo to go in the tops. Millicent can give you some cash, OK?'

Kev nodded, and taking a sip of his tea, he sat back and allowed the flow of conversation to wash over him, basking in the sensation of being a part of the crew once more and wondering what kind of cargo he could come up with to camouflage the shipment of guns.

CHAPTER 14

Kev was feeling pleased with himself as he stepped back aboard the *Elizabeth Anne*. It had taken him some time to find a cargo to fill the top of the gun crates Phineas and Jonas were busy constructing, but finally, he had managed to find something in enough quantity to fill the spaces.

He was about to go and report in to Phineas when the sound of excited chittering accompanied by Millicent's furious tones stopped him in his tracks.

In the days since Norman's arrival aboard, the crew had discovered why the circus ringmaster had been quite happy to rid himself of the clockwork monkey. Norman had an unfortunate penchant for other people's property, and nothing they had tried had been effective in reducing this yearning in the slightest. Not only was he irresistibly drawn to anything not belonging to him – which meant virtually everything – but also, he was a skilled lock picker, so no matter how diligently items were locked away from him, Norman was able to use his deft metal fingers to break in and filch whatever the crew tried to hide from him.

He would gleefully sit and chitter away to himself as he turned the purloined items over and over in his cunning little hands as he assessed their size and shape. If he was satisfied with this assessment, he would then proceed to swallow the item whole.

For reasons unknown, Norman's mysterious creator had given the little automaton a rudimentary form of digestive tract, and once

Norman had swallowed something, the only thing to be done was to let his internal workings do their job and await the arrival of the subsequent deposit. Fortunately, as Norman was clockwork, everything he swallowed was returned exactly as it had disappeared.

The discovery of this unusual talent had at first captivated and enthralled the children of the *Elizabeth Anne*, and they had spent many fascinated hours feeding Norman all manner of objects and waiting for them to reappear. As this process took several hours to complete, eventually, even Sherlock grew weary of this, and the novelty wore off.

The only time the crew were able to feel their personal property was safe from Norman's prying fingers was when he was happily ensconced on Mina Myra's shoulder. Mina Myra was besotted with her pet, and Norman too appeared to be very attached to Mina in turn, grooming her hair and chattering softly into her ear.

Now Kev watched as Norman rocketed onto the deck, followed by a livid Millicent, clutching her trinket box and waving a fistful of dismantled jewellery. A distraught Mina Myra trailed behind.

'This is the end. The absolute living end. Not the penultimate ending but the literal end!' exclaimed Millicent furiously, waving her fistful of beads. 'Just look what this . . . this plunderous, sticky-fingered miscreant of a monkey has done to my necklace!'

Norman had clambered up into the rigging, where he hung by one hand, screeching and chattering, baring his fangs at Millicent. Mina Myra stood wringing her hands and calling up to him in the attempt to bring him down – to no avail.

'This can't go on, Mina Myra,' admonished Millicent. 'I know you love him, but this has gone too far. You'll have to get rid of him or let him wind down.'

Mina Myra's lower lip trembled. 'Please, please, please, Millicent, I'll try harder to keep an eye on him, but please, please don't make me get rid of him.'

Millicent sighed. 'I'm sorry, Mina. I truly am. But we just can't control him. I suspected he was defective, and I was right. This kind of thing will just keep on happening. We're not equipped to deal with a naughty monkey. I'm worried one day he'll destroy something really important.'

Mina Myra hung her head. Unable to come up with an argument.

Kev had watched all this with interest and not a little amusement, and he stepped forward now to offer his solution. 'Maybe I can send a message to Nellie Sprocket, Millicent. She may be able to fix Norman for us, and then Mina won't have to give him up.'

Millicent thought it over. Looking at Mina Myra gazing up at her beseechingly, she sighed and gave in. 'All right. Let's see if Nellie can help out, but you need to come up with a way to keep him under better control in the meantime.'

Mina Myra nodded happily. 'Oh, I will, Millicent,' she reassured her. 'You'll be *dazzled* by how well I'll manage him. I promise.'

Millicent only sighed once more. 'Somehow I get the feeling I will live to regret my benevolence, but I suppose it's only fair to give you another chance with him, and maybe Nellie will be able to fix him for you.'

Seeming to sense the crisis had been diffused, Norman allowed himself to be coaxed down from the rigging and into Mina Myra's arms, where he lay on his back, eyes half closed as she rubbed his furry belly soothingly.

Kev and Millicent watched for a while before Millicent sighed yet again and turned to Kev. 'I hope Nellie can help us, Kev. I can see how much that pilfering contraption means to her.'

Kev nodded. 'I know. Personally, I can't see the attraction.'

'Me neither, Kev,' replied Millicent with feeling. Looking at the ruins of her necklace in her hand, she continued, 'Well, I need to go and see if I can restring this. Have you had any success tracking down a suitable cargo for the crates, Kev?'

Kev nodded. 'Yep. I reckon I've cracked it. I'm just off to let Phineas know.'

Millicent chuckled. 'I have missed your funny little sayings, Kev,' she told him before heading back to her cabin.

Following the sounds of hammering and sawing, Kev went to find Phineas and Jonas. Looking up at his approach, the men put down their tools and waited for him to speak.

'I've found suitable goods to go in the top of the crates,' he told them.

Phineas nodded. 'Good. The tide's about right in the next couple of nights for the retrieval of the guns. Excellent timing. Give us a hand, Kev, will you? We're almost done here.'

Kev nodded and picked up a hammer. The men set to it in companionable silence, and soon, the sounds of hammering were all that could be heard.

The soft sounds of water lapping against the sides of the skiff, the soft plash of the dipping oars, and the call of the ruru were the only sounds to break the stillness of the night as Phineas and Jonas rowed up the Kauaeranga River. The incoming tide helped to push their boat along faster, and they were making good progress towards the hidden cache of guns. Millicent sat in the bow, watching ahead through night-vision goggles and focusing her eyescope to search out the landmarks Jebediah Strangewayes had given them.

Earlier in the day, Kev and Jonas had gone with a wagon to load their legitimate cargo into the crates, and these now sat aboard the *Elizabeth Anne*, awaiting the arrival of the guns. Everyone had gathered on deck when the men had arrived back, interested to see what Kev and Jonas were bringing back. Jonas had said very little when queried by Phineas as to what the goods were and merely shrugged when asked if they were going to be adequate camouflage for the guns.

Phineas had prised the lid off one of the crates, and the crew had craned their necks to get a glimpse of what was nestled in the thick bed of straw within.

'Teapots!' exclaimed Phineas incredulously. 'We're shipping teapots?'

Kev shrugged a little sheepishly. 'You have no idea how hard it is to find anything of a suitable quantity in Grahamstown,' he explained defensively. 'These were the only things I could find in enough numbers to fill all the crates, and to be honest, the guy was really happy to be rid of them. I was able to beat him down on the price.'

Millicent bent over and pulled out a teapot, holding it up for closer inspection. 'I'm not surprised he wanted rid of them,' she said, a quiver of amusement in her voice. 'I've never seen such ugly teapots in all my life.'

Indeed, the teapots were uniformly unattractive, being thick, misshapen, and coloured an unredeeming brown. Purchased by a merchant who had vastly overestimated their appeal to the housewives of Grahamstown or indeed even the miners – who, while less exacting on aesthetic appeal, preferred something sturdier than pottery – the teapots had languished in the back of his shop until Kev had arrived and struck a deal to suit both parties.

Shaking his head, Phineas replaced the lid of the crate. 'I suppose it hardly matters what we're carrying to hide the guns, but I had hoped for something we could resell afterwards, to be honest. I can't imagine who would want to buy these.'

'Never mind,' said Millicent soothingly. 'The main thing is to hide the guns. We'll think of something to do with them once we're finished, I'm sure.'

Now having left Kev guarding the *Elizabeth Anne*, Phineas was leading the expedition for the guns. The tide was perfect for a run up the river, and by the time they had loaded the guns, they would only have a short wait until the ebbing tide would help carry them back down again. In the bow, Millicent raised her hand, signalling for the men to slow down. Phineas and Jonas shipped their oars and allowed the skiff to drift on the currents as Millicent searched out the marker on the bank. Finding it, she indicated with her hand, and Phineas steered the boat towards the riverbank.

Jonas clambered out and, catching the rope tossed to him by Phineas, secured the skiff and waited as Phineas and Millicent climbed ashore. Millicent had changed from her skirt into close-fitting trousers, something that Phineas insisted showing his appreciation for by slapping her on the bottom every chance he got.

Pushing their way through the bush, they found the cache of guns, well wrapped in oilskins, where Jebediah had told them they would be. Quickly unearthing them and transporting them to the boat, Phineas and Jonas soon had them safely stowed, while Millicent kept watch through her night-vision goggles.

The last of the guns had just been loaded when the splash of oars and the sound of muffled voices drifted up the river towards them. Exchanging glances, the trio quickly untied the skiff.

Placing her lips to his ear, Millicent whispered to Phineas, 'Head upstream, Phin. I'll hide here and see what develops. I bet they're after the guns too. Hide around that bend in the river 'til you hear the all-clear.'

Phineas wasn't happy about leaving Millicent on her own, but as there was no time to argue and he knew she could look after herself, he motioned to Jonas, and the two men swiftly and silently rowed themselves and their contraband upriver and out of sight.

Millicent returned to where the guns had been hidden and, concealing herself in the dense bush, waited quietly, schooling her breath and adjusting her eyescope.

From the riverbank, she could hear the sounds of a group of men as they tied their boat and came ashore. While they weren't being overly noisy, neither were they attempting to cover their presence in any way, confident they were alone in the night.

Millicent waited in her hiding spot and listened as the group of men approached. They were most definitely after the cache of guns, and Millicent thanked her lucky stars they had got there first. Peering carefully through the foliage of her hiding spot, Millicent could see the group easily. They were enforcers from the Grahamstown station. They searched around until they found where the guns should be. Finding the leaf litter disturbed and the guns already gone, the sergeant in charge swore in displeasure and turned to backhand another of the group Millicent hadn't noticed before.

'They're gone, you idiot!' he exclaimed. 'Who else knew about this cache?'

The man shook his head miserably. 'I don't know. I swear. I don't know who Strangewayes might have told. He don't have to tell me nothing.'

Millicent sharpened the focus of her eyescope on the man. Her heart sank as she recognised Jebediah's first mate, Frankton Palmer. This would hit Jeb hard, she knew. The sergeant grunted, obviously angry but unable to refute the argument. He settled for cuffing the man once more before ordering his men back to the boat.

Millicent waited until the sounds of the men forcing their way back through the bush and the distant noises from the river told her the men had left to go back to Grahamstown before slipping out from her hiding spot and creeping back to the riverbank.

There was no sight or sign of the enforcers when she had arrived back at the river, but even so, she waited a bit longer before she whistled a soft alert and waited as Phineas and Jonas made their way back down the river. Quickly, she filled them in on what she had seen.

Phineas leaned on his oars and thought for a while. Sighing, he turned his attention to the river, trying to sense if they were in danger of discovery if they left so soon after the enforcers. Slack tide had ended, and the current was beginning to pull the skiff back down towards the mouth of the river. Deciding that if they went slowly and kept an ear out, they should be fine, Phineas motioned for them to get on their way, and carefully, they made their way back downriver, the guns beneath their feet.

As they neared the mouth of the Kauaeranga River, where it spilled into the Firth of Thames, Jonas and Phineas slowed the skiff still further and, hugging the mangroves at the riverbank, edged carefully towards the land docks.

Millicent raised her hand, indicating for them to stop. Holding the boat still by grasping the mangroves and back-paddling, the men waited for the all-clear. Millicent adjusted her eyescope and focused on the group of enforcers clambering onshore ahead of them and making their way back into town.

When Millicent indicated it was safe to do so, the men pushed out into the current and allowed the skiff to drift past the enforcers' tethered boat farther down to where the land docks jutted out into the firth and the *Elizabeth Anne* was tethered.

Moving as quickly and silently as they could, the trio tied the skiff to the pilings beneath the docks and began unloading the guns, passing them hand to hand until they were piled in the shadows beneath the *Elizabeth Anne*'s lifting platform.

Once the guns were unloaded, Phineas climbed back down and cut the skiff free, watching as the current caught it and, spinning lazily, it was pulled out by the tide into the firth. Clambering back up, he stood, regarding Millicent for a moment. 'So who was it, Millie? Did you see? Who's the rat?'

Millicent nodded, compressing her mouth into a tight line. 'Frankton Palmer,' she said in a hard voice.

Phineas's own mouth settled into a grim line, and his eyebrows pulled together into a fierce scowl as Millicent named Jebediah's first mate. 'This is a bad business, Mill,' Phineas muttered, almost to himself, 'a real bad business.'

Millicent nodded. 'I know, Phin,' she replied. 'This will break Jebediah. I know it. He's treated Frankton as a brother for more years than I can remember.' Anxiously, she slipped her hand into Phineas's. 'What's happening to us, Phin?' she asked. 'We used to be such a happy community. Who's doing this to us?'

'I wish I knew, Millie,' Phineas replied. 'If we knew that, we might have a chance at fighting back. As it is, it's like trying to wrestle a shadow that's always moving and shifting shape.'

Millicent nodded unhappily. 'I know, Phin. We appear to have an enemy we haven't realised we have until now. I only hope it's not too late to stop whatever plan he or she is hatching against us.'

CHAPTER 15

Kev and Persephone sat on deck, sipping the cups of tea Persephone had brought out to help keep them warm while Kev was on sentry duty. He was waiting for Jonas to come and relieve him, and Persephone had come to keep him company.

Slowly, they were rediscovering the easy rapport they had enjoyed before Kev had left to return to his own world. They had yet to become lovers, which brought its own frustrations, but they both sensed they needed time to re-establish their relationship.

As each day passed, they found they were becoming more relaxed with each other, and the distress that had marred their final days together was fading into a very dim memory.

They had always been good friends, and now the deeper feelings of love and romance were beginning to blossom once again, this time without the thorns, and the sweetness of this was something they were both reluctant to disturb. So they walked the fine line of unrequited passion and allowed their relationship to take its own course.

They sat chatting and sipping their tea, laughing and flirting a little, stealing the odd chaste kiss and waiting for Jonas so they could go off together.

As they waited, Kev spotted a party of enforcers making their way towards the airship along the docks. Phineas and Millicent had filled the crew in on the happenings of the previous night and warned that they may not have heard the last of it before they had a chance to leave with the guns.

'This can't be good,' he remarked as he watched them approach.

He noticed several other groups preparing to board other airships in port and realised the *Elizabeth Anne* wasn't the only target. This was good news. It meant the enforcers had no clear lead as to who might have the guns.

Persephone left to alert Millicent about the enforcers, and by the time the women got back, the party was already on board. Millicent greeted them blandly and held out her hand for the proffered warrant.

'We have a warrant to search all the airships in port,' the sergeant in charge informed them. 'Do you currently have cargo aboard?'

Millicent nodded. 'A consignment of teapots,' she told the enforcers, 'in the hold.'

'I'm sure you have nothing to hide, but we will need to search this ship and inspect the cargo.'

Millicent nodded again. 'Of course, officer' was all she said, and she led the way to the cargo hold.

Millicent and Kev stood and watched the enforcers inspect the ship and begin the task of looking in every crate. They didn't look enthralled at the idea of having to search each crate, Kev thought thankfully. It was one thing to suggest a plan on the strength of seeing it on TV, but in reality, he had no idea if it would actually work in the real world.

At that moment, Mina Myra trailed in. Never one to let the opportunity to poke her curious nose into adult affairs pass her by, she had gathered Norman onto her shoulder and dragged Rosalind along in the hope that something exciting might be happening.

Mina Myra was convinced that all adults conspired to keep the interesting things away from children in an attempt to make their lives as dull as possible. Nothing anyone could say and no amount of intriguing activities could convince her otherwise, and as soon as she felt the grown-ups were trying to keep her out of things, she made a point of inserting herself right back in, determined not to miss out on the slightest bit of entertainment.

Millicent sighed. 'That's all I need,' she muttered to Kev as she moved to shoo the girls away.

Kev held her back with a hand on her arm, a speculative look on his face. 'Leave them be, Millicent,' he said. 'They can't do any harm, and they will be a distraction, in a way.'

Millicent frowned but nodded and let the girls stay to watch – not that either girl was content to just watch.

Rosalind wandered over to where the men were beginning to lever off the top of one of the crates with a crowbar. This clearly offended her as she shot Millicent and Kev a look of outrage as if to ask them why they were allowing such a desecration of their property. Turning back to watch the enforcers with a disapproving frown creasing her brow, she fixed them with such a glare of open hostility that for a moment, they actually paused in their task and looked around to see if it was OK to continue. The sergeant motioned them back to the job with an impatient wave of his hand, and so they turned back to rummaging through the tightly packed straw.

Rosalind obviously felt the enforcers were not to be trusted as she hovered around them, watching their every move with such intensity that the men began to hasten through their task, giving each crate a cursory glance at best, eager to escape the odd little girl with the forbidding stare.

Mina Myra, meanwhile, was attempting to engage the sergeant in conversation. Being a complete stranger, he was fair game. Mina had long since figured out that most adults would try to disengage from conversation once they got to know her and so was relishing the prospect of a new unwitting conversational partner.

Mina Myra didn't need for anyone to reply to her conversation as she was well able to keep up a never-ending flow all by herself, but she did expect unwavering attention while she did so. Every time the sergeant's attention looked like it may be shifting, she gave him a sharp tug on his sleeve to draw it back to herself. Norman too appeared to appreciate an audience as he began to hoot and chatter, climbing up onto Mina Myra's head and proceeding to show off in a shameless manner. This was very distracting for everyone except Mina Myra, who appeared unperturbed by her pet's antics.

The final straw came when Norman leaped from Mina Myra's head onto the sergeant's shoulder and gave him a hefty nip on the ear.

'Argh!' exclaimed the sergeant in outrage. 'The bloody monkey bit me!'

He grabbed for Norman, who leaped back onto Mina Myra's shoulder and began scolding the sergeant as if it was his own fault he'd been bitten. The sergeant raised his hand to his stinging earlobe to discover Norman had bitten him hard enough to draw blood.

'I'll have that moth-eaten mammal's guts for garters!' he threatened.

Mina Myra gave him a withering stare. 'He's "not" even alive,' she said, lifting her arms out at waist height as she spoke and crooking her index and middle fingers in funny little beckoning motions. 'He has no "guts" to make into anything. You can't make garters out of cogs and gears. It won't work, and "you'll" just look silly,' she declared, unaware she was looking a little odd herself.

'What is she doing?' asked Millicent in bewilderment.

Kev looked hard at Mina, and a light dawned. 'Ah, I think she's using air quotations,' he explained.

'Air what?' asked Millicent in confusion.

'Air quotes,' reiterated Kev. 'You know, to indicate irony or sarcasm. It's a thing. At least where I come from. I used them one day in front of Mina and had to explain myself. It obviously made an impression.'

Millicent shook her head. 'I'm not sure if she quite understood the concept, Kev,' she said.

Indeed, Mina Myra's fingers appeared to be placing quotations around random and unrelated words and phrases. This had the effect of making her conversation even more confusing than usual, and the sergeant had obviously had enough. Holding his handkerchief to his throbbing ear, he beckoned to his men. Gratefully, they stopped searching the crates and followed him back onto the deck.

Millicent, Kev, and the girls watched as the party boarded the lifting platform and let themselves back onto the docks below.

'Goodbye and thank you for "coming",' sang out Mina Myra after them. 'Be sure to "call in again" sometime. It was lovely to "have you".' Turning to Millicent and Kev, she declared smugly, 'It's so nice to have new people to talk to.'

Phineas came up on deck to stand beside Millicent and Kev as they watched the enforcers getting into the lifting platform of the next-door airship. 'All good to leave?' he asked.

Millicent nodded. 'Yes, we're in the clear. The sooner we get rid of these guns, the better. We'll set sail as soon as we can.'

Phineas nodded, as anxious as Millicent to be rid of the guns in the hold as soon as possible.

CHAPTER 16

Cornelius Xavier Blackwater III was a remittance man. Sent to the colonies by his wealthy family on the understanding that he never return to Mother England, he had set about turning his monthly stipend into a lucrative bootlegging business.

He had ceased needing to rely on this stipend many years ago, but that didn't stop him from feeling a certain satisfaction at taking it off his family's hands all the same. In fact, compared to his current income, it was a paltry amount and barely made a splash as it hit his coffers and got swallowed up by the tidal wave of money he made from bootlegging, but nothing could induce him to stop accepting it either.

It was a form of revenge on his part to insist on being paid, and if, at the odd time, his family had written to query if the money needed to be sent any longer, he would write back threatening to reappear at the family dining table should they stop the payments.

He looked out from his hideout in the shadow of Mount Moehau, on the northern tip of the Coromandel Peninsula, and watched his airships as they wove through the air, their massive gossamer wings harvesting the aether from the atmosphere, and reflected on just how far he had come and how powerful he now was. He gave mental homage to his perspicacity in recognising the potential of bootlegging aether.

He felt no reverence for the aether itself, that delicate and mysterious substance that bound all things together. It was merely a commodity, one that had made him incredibly wealthy, the wealth, in its turn, buying him the power he now wielded and craved. It was a costly business, extracting aether from the atmosphere, but the phenomenal returns made it a worthwhile investment, one the government had been quick to see the benefits of too.

The government kept its iron fist tightly wrapped around the distilling of aether for many reasons, not the least of these the uncertainty of how long the resources of aether would last if harvested indiscriminately. Cornelius knew the government's concern for the aether levels had little to do with the consequences of them running out and everything to do with reaping the financial rewards until they did so and had no qualms about setting himself up in opposition. He had been born with an intense dislike for any authority other than his own. He was always on the alert for times when those wielding authority looked as though they were overstepping their bounds, so he could make a point of thumbing his figurative nose at them.

He had established himself very well as the distiller and seller of illegally harvested aether, enjoying the fact that he was making a fortune beating the government at its own game. There was an enormous niche on the black market for his product, naturally enough, which Cornelius had filled exclusively, there being a vast and varied group of consumers eager to sidestep the government's strictly enforced regulations.

In the distance, he could see the *Taniwha* approaching. He had been intrigued on receiving a message from Huia, Queen of the Skies, wishing to meet with him but giving no indication as to why. He knew of Huia, of course, the airship community of the Coromandel, on both sides of the law, being a small one, but their paths rarely crossed as Huia never ventured this far north on a raid.

He watched as the *Taniwha* halted some distance from his lair and deployed her sky hooks. Although he assumed this to be a friendly visit, Huia herself was obviously not taking any chances. He wondered if she would come alone. This question was answered as he spied the shape of her Pegasus as it lifted from the deck and headed towards his hideout.

Turning from the window, Cornelius cast his eye critically over the table set behind him. He had had it strategically placed so the diners would be able to look out the window and take in the vastness and efficiency of his enterprise. He had also ensured that the room was well decorated with the luxurious items his wealth had obtained and set a menu designed to be sophisticated as well as appetising. He was out to impress.

There were very few people in the Coromandel who could match him in terms of influence and power, but Huia was one of them. She was as well born as he was. She had created wealth almost equal to his, and she was a leader who had earned the same respect his men afforded him. He found he was anxious not to appear the lesser of the two of them.

As he repositioned a piece of cutlery which didn't require rearranging and waited for Huia to arrive, he wondered once again why she had requested to meet with him. He had suggested they meet in his domain, knowing it to be remote from prying eyes with a secure air space, but he had been a little surprised Huia had agreed to it. Whatever was prompting her visit was obviously enough of a concern for her to forgo her natural instincts. Going out onto the landing platform he had built into the side of the mountain, he waited for Huia to come swooping down on her flying horse.

The Pegasus landed, its metal hooves touching down delicately, and Huia swung herself from its back and strode towards Cornelius, looking every inch the warrior queen she was. She had dressed for the dinner invitation he had issued in a satin evening dress of azure blue, over which she wore a korowai.

Damn, but she's one fine-looking woman, he thought as she approached him, the tassels of her korowai rippling like water. Ruefully, he reflected that she was as unlikely to look at him with any more favour than the blushing debutantes who had spurned him back in his misspent youth, his good looks not enough to outweigh his status as a younger son or his reputation as a wastrel and ne'er-do-well. Huia stopped before him and nodded in greeting.

Cornelius smiled. 'Huia,' he said in way of greeting and swept a hand out to indicate she precede him inside.

Back in the room set aside for their meeting and seated at the table, they waited in silence as Cornelius's men served them with food and wine. Once alone again, Cornelius gave Huia a moment to admire the view of his airships busy at work before broaching the reason for her visit.

'And to what do I owe the honour of this visit, Huia?' he queried as they both savoured the meal in front of them.

Huia took a sip of her wine. Placing the glass carefully on the table, she looked up and fixed him with her direct stare. 'We have a problem, Cornelius. It's Elmstone. He's beginning to spread his tentacles out onto my side of the Waihou, and I believe he has designs on Grahamstown as well.'

Cornelius sat back in his chair and regarded Huia thoughtfully. 'I don't see how this information has anything to do with me, to be honest.'

Huia leaned forward over the table, her meal forgotten. 'You might think yourself too far away from what's going on in Grahamstown for concern, Cornelius,' she told him, 'but you'd be a fool to underestimate Silas Elmstone. He's a vile, ill-favoured sneak thief, but he's been gaining strength in that swampy stronghold of his, and if you think you'll escape his notice for much longer, you're deluded. I know for a fact he has got the enforcers of Grahamstown in his pocket. We need you, Cornelius, and even if you don't think so, you need us too. The only way we can defeat Elmstone and protect our way of life is to work together.'

'What way of life, Huia?' challenged Cornelius. 'You might believe you're a part of one big happy family, but I assure you, I do not. Nor do I want to be a part of one.'

'Maybe not,' Huia replied. 'At least, not now. But how long do you think all this will last once Elmstone sets his sights on you?' she continued, indicating his airships with a wave of her hand in their direction.

'You really think Elmstone is strong enough to be a threat to me?' queried Cornelius in disbelief.

Huia shook her head. 'Maybe not yet,' she admitted, 'but I never took him seriously as a threat either until recently.'

Quickly, she related the theft of her taonga and the discovery of how Silas Elmstone had managed to plant a spy on board her ship.

'We have to act now, Cornelius,' she insisted, 'before he gets any stronger. If we strike now, we have a chance.'

Cornelius didn't reply at once but instead looked out over his empire and weighed Huia's words in his mind. As much as he didn't want to admit it, her revelations had unsettled him. It was true that he believed himself untouchable, but something of what Huia was telling him rang true. Elmstone might not be able to touch him right now, but he would be foolish to ignore the threat he presented. 'What do you want from me?' he asked finally, returning his gaze to Huia.

She looked back at him, her gaze unwavering. 'I need you to reach out to Grahamstown's airship community. You're the bridge, Cornelius, between them and me and my kind. You can bring us together. They won't trust me. I've raided too many of their runs and taken too much of their cargo for them to believe or trust me. But you, they'll listen to.'

Slowly, Cornelius nodded. 'If you're right and Elmstone is becoming a real threat, then I agree with you. If a toad like him can grow in power enough to rattle your cage, my dear, I would be a fool indeed to take no notice of your warning. As luck would have it, I'm expecting a shipment of guns from Grahamstown at any moment. That will be my chance to give warning there. How will we make contact with you?'

Huia smiled and slipped a tiny metal cylinder out of the sash of her evening gown, pushing it across the table towards him. 'Use the Network,' she told him. 'You can make initial contact through its head agent, Nellie Sprocket. The details on how to reach her are in the cylinder.'

Cornelius nodded and, reaching for the cylinder, slipped it into his pocket. 'Very well, Huia,' he said. 'And now that business is concluded, let us enjoy this fine meal and excellent wine. It's very rarely I enjoy such an illustrious and beautiful guest such as yourself.' So saying, he inclined his head with a smile and raised his wine glass in a silent toast in Huia's honour.

CHAPTER 17

J ebediah Strangewayes was seated once more at the galley table of the *Elizabeth Anne*, sharing a pot of tea with Millicent, Phineas, Jonas, and Kev. Before setting off to deliver the shipment of guns to Cornelius, Millicent had felt it important to inform Jebediah about the identity of the spy aboard his ship. As expected, he had taken the news of his first mate's treachery badly. At first, he had been angry and inclined to deny the truth of what Millicent and Phineas had to tell him, but eventually, as both of them calmly insisted on the truth of their revelation, it was beginning to sink in, and the depth of the betrayal was deeply felt, not just by Jebediah himself but by the crew of the *Elizabeth Anne* as well.

Millicent herself found it almost inconceivable to comprehend such a betrayal. She thought of each of her crew and tried in vain to imagine how she would cope if she was standing in Jebediah's shoes. It was a sobering and disturbing thought that someone had managed to infiltrate their community and begin to set them against one another without anyone the wiser until now, and she wondered just who their hidden enemy was and what he or she was hoping to achieve.

Jebediah rubbed his hands over his face in an effort to clear his thoughts. 'It was a lucky thing, you getting to the guns first,' he declared. 'No doubt, the enforcers would have used those guns against me, especially with Palmer's testimony, and maybe even have had a chance at tying Cornelius into it as well.'

Phineas nodded. 'We've held off delivering the guns because it occurred to me that Palmer may well have known of the rendezvous site with Cornelius and we could have been flying into a trap.'

Jebediah looked at Phineas with anguished eyes. 'Oh aye,' he said bleakly. 'I don't doubt that either. Palmer knew all the details. The only thing I've kept from him, thankfully, was reaching out to you.'

Jonas, as usual for him, had been content listening to the conversation, but now he leaned forward. 'I know you'll be wanting to interrogate Palmer before giving him the end he deserves, but I think it would be better if you held off on that for now.'

'Why?' queried Strangewayes incredulously. 'I can't wait to rid myself of the canker in the soul of my crew. I can't abide the notion of having him around for a moment longer!'

'I understand how you feel, Jeb,' said Jonas, 'but think about it. We have no idea who managed to turn him against you or for what reason. If we keep him close, maybe we might be able to watch him and see who he's in contact with. It would be to our advantage to find that out at the very least, and maybe once we know that, we can use Palmer to feed misinformation back to this mysterious enemy.'

Phineas nodded. 'Jonas is right, Jeb,' he said. 'By holding our hand for a time, we may just be able to find out who's behind this mischief. That would be good knowledge to have.'

Jebediah nodded reluctantly. 'Aye. Happens you're right. As much as I detest the thought of harbouring that snake in my bosom, I'll hold off on dispatching him for now, but as soon as we find out who's behind this, I'm ridding myself of him.'

The group around the table fell into a gloomy silence, all of them contemplating the troubles that were besetting their tight-knit community. Lenore pushed her way through the galley door, her arms laden with packages from her trip into town to buy provisions. Kev jumped up to help her unburden herself, taking the bags from her and placing them on the galley bench.

'Thanks, Kev,' she said, easing her shoulders and rummaging through one of the bags and presenting him with a brown paper–wrapped parcel. 'This was waiting for you at the post office.'

Taking the parcel from Lenore, Kev turned it over curiously. It had no return address or indication as to who had sent it. By the time he sat down at the table again, everyone's interest had been piqued, and all attention was on him as he cut the string and unwrapped the parcel.

Inside was a plain wooden box, and Kev lifted the lid to reveal a small brightly enamelled bird. Carefully, Kev lifted it out and placed it on the galley table. It was beautifully made, each metal feather individually crafted, and with eyes of jet. From its back, a small key protruded, and Kev realised it must have been sent by Nellie Sprocket.

Gingerly, he grasped the key between his thumb and forefinger and carefully wound up the bird's clockwork mechanism. Letting the key go, Kev sat back, and everyone watched as the little bird began to chirp and trill, its tiny metal beak opening in song and its head tipping from side to side in an endearing manner.

Suddenly, without any warning, the little bird gave a loud and discordant squawk, its beak gaping open. Every one of its feathers stood out from its body, and its black eyes stood out on tiny stalks. From under its tail, an aperture opened, and a tiny blue enamelled egg popped out and fell onto the table.

Kev picked up the egg. Seeing it was hinged in the middle, he flipped it open and drew out a minute scrap of paper, on which was written,

Clockwork Owl
Tomorrow, anytime

'Well,' declared Kev, 'I think that's Nellie's way of telling us she can help out with Norman.'

'Thank goodness!' exclaimed Millicent. 'I've had about all I can take of that misbegotten monkey.'

'Whereabouts is the Clockwork Owl?' queried Kev. 'I've not noticed it around town.'

'It's up the coast a way,' Phineas informed him. 'It's a respectable enough establishment, I think.'

'It's a wee hike to get there,' explained Millicent, 'but you can take the perambulator.'

'Dear lord, Millie!' exclaimed Phineas as Jonas gave a barely concealed snigger. 'Don't make the poor lad take that contraption. We can hire him a pony trap.'

'Nonsense,' announced Millicent emphatically. 'There is nothing wrong with the perambulator. It's a perfectly adequate conveyance. I don't understand your aversion to it, and it is better than having Sherlock doing multiple trips in the Hummingbird to get everyone there and back again.'

Feeling bemused at finding himself in the midst of an ongoing argument he had no knowledge of and with visions of baby carriages floating through his mind, Kev quickly reassured Millicent he'd be happy to use the perambulator, and it was settled that he would escort Mina Myra and Norman to meet Nellie in the hope she would be able to help them.

The following morning, Kev and Mina Myra, with Norman in his usual spot on her shoulder, followed Millicent down onto the land docks to a shed tucked away behind the warehouses and trading posts that clustered around this end of town. Unlocking and opening the door, Millicent let them in and drew a dust cover off a vehicle parked in the middle of the shed.

Kev surveyed the perambulator with interest, intrigued as to why Phineas objected to it so strongly. It was a high-sprung three-wheeled vehicle, big enough to seat two comfortably side by side. It was elegantly constructed, and Kev could tell it was well made, obviously expensive, and, most definitely, overwhelmingly feminine.

'I bought this so I could go out on little trips when I was in port,' explained Millicent, polishing the handrail lovingly with her sleeve, 'but Phineas refuses to be seen in it.'

Looking at the lacy canopy and ornately scrolled embellishments, Kev began to get a glimmer of Phineas's objections to the perambulator.

It was a vehicle designed to carry a lady around a park on a morning or afternoon out taking the air. As a practical means of transportation, it was somewhat lacking, and Kev could imagine Phineas's horror at being paraded around town in it by Millicent.

Millicent showed Kev where the key was to wind it up, and he clambered aboard. Mina Myra sprang up beside him. The perambulator had a tiller of sorts, by which it could be steered by turning the front wheel in the direction you wished to go.

'Can I have a turn, Kev?' asked Mina Myra eagerly.

Catching sight of Millicent's disapproving frown, Kev shook his head but leaned in and whispered, 'On the way home.'

Mina Myra, understanding the need for secrecy, settled herself without further argument, and Kev wound the perambulator and disengaged the brake. Millicent stood in the doorway, waving them off as the perambulator took off down the street at a very genteel speed.

As the perambulator only had one speed and it frequently needed rewinding, the trip up the coast to where the Clockwork Owl perched on a narrow strip of land between the firth and the steep plunging sides of the ranges took a considerable length of time.

Pocketing the key and enduring the sniggers of a scattering of drinkers sitting on settles outside the inn, Kev found himself in solidarity with Phineas over the perambulator. He resigned himself to the tedious trip back home again and decided this would be the last time he'd be using it.

Leading the way, he escorted Mina Myra inside the inn and waited as his eyes adjusted to the dimness. Spying Nellie sitting in a corner facing the door, he led Mina Myra and Norman over to sit across from her. She had a tankard of ale and a loaf of bread in front of her. A heel of hard cheese lay on a plate beside the loaf, and Nellie began cutting off hunks for them as they took their seats.

Nellie returned Kev's greeting, looking pleased to see him again, and nodded welcomingly to Mina Myra, who appeared very taken with Nellie and insisted on sitting as close to her as was possible.

Nellie observed Norman sitting on Mina's shoulder thoughtfully. 'So this is the errant monkey, is it?' she asked. Kev nodded, and Nellie patted the table in front of her. 'Put him down here,' she instructed.

Mina Myra placed Norman on the table, where he proceeded to poke his fingers into the lump of cheese. Nellie pulled a jeweller's loupe out of her pocket and, bringing it to her eye, peered behind Norman's ear at the small metal stud embedded there.

'Ahhh, I thought as much,' she breathed in awe. 'He's a Drosselmeyer.'

'He is!' exclaimed Mina Myra, her eyes growing round as she caught onto the reverence in Nellie's voice. Turning to look at her pet, she stroked his furry back. 'I thought he was a monkey.'

Nellie chuckled. 'And so he is, my sweet. A very special monkey. He's very old and very valuable. He was made by a genius automaton maker many, many years ago.'

'Can you fix him?' Kev asked.

Nellie looked at him as though he had uttered a particularly foul blasphemy. 'Fix him? Fix him? You don't *fix* a Drosselmeyer, Kev.'

'Well, he's defective,' insisted Kev. 'He keeps stealing stuff and eating it.'

'Oh,' declared Nellie, a light going on in her head. 'I see the problem.'

'Good,' said Kev, feeling relieved. As much as he didn't like the monkey, he knew how attached Mina Myra was to him, and he hated to think how heartbroken she would be if she had to let him run down.

'Unfortunately, I can't do anything to rectify that problem for you.' Seeing Kev's consternation and Mina Myra's distress, she went on. 'You see, Herr Drosselmeyer was, in every respect, a genius. A very clever man with a great vision. His automatons are the most exquisitely manufactured automatons you can buy. No one has been able to surpass him in skill or invention before or since. Believe me, many have tried, all to no avail, and a Drosselmeyer automaton remains the pinnacle of achievement to this day. Every new invention he brought out became more and more sophisticated and lifelike until it became almost impossible to tell at first glance they were not alive. Eventually, Herr Drosselmeyer invented a line of automatons that could be imprinted by their owners with any behaviours and habits they desired. Your little fellow is one such example. Once the imprinting process was complete, it was also irreversible. It would seem that Norman's first owner bought him to be exactly what he is – a petty thief – and he has been imprinted to behave thus.' Gazing at Kev and Mina Myra sadly, Nellie concluded, 'even if I had the skill to alter his early programming, I would not. He is what he is, a fine example of one man's skill and vision. It would be sacrilege to tamper with him.'

Mina Myra's eyes brimmed with tears. 'If you can't fix him, then Millicent will make me get rid of him or worse – let him run down.'

Nellie shook her head regretfully. 'I wish I could help you, sweetie, but I can't change him to be what he is not. You must all learn to accept him as he is and learn to adapt to his shortcomings.'

Mina Myra gulped and wiped her eyes, looking at Kev and Nellie earnestly. 'Well, I love him as he is, and I will protect him and look after him,' she declared bravely.

Kev's innate kindness was stirred, and he patted Mina Myra reassuringly on the shoulder. 'Don't fret Mina,' he told her. 'We'll think of something.'

Mina Myra sniffed, and pulling Norman to her, she wrapped her arms around him. She buried her face in his fur, while Norman chattered away and ran his fingers through her hair, for all the world as if he were offering her comfort.

'I'm sure it will work out somehow, Mina,' Kev said, not quite believing it but wanting to be encouraging.

Nellie nodded. 'Kev is right,' she said. 'Sometimes the things that cause us the most difficulty turn out to be the things we need the most. Don't give up on Norman just yet, sweetie. He may be the very thing you all never knew you needed.'

CHAPTER 18

Persephone nodded to her colleague, Dr Wilton Barry, and watched as he slipped the hypno-goggles over their patient's eyes. Persephone was interested to see if Wilton's newest invention would do what he claimed it would.

Persephone was a skilled surgeon, and thanks to her intervention, many of the grateful miners of Grahamstown had been able to recover from catastrophic accidents that would have left them maimed or even dead. Her skill at integrating mechanical body parts into the human body was unsurpassed, even by surgeons with more years of experience under their belt, which meant her patients recovered more quickly and returned to their normal lives in a shorter time frame than usual. But even so, Persephone was aware that the trauma experienced by her patients and the psychological effect it had on them, as much as the physical, could impede their recovery.

Wilton Barry had theorised that by using hypnotic suggestions before patients went under anaesthetic, their recovery would be quicker. Persephone had agreed to let him trial his new goggles on her patients to test his theory.

Persephone watched with interest as Wilton adjusted the goggles and then, sitting close by the patient's head, began talking in a low monotone voice. As she readied herself to repair the damage down to the miner's leg by an unfortunate slip of the pickaxe he had been wielding, Persephone thought briefly of the crew of the *Elizabeth*

Anne, knowing they would be well on their way to rendezvous with Cornelius.

Kev had arrived back from the trip to the Clockwork Owl in a pensive mood. He had briefly reported on what Nellie had told him regarding Norman, but it had been her words to him as she farewelled them that had given him pause for thought. She had also slipped him a small cylinder, instructing him to open it only on return to the *Elizabeth Anne*.

Nellie had confirmed that there was indeed an enemy with designs on Grahamstown and that if the airship community wished to escape his nefarious plans, they would need to band together and even join forces with their erstwhile enemies. Inside the cylinder had been coordinates for a new rendezvous point with Cornelius, who was also going to fill them in on who the enemy was and how they would proceed.

She had also cautioned Kev not to reveal any of this to anyone else in Grahamstown as there were an unknown number of spies in the town, and until they had all been identified, secrecy was vital.

Everyone on board felt edgy and ill-equipped but, knowing for many reasons that they were the only ones able to meet with Cornelius at this time, prepared themselves and the ship for the trip to meet up with him.

Persephone had remained behind as she had a busy operating schedule at the hospital, but she couldn't help wondering how they were getting on. As Wilton neared the end of his hypnotic suggestions and began to administer the ether, Persephone schooled her thoughts and allowed herself to be absorbed in the task at hand.

Kev and Jonas hauled on the ropes that tethered the *Elizabeth Anne* to her berth in the docks. Phineas had been stoking the engines and bringing the boilers up to full steam, and they were ready for departure. Millicent was watching from the wheelhouse as Orson and Sherlock brought the ship around and headed her off in the direction of Auckland. Millicent had plotted a circuitous route to the rendezvous point, not knowing just who was watching them.

The morning was cold and clear after a night of rain, and the misty clouds still wreathed themselves through the steep-sided valleys between the ranges behind the town as the *Elizabeth Anne* sailed up the Firth of Thames and out into the Hauraki Gulf.

The ocean slipped away beneath them as they sailed full steam ahead, and before long, the waters of the Tamaki Strait lay beneath them, but instead of turning and following the strait into Auckland, they kept sailing until the island of Tiritiri Matangi was beneath them. Turning the *Elizabeth Anne* so she was travelling out into the gulf once more, towards a spot somewhere off Cape Colville, Millicent headed her ship to the rendezvous point.

Standing in the bow and adjusting her eyescope, Millicent kept a lookout for Cornelius's airship. At first, it appeared as a speck on the horizon, but as they drew nearer, the shape of his pleasure ship, the *Oracle*, became ever more distinct.

The engines stilled, and Kev and Jonas deployed the skyhooks as Phineas joined Millicent at the bow rail.

'I wouldn't mind getting a good look on board that ship,' he said. 'I hear no expense has been spared.'

Millicent merely snorted. 'I daresay,' she replied, 'I sometimes think Cornelius has more money than sense.'

Phineas chuckled and shrugged. 'You may be right, Millie, but you can't tell me you're not just a tiny bit curious to see how the other half lives.'

Millicent shook her head. 'No, I honestly don't care if I do. I've never been too worried how other people live so long as they leave me alone to live how I like. You know that, Phin.'

Phineas wrapped his arms around her from behind and hugged her tight. 'Ah, Millie,' he declared, kissing the top of her head fondly, 'that's one of the reasons I love you so much. But if I get a chance to go aboard, I'm taking it.'

Millicent laughed. 'Fair enough, Phin. I won't stop you,' she replied, hugging his arms where they circled her waist.

Standing thus, they watched as a small aircraft lifted off the *Oracle*'s deck and headed towards them. By the time Phineas and Millicent had wandered over to where Cornelius had landed his craft on the deck, the rest of the crew had gathered to admire it.

'Nice,' murmured Sherlock, running a hand over the sleek sides of the craft.

'It's the newest model of Swallow,' Cornelius informed him. 'Faster and more manoeuvrable in the air than its predecessor and a delight to fly.'

'I bet,' remarked Sherlock enviously.

Cornelius smiled and, much to Sherlock's disgust, tousled his hair as he passed. Noting Sherlock's outraged expression with amusement, Millicent offered Cornelius her hand, which, instead of shaking, he raised to his lips and kissed gallantly.

Millicent threw back her head and laughed in delight. 'Really, Cornelius,' she admonished, 'do you take me for some green girl?'

'Never!' protested Cornelius, an answering grin tugging at the corners of his mouth. 'But old habits die hard, and I'm always out to make a good first impression.'

'Well, save your charm for someone who appreciates it,' Millicent informed him. 'Come along and have a cup of tea. I understand we have problems to discuss as well as guns to deliver.'

Once they were all seated around the galley table, Cornelius quickly filled them in on everything Huia had told him. Phineas whistled a low whistle once Cornelius's story was finished.

'Silas Elmstone, eh?' he said, shaking his head disbelievingly. 'I never would have guessed he was the source of our troubles. He always seems so ineffectual. I doubt any of us have taken him seriously.'

Cornelius nodded. 'I feel the same, Phineas, to be honest with you. When Huia told me about him, I was incredulous. But if she's right – and I have a feeling she is – we can't afford to dismiss him any longer. Somewhere along the way, he's gotten more powerful than any of us gave him credit for.'

'It never pays to underestimate an enemy,' Phineas pointed out, 'and it seems we've all been guilty of this as far as Elmstone's concerned. Let's just hope we've come to our senses in time.'

Kev adjusted the light from the lamp before him on the table as he tried to work on the harness he had designed, with Persephone's help, to keep some measure of control over Norman. Millicent had shaken her head at him when he had explained Nellie's verdict on the little monkey but had only sighed and given in to his insistence that he would come up with a way to stop his pilfering.

As Norman was very attached to Mina Myra – who, for the most part, was able to keep him out of mischief when in direct control of him – Kev decided if they could keep him tied up when not with Mina, it should ensure an end to his thieving and destructive ways.

Kev was busily sewing bits of leather into a close-fitting harness which would buckle securely behind Norman's back where his clever little fingers could not reach to undo it. For good measure, they intended to padlock him into it – just to be on the safe side. This would mean Norman could, in theory, be tied securely in one spot and thus be prevented from wreaking havoc as soon as Mina Myra's back was turned.

Kev was enjoying the peacefulness aboard the ship as he concentrated on his task. The children were all abed, and the adults had been invited aboard the *Oracle* for a night's entertainment. Kev had been happy to volunteer to stay behind in a reprisal of his childminding duties as he could see Lenore was as curious about the *Oracle* as any of the others, and he had no heart for it without Persephone.

As he tied off the thread to the last bit of sewing and held up the harness to see how it was looking, he heard the sound of the others returning from their night out. Puzzled at the lack of chatter to accompany the sound of their feet, Kev looked up as Lady Elspeth stalked in, followed by Jonas. She was obviously out of sorts and went to the sink for a glass of water, while Jonas hovered uncertainly behind her.

'I'm going to bed' was all she said before going out and leaving the two men staring at each other.

Kev felt ill-equipped to breach the uncomfortable silence and was relieved when Lenore came in, hoping she would take charge and diffuse the atmosphere for him. Lenore, however, declined to speak but kept shooting Jonas meaningful looks, which he was doing his best to ignore.

Kev decided it was time to retire to his cabin and, feeling slightly disappointed the others weren't about to follow their usual habit of congregating in the galley to go over the evening in detail, hastily bade Jonas and Lenore a good night while clutching his work bits to him before exiting the galley hurriedly.

Once Kev was gone, Lenore turned to Jonas in exasperation. 'Really, Jonas!' she exclaimed, her voice vibrating with frustration. 'This can't go on. You have to talk to Elspeth and tell her why you don't want to marry her.'

Jonas looked shocked.

Lenore sighed. 'If you think the others have no inkling on what's up between you, you're very sadly mistaken. Even Kev's aware, and we all know he's not always the quickest to pick up on these things.'

Jonas shook his head sadly. 'I've tried, and I thought we'd come to an understanding about why I can't take the next step.'

Lenore snorted, a habit she had picked up from Millicent, and folded her arms across her chest. 'Well, it's obvious your idea of understanding and Elspeth's are more in the nature of parallel lines than intersecting ones. I daresay you skirted around the issue and thought she had picked up on all the things you *didn't* say and felt you had done enough to put her mind at rest.'

This was so close to the truth, Jonas could only look at Lenore sheepishly while running the palm of one hand up the back of his neck.

Lenore sighed again and, reaching out, laid a comforting hand on Jonas's arm. 'You need to tell her everything, Jonas. If she loves you – and I'm convinced she does, otherwise, this wouldn't bother her so much – she will come to understand.'

Jonas shook his head. 'It's not that I don't want to tell her. It's that I can't. And it's not that I'm afraid she'll think less of me if she knows the truth – or, at least, not entirely. I'm bound by oath not to reveal to anyone my secret status, and I'm bound by those same oaths to serve until my death.'

Lenore sat down heavily at the galley table. 'Oh, Jonas,' she commiserated, 'I'm sorry, but do you really think the ministry will be any the wiser if you tell one person? You know as well as I do Elspeth's entirely trustworthy. Besides, I kind of know, and the sky hasn't fallen.'

Jonas sat opposite Lenore and placed his hands over hers, giving them a little shake for emphasis. 'But I'd know, Lenore. I may not have much honour in other people's eyes, but I have my own sense of right and wrong, and breaking an oath goes against my deepest nature. I wouldn't be betraying the ministry, which I know full well sees me as dispensable, as much as I would be betraying myself.'

Lenore shook her head. 'I don't understand you, Jonas. You're willing to risk losing the woman you love for the sake of a ministry you admit yourself sees you as no more than a pawn in its own murky game.'

Jonas winced but held firm. 'I'm hoping for an answer to my dilemma, Lenore. I'm convinced a way out lies out there somewhere. I just haven't thought of it yet, that's all, and then Elspeth and I can get on with our lives.'

Lenore only shook her head at him. Discouraged, she stood up and went to the door. Turning to look back at Jonas, she said, 'I only hope you're right, Jonas. It's an awful lot to risk on a hope for things to work out OK in the end.'

Jonas didn't reply but watched as Lenore opened the door and went out before slumping forward and resting his forehead on his folded arms, Lenore's words echoing in his mind, ringing more truthfully than he was comfortable admitting.

Lady Elspeth ripped off her jewellery angrily and shoved it into her trinket box in an untidy jumble that would have her cursing in frustration the next time she tried to untangle it. She shook out her auburn hair and picked up her hairbrush, dragging it through her tresses with harsh, staccato jabs.

She had behaved badly this evening and knew it. As much as she attempted to mentally pass the blame to Jonas and his persistent reticence, she was well aware that there was no excuse for the way she had acted on board the *Oracle*.

It had started out as a wonderful evening. Cornelius's luxurious airship surpassed everyone's expectations, and even Millicent had been wooed by the softness and elegance of her surroundings.

Phineas and Cornelius had quickly ironed out the details of the gun exchange, and then the rest of the evening had been given over to fine wine, food, and entertainment. Cornelius, it turned out, was an excellent piano player with a passable tenor voice and had been more than happy to show off his skills for them.

Lenore too had been coaxed into singing, accompanied by Cornelius, and Lady Elspeth herself had been thrilled to add to the evening's programme by having her turn at the keys.

The trouble had begun after that as, flushed with the heady feeling of accomplishment, she had allowed Cornelius to monopolise her attention and flirt with her to the exclusion of the others. She suspected that a not-so-dormant desire to flout conventions lay at the root of Cornelius's behaviour, and she could have quite easily steered them back into the general conversation. But a small rebellious part of her had wanted to use the situation to prod Jonas into taking some kind of action to break the stalemate they seemed to be in.

Jonas, however, didn't become angry or even appear to be jealous in any way and calmly refused to pick up the figurative gauntlet, leaving her feeling put out and vaguely ashamed of herself no matter how she reasoned to herself that she wasn't doing anything wrong.

At one point, she caught sight of her reflection in the mirror over the mantle – her cheeks blushing prettily and her eyes sparkling as she threw her head back to laugh delightedly at some nonsense Cornelius was saying – and realised she had crossed a line.

She looked around and noticed the others for what felt like the first time. Jonas looked perfectly composed, much to her chagrin, and neither Millicent nor Phineas were giving any indication that she was behaving in anything but the utmost ladylike manner as they chatted amiably with Jonas, but Lenore caught her eye and shot her a warning look that stung her.

Not liking how she was feeling, she gracefully excused herself and went to powder her nose. When she returned, she discovered Millicent had firmly taken charge and begun the process of wrapping up the evening. She was standing, shaking Cornelius by the hand and thanking him for his hospitality, impervious to Cornelius's entreaties to stay for a bit longer and partake of supper.

Millicent had smiled and, shooting Lady Elspeth a look that told her her actions hadn't gone completely unnoticed, politely turned him down, and they had all been ferried back to the *Elizabeth Anne* in silence by one of Cornelius's crew aboard one of medium-sized craft he kept for ferrying people to and from his pleasure craft.

Lady Elspeth would never have considered herself spoilt, having had to work hard to make her way in the academic world she had chosen as her life's pathway. But she realised she had underestimated the influence of the privileged upbringing she had had and that she had much to learn about how to behave gracefully when not getting what you wanted, something that, until now, had never occurred thanks to her wealth and hard-working habits.

Having brushed her hair until her scalp tingled, Lady Elspeth realised she had no idea how to cross the widening breach that was developing between her and Jonas and that there was very little she could do to coerce Jonas into behaving in a way she considered acceptable. This realisation depressed her as she wondered if she was capable of not pushing Jonas until she pushed him beyond reach.

Turning out her lamp, in a vain attempt to try and sleep, she tossed and turned, scrunching her pillow beneath her head. Trying to still her mind enough to rest, she realised for the first time in her life that she was going to have to stop pushing for what she wanted if she was going to salvage her relationship with Jonas.

Like many quiet people, he possessed a stubborn streak of formidable proportions. No amount of trying to edge conversations and decisions along the path she wanted to go had been remotely effective. All she was doing was pushing him further into his shell.

Sighing, she wondered if perhaps she wasn't being a little bit of a bully. This was an uncomfortable thought. Coming to the conclusion that she needed a change of tack for her own sake as much as Jonas's, she decided she would just let the whole subject drop and allow things to develop – or not – as they would.

Having reached this decision, a lovely sense of relief and calmness of mind fell on her, and at long last, she found her eyes were growing heavy, and she sank into the best sleep she had had in many weeks.

CHAPTER 19

Cornelius watched as his men began the careful task of packing the tiny vials of distilled aether into the padded boxes for transportation. In this state, the aether was highly volatile as it was constantly seeking to return to its natural state. By storing it in dark glass vials and keeping it well insulated from heat and sudden bumps, it was possible to store it safely, but it was a tricky business, and Cornelius preferred to oversee the packing and transportation of the aether himself.

The last thing he needed was an unfortunate accident that would destroy the many months of hard work spent harvesting the aether. Not only would he lose his profit, but also, that kind of explosion would alert the authorities to his clandestine endeavours. He watched his well-trained men in their gauntlets and goggles as they gingerly inserted each tiny vial into its own padded slot in the boxes and thought of the shipment of guns stashed securely in his hideout.

The demand for aether far outstripped his ability to supply it, and he had been hoping to take on extra men to harvest and transport the aether to those waiting on it. But after Huia's visit and his subsequent conversations with Nellie Sprocket and the crew of the *Elizabeth Anne*, he realised he was going to have to postpone those plans for now. He couldn't risk hiring one of Silas Elmstone's spies. The idea of harbouring one in his crew filled him with horror.

Nellie had confirmed his role as the bridge between the pirates and the airship community of Grahamstown. She had filled him in on some of the troubles she suspected Elmstone of causing, and he was coming to realise they were all fighting for high stakes.

Cornelius had little regard for the letter of the law and no respect for the government with its intrigues and politicking. He knew there were as many privateers sailing the skies as there were pirates and that the government would be aware of Silas and his growing ambitions and, as yet, had not attempted to rein him in.

They could expect no help from the authorities. In fact, he suspected they were probably aiding Elmstone for their own ends or, at the least, passively watching the outcome. If they wanted to defeat Elmstone and bring his plans to an end, they were on their own and would need to put aside their differences and grudges if they stood any chance of victory – a troubling thought.

Once the aether was safely stowed, Cornelius left the delivery to one of his captains and returned to his eyrie. Entering his study, he found a messenger from Nellie sitting on the windowsill in the form of a large black clockwork bird. As he watched, the bird disgorged a small metal cylinder from its innards, which he picked up and, unscrewing the lid, shook the piece of rolled paper nestled inside, out into the palm of his hand.

It was a list of confirmed spies aboard every airship sailing into Grahamstown. The only vessel not affected was the *Elizabeth Anne*, which made Millicent an excellent point of contact.

He realised, reading through the list, that Silas had been playing a long game. His managing to infiltrate the airship community in this way without anyone being the wiser until now was disturbing.

Sitting down at his desk, he drew a piece of paper towards him and began the painstaking task of encoding a message to Nellie for forwarding onto Millicent. The sooner they got themselves organised and a had a plan of attack, the better.

CHAPTER 20

Merton Wells stepped through the door of the Junction Hotel onto the street. An unusual wave of optimism flowed over him. As he was not normally a man to see the glass as half full, this unexpected feeling caught him unawares, and he blinked a few times, unsure of what to do with it. In a brief life yet to reach its third decade, he had no experience of looking on the bright side, and the gloom caused by his catalogue of disappointments and missed opportunities hovered over him like the threat of rain on a sunny day. To be overcome by the opposite emotion – and so unexpectedly – was both exhilarating and unsettling.

Having decided nothing good could come from the feeling, he managed to coerce his mind into its habitual pessimism and immediately felt better. On returning to his comfort zone, he pondered the mystery of why his life hadn't reached the pinnacle of success he felt it should have by now. It wasn't from want of trying, he knew that. But somehow, no matter how much effort he put in, he never seemed to reach his full potential, unaware he was a self-fulfilling prophecy.

Pulling a creased and grubby piece of paper from his pocket, he studied it thoughtfully before lifting his head to get his bearings. At last, he felt a shifting in the aether, and he knew he was on the cusp of something different.

He was getting close. He was convinced of it. He could feel it in his bones. Ignoring the inconvenient fact that his bones had quite often misled him in the past, he set off for the airship docks, buoyed by the return of the unfamiliar sense of optimism.

His plan was to scout out the docks and survey the ships in port. He was certain his target was on board one of the vessels that docked here on a regular basis. As yet, he had no firm plan on how to apprehend the man he sought, but he was sure something would come to him.

Finding himself a secluded spot, he settled down and took out a small pair of brass binoculars. Lifting them to his eyes, he made himself comfortable, watching the comings and goings from the airships with interest.

⧗

Lady Elspeth pushed against the store door with her shoulder, her arms full of parcels, and stepped out onto the street. She shifted the load in her arms to make it easier to carry back to the airship.

Millicent had sent her into town to buy supplies for the party she was hosting, ostensibly for her birthday but really to create an occasion to get all the airship captains in one spot and fill them in on the information passed on by Huia via Cornelius.

Lady Elspeth was wishing she had thought to bring a wheeled basket when she spotted Jonas up ahead, stepping out of the Junction and heading up the street ahead of her.

'Jonas!' she cried, trying to get his attention so he could help her with her burden.

He didn't appear to hear her and carried on up the street, oblivious to her plight. Picking up her pace as best she could, Lady Elspeth hurried after him, closing the gap a little.

'Jonas!' she shouted again, but once more, he ignored her and took off ahead of her, much to her annoyance.

Her arms were beginning to ache, and she had to slow down and rearrange the parcels. By the time she looked back to the street, Jonas had vanished, and she huffed bad-temperedly before setting off in the direction of the docks.

She stepped back aboard the *Elizabeth Anne* with relief and hurried to the galley to unburden her sore arms. Stepping through the galley doorway, she found Kev, Persephone, Lenore, and Jonas seated at the table, just ready to pour a cup of tea. Thankfully, Lady Elspeth dropped her parcels onto the bench and joined the others. Lenore poured her a cup of tea and passed it to her without comment.

'Thank you!' she exclaimed feelingly. 'That's just what I need.' Taking a fortifying sip, she turned to Jonas. 'Did you not hear me calling to you before?' she asked tartly. 'I could have done with a hand with those parcels.'

'Before when?' queried Jonas, feeling a little baffled.

'Before now, in town,' explained Lady Elspeth. 'You just ignored me, I'm sure of it.'

Jonas shook his head. 'But I wasn't in town,' he insisted. 'I've been aboard all morning.'

Lady Elspeth looked at him unbelievingly. 'Nonsense, Jonas,' she declared. 'I saw you with my own eyes.'

'You can't have done,' replied Jonas calmly, 'because I was here.'

Lady Elspeth frowned and was about to argue further when Kev interjected. 'It's true. Jonas has been here with me all morning. He's been giving me more training in hand-to-hand combat.'

Lady Elspeth wasn't convinced. 'Well, who did I see then? It was you. I'm certain of it.'

'Well, I've heard we all have a doppelganger,' suggested Kev. 'Maybe it was someone who looks like Jonas from a distance.'

Lenore looked thoughtful. 'You could be right, Kev,' she said. Turning to Lady Elspeth, she continued, 'I had a similar experience, actually, just the other day. I thought I saw Jonas too, but then I realised it couldn't have been him because he'd gone up to the mine to visit Edgar.'

Lady Elspeth didn't feel convinced but decided to drop the subject. Sipping her tea, she listened as the others began to discuss arrangements for Millicent's party. She admitted to herself that it wouldn't be like Jonas to deliberately ignore her. Maybe Kev was right and he had a double out there.

Millicent came in carrying a wad of envelopes in one hand. 'Ah, excellent timing,' she said cheerfully. 'I need one of you to hand-deliver these to each of the airships in port and leave the rest with the harbourmaster for delivery.'

'I'll go,' volunteered Jonas. 'I take it these are the invitations to the party?'

Millicent nodded. 'They are, indeed,' she replied. 'It seems a frivolous way to get the airship captains together in one spot under the circumstances, but that may just be the kind of red herring we need so as not to alert any of Silas Elmstone's spies.'

'I think it's a fantastic ploy,' reassured Persephone. 'I'll invite some of the other doctors from the hospital if you like. That should really throw any suspicious watchers off the scent.'

'That's an excellent idea,' approved Millicent. 'I'll make up some more invitations.'

'Do you think everyone will come?' asked Kev worriedly.

'Oh yes,' declared Millicent with some satisfaction. 'My parties are legendary. There won't be a single "with regret", I promise you.' So saying, she handed Jonas the invitations and left to write out more invitations for Persephone to take to the hospital.

Jonas stepped back aboard the *Elizabeth Anne*. It was far later than he had originally intended to stay out, and the night was well advanced. He was reluctant to admit to himself that it was easier to stay away than to endure the continuing tension between him and Lady Elspeth.

He had found himself aimlessly wandering the streets after delivering Millicent's invitations until he had eventually found himself on Edgar and Morag's doorstep. He had happily accepted their invitation to stay for dinner, and the rest of the afternoon and evening had been spent very pleasantly in their company, and for a while, he had been able to forget about his own troubles.

Now on his return, he could feel the tension begin to stir in the pit of his stomach again, and he hoped Elspeth was already asleep. The thought that she might be awake and waiting up for him caused his spirits to sink a little, and he began to feel worried that he might not be able to find a way to resolve this difficulty between them.

As he turned to lock the lifting platform in place, he froze, feeling a tiny shift in the air behind him that caused the hairs on his neck to lift. Taking a steadying breath, he silently and almost undetectably slipped the dagger from his sleeve, where he kept it in a holster strapped to his forearm.

As he did so, he felt another infinitesimal disturbance in the air behind him. In one smooth practised movement, he ducked and, using the momentum of his own body, rolled to the deck. His body weight took him gracefully to his feet once more, and he heard a soft grunt behind him as his hidden attacker swung and found nothing but air.

All his senses on high alert now, Jonas stepped towards the grunt in the darkness, closing his eyes as he did so and engaging his other senses as he brought his arms up and around while bringing one leg out in an arc, sweeping his attacker's legs out from under him and sending them both crashing to the deck. Twisting his body as they fell, Jonas ensured he was on top, with the unknown assailant trapped beneath him.

Once more, using the weight and momentum of his own body, Jonas pinned his attacker to the deck, knees pinning his arms, one arm across his throat. The man struggled fiercely, but as Jonas's dagger under his chin drew blood with every lurch, he soon gave up and lay still.

The commotion of their bodies hitting the deck and the mystery attacker's subsequent struggles had aroused the rest of the crew, and Jonas could hear the sounds of their footsteps pounding onto the deck.

'What the hell's going on?' demanded Phineas, his face creased from the pillow and his night shirt on back to front. He lifted the lantern he held higher to illuminate the two men sprawled on the deck.

The rest of the crew were also in similar states of disarray and had the dazed look of those awoken from deep sleep. Phineas stepped forward and kicked the man's knife from out of his trapped hand and sent it scudding across the deck.

Carefully, Jonas moved his body weight until he was able to drag the intruder up off the deck, keeping his dagger to the man's throat as he did so, and light from Phineas's lantern illuminated them fully for the first time.

Jonas noticed the others blink and do double takes. Small exclamations of surprise littered the air. Puzzled, Jonas looked to the crew and then back to the man he was holding onto so tightly. Letting go of his grip slightly now that he was assured Phineas and Kev had him covered, Jonas got a glimpse of his assailant for the first time.

'Well, I never,' murmured Jonas to no one in particular.

'It's uncanny,' breathed Millicent, gazing from Jonas to the stranger in amazement, while Phineas rubbed his eyes and took another look.

Jonas looked at his captive, who could, for all intents and purposes, pass as his twin brother, an idea beginning to form in his mind. Slowly, a small smile tugged at the corners of his mouth as he realised this could be the end of all his problems.

CHAPTER 21

The crew sat around the galley table and regarded the man tied to a chair in front of them. It had taken some time to settle the children and send them back to bed, but Millicent had been adamant, and eventually, they had all been coerced into obedience, albeit unwillingly, and Lenore was only now settling an overstimulated Mina Myra, while the others were keeping their eyes on their captive.

The man had appeared to accept his capture with a weary resignation and had offered no resistance. He was an object of intense curiosity to the crew given his close resemblance to Jonas, and they had all been speculating about him quite audibly, but until now, he had not offered any explanation as to what he had been up to.

Millicent was highly offended that he had come aboard her airship with what was obviously sinister intent, and she was watching him with open hostility. The others, however, were deeply intrigued by his resemblance to Jonas, and differing theories as to why this should be were being offered and dissected avidly.

'Do you think he's a long-lost relative?' asked Persephone. 'The resemblance is uncanny. What do you think?' she continued, turning to Lady Elspeth.

Lady Elspeth shook her head. 'I wouldn't know. I don't think he looks that much like Jonas, to be honest. There's a definite likeness – you could be fooled from a distance – but up close and together like this? I can't see it myself.'

'Well, you know Jonas so well,' said Kev, 'but I reckon they look more alike than some real brothers do.'

Lady Elspeth shrugged and turned to look at Jonas and then the man in the chair. It was true that they looked incredibly similar – eerily so, in fact. It was certainly a mystery, as was the reason the stranger had turned up on board the *Elizabeth Anne*.

Jonas remained silent but continued to watch the man closely from behind his dark glasses. He only half-listened to what the others were discussing, much more intent on refining the plan he was hatching. He needed to somehow get the stranger on side and convince him to go along with it, and he was weighing up the chances of this to himself. As interesting as it was to come across someone who could pass as oneself, Jonas was way more interested to find out if he could persuade the man to cooperate in his scheme than in his unknown parentage.

Having never known his father, his mother being a respectable 'widow', Jonas surmised that the likelihood of having any number of unknown siblings was reasonably high. But regardless of the origins of the stranger's uncanny resemblance to himself, he recognised it as a perfect opportunity and intended to use the situation to its full advantage.

Lenore came in through the door and took her place at the galley table. Phineas looked at Millicent, who nodded to him, and he rose and stood over the stranger, hands on his hips.

'It's time for you to explain just what you're doing aboard this ship,' he demanded. 'Are you working for Silas Elmstone?'

The man sighed deeply and shook his head. The overwhelming impression was of a disheartened man. Phineas found this rather disconcerting, having expected defiance or insolence, maybe even an attempt to bargain his way out of the situation. The man's depressed spirits took him by surprise, and he was unsure of how to proceed, feeling reluctant to use forceful means under the circumstances.

The man merely indicated his pocket and said, 'In there.'

Puzzled, Phineas reached in and drew out a piece of folded paper. Having unfolded it, he raised his eyebrows and handed the paper to Millicent, who whistled and looked at Kev.

'Really?' she asked, handing the paper to Kev.

'What?' exclaimed Kev, showing the paper to Persephone.

Taking the paper from Kev, Persephone looked as though she wasn't sure whether to laugh or cry.

The stranger nodded towards Kev. 'I'm after him,' he explained. 'I'm all above board. I'm a bounty hunter, bottom fact – got a licence to prove it and all.'

At this, Jonas held out his hand for the paper, which Persephone relinquished. 'There's some mistake,' she said as she did so.

Jonas perused the paper. He already had an inkling of what was on it. Sure enough, it was a copy of the same identikit drawing of Kev the Ministry of Secret Affairs had sent out prior to Kev's return to his own world. He experienced a sinking feeling in his gut. This would complicate his plans somewhat. Now he was going to have to get the man off side, as it were, before he could bring him on side. His mind raced as he tried to adjust his plan to accommodate this unfortunate turn of events. Jonas was intrigued as to how a bounty hunter had managed to get hold of a copy of an internal ministry document and wondered how much the man knew about the ministry and its network of secret assassins.

'So what's your name, friend?' he asked him.

'Merton Wells, at your service,' he answered, 'and I aim to apprehend one Obadiah Effington and take him into the crowbar hotel for questioning relating to the charges you see there before you.'

At this, the entire crew began to protest at once. The resulting cacophony of voices rose in an ascending crescendo of disbelief, denial, and outrage as everyone tried to convince the bounty hunter of Kev's innocence. The uncomfortable fact of Kev having posed as Obadiah Effington in a daring rescue mission to free Sherlock from jail was not forgotten, but they all hoped by talking loud enough and for long enough, the bounty hunter could be bamboozled into going away. This was not having the desired effect. Jonas could see by the stubborn set of the man's jaw and the suspicious looks he shot them from beneath his brows that he wasn't buying a word they were saying.

Jonas raised his hand to quiet everyone down, and one by one, the crew fell silent, watching him curiously. Jonas had no clear idea of what he was going to say, but he knew he had to convince Merton Wells that Kev was not the man he was looking for.

'This man is not Obadiah Effington,' he said, indicating Kev with a small gesture. 'His name is Kev, and he's a member of this crew and has been for some time.'

'I know my own eyes and what I see,' replied the bounty hunter stubbornly. 'It doesn't matter what moniker he goes by. He's the man on the poster – the spitting image. So don't you try and sell me a dog.'

'Fair enough,' replied Jonas. 'If this man is indeed Obadiah Effington, then I am Merton Wells.'

'Don't make a stuffed bird laugh,' replied Merton Wells. 'You know that's ridiculous.'

'Is it?' queried Jonas. 'Can you prove I'm not?'

'Of course, I can, you lumpkin. I'm Merton Wells. I just said as much.'

'Ah, but how do you know I'm not Merton Wells?'

'Because I'm Merton Wells!'

'I have no doubt you are. But I say I'm Merton Wells.'

The man was beginning to grow red in the face with frustration, and the rest of the crew were watching with increasing puzzlement, all of them wondering what Jonas was trying to achieve.

'Look here,' demanded Merton irately. 'You can say you're me until the cows come home, but I know you're not.'

'Perhaps,' conceded Jonas, 'but as I look exactly like you, can you, in fact, prove to someone else that I am not you?'

'Of course. Everyone who knows me will be able to tell you're an imposter.'

'But we don't know you, so who's to say I'm not you?'

'Your crew mates, for one,' declared Merton triumphantly.

Jonas turned to the others, who were all looking at him with varying degrees of bewilderment, and raised his eyebrows. 'Who am I?' he asked them, wriggling his brows in what he hoped was a meaningful way.

'Er . . . Merton Wells?' offered Lenore tentatively.

Jonas slapped his thigh triumphantly. 'Yes! That's exactly who I am.'

The rest of the crew were beginning to look at Jonas as though he were losing his mind.

Turning back to Merton, Jonas shrugged and raised his hands in a gesture of helplessness. 'There we have it. You can't prove I'm not Merton Wells. Even my crew mates believe me to be him.'

'I have no notion what you're trying to prove,' stated Merton wearily, 'but I'm getting tired of this conversation.'

'I'm just trying to point out that it's very easy to say someone is who you think they are, but there isn't any way to prove it.'

'Yes, there is!' exclaimed Merton angrily. 'I have a picture of a man calling himself Obadiah Effington whose fizzog looks just like this man here, and unless you've got a better argument than this ridiculous "Who am I?" game, I'm taking him in.'

'Just because someone looks like someone doesn't mean they are them,' insisted Jonas, beginning to feel a little confused himself.

'I can admit the rightful truth of it,' admitted Merton, 'but that's not my concern. All I have to do is bring him in. If he's innocent, it will be proven. You can call him Kev for as long as you like, but he could just be calling himself Kev the same way you're calling yourself Merton.'

By now, the crew were listening and watching the exchange between Jonas and Merton with interest, especially Kev, who, naturally enough, had much more at stake in the outcome.

'Or maybe,' continued Merton, 'he really is Kev but called himself Obadiah.'

Jonas sighed inwardly as Merton unwittingly hit upon the inconvenient truth. He was going to have to use his plan B, which maybe should have been his plan A all along, as much as he hated revealing too much about himself.

'This man is Kev, not Obadiah Effington, in spite of resembling him closely,' he stated clearly.

Merton Wells's chin jutted stubbornly. He was clearly frustrated by this continuing conversation and beginning to lose his patience for it. He pulled against his bonds as he tried to use his hands to emphasise his words. 'I don't care who you *say* he is. Unless you're going to do me in, you cannot keep me from taking this man into my custody.'

Jonas slipped his hand into the inside pocket of his jacket and drew out a small leather wallet. Flipping it open, he revealed the tiny identification badge inside, knowing that Merton Wells was likely to recognise it if he was aware enough of the ministry to be able to intercept its aether mail. Sure enough, Merton Wells's eyebrows shot upwards, and he gave Jonas a searching stare, tinged with a blossoming respect and a smidge of envy.

'This man is not Obadiah Effington,' stated Jonas. 'He never was and cannot possibly be because I dispatched the real Obadiah over a year ago.' Slipping the wallet back into his pocket, he fixed Merton with a hard stare. 'I hope you realise what this means, Mr Wells.' To the surprise of the rest of the crew, who were only vaguely following what was happening, their captive groaned and slumped against his bonds.

'Well, if that don't just beat the Dutch! If this ain't just the story of my life!' he declared somewhat melodramatically. 'Turns out I got the wrong pig by the tail. I'm forever shooting into the brown. I'm nothing but a foozler. I may as well just hang up the fiddle and become a greengrocer.'

'So does this mean Kev's not a wanted man?' asked Persephone tentatively.

Jonas looked over to where she sat at the galley table. Kev had his arm around her, and they both looked anxious. Jonas smiled and nodded. 'It's all right, Persephone. This little misunderstanding has been all cleared up. Mr Wells realises he has been chasing the wrong man.'

Jonas was disturbed to see Millicent – who knew full well that Kev had posed as Obadiah Effington and that he had done the things cited on the warrant – was regarding him thoughtfully, maybe even suspiciously. His heart sank. He didn't want to have to confess to the crew.

'What say we all have a lovely, restorative cup of tea?' announced Lenore, leaping up and bustling about the galley.

Jonas was grateful. He realised she was attempting to take the focus off him.

Millicent shook herself. Lenore's busyness distracted her, and she rose to help set out the tea things. Turning to Phineas, she said, 'Please escort Mr Wells off my ship. I think I've had enough of him for one night.'

Jonas stood up and lifted a hand to halt Phineas. 'Sit down, Phineas. I'll take care of Mr Wells.'

Phineas shrugged and sat back down again as Jonas released the bounty hunter from his bonds and ushered him out of the galley.

CHAPTER 22

Merton Wells held out a conciliatory hand to Jonas as the two men stood by the lifting platform. 'I'm conscience struck over this bag of nails, Mr Emerson. I'm willing to acknowledge the corn when I'm wrong.'

Jonas took Merton's proffered hand and overture of peace. 'No harm done,' he told him, thankful Merton didn't appear to be the kind of man to bear a grudge, needing to keep him on his side if his plan was to succeed. 'I'm interested to hear your story,' he said as the two men shook hands. 'Do you have time for a quick drink?'

'I've been known to bend the elbow on occasion,' Merton informed him.

Jonas nodded. 'Excellent. Meet me in Irishtown in half an hour. There's a sly grog there.'

Merton listened to Jonas's directions and stepped aboard the lifting platform as Jonas turned on his heel and returned to the galley. Slipping back in through the door, hoping to evade any questioning from Millicent, Jonas slid in beside Lady Elspeth. Feeling pleased with how his plan was working out, he leaned over and placed a quick kiss on her cheek. She turned, surprised, and gave him a hard look. Catching the expression on his face, her own features softened, and she took his hand in hers under the table.

Noticing the sense of rapport between them, Millicent decided not to spoil it by questioning Jonas. She was certain he knew more about the situation than he was saying, and she wanted to get to the bottom of it. But as much as the suspicions and questions gnawed at the edges of her mind, her natural kindness prevented her from ruining this rare moment of accord between Jonas and Lady Elspeth.

Things can wait, she told herself.

Jonas edged quietly through the door of the sly grog and waited until his eyes adjusted to the smoky gloom inside. It was nothing more than a rough lean-to tacked onto the back of a cottage.

The owner was a miner's widow trying her best to make the ever-widening gap between her ends meet up, and Jonas often drank here out of pity and not for the quality of the liquor, which describing as rough would have been a misleading understatement.

Taking his shot of the potion on offer, Jonas looked around for a spot to watch and wait for Merton Wells. Spying an empty table in the corner, he made his way over to it with satisfaction. Depositing his glass on the sticky surface of the table, he sat back to wait.

He didn't have long. He'd only just screwed up the courage to take the first sip of his drink when Merton appeared in the doorway. Jonas watched as he shouldered his way to the bar, murmuring, 'mind the grease,' as he did so.

Having procured his own drink and given it a suspicious sniff, Merton looked around for any sight of Jonas. Eventually catching sight of him, he made his way over and, angling his chair so as to be able to keep one eye on the door, sat down.

Jonas raised his glass to Merton, who returned the gesture, and the two men took a sip. Jonas was somewhat prepared for the fiery assault on his senses, but Merton was not.

'Bloody hell!' he wheezed, eyes watering. 'It wouldn't take much of that to get you chirping merry.'

'Indeed,' murmured Jonas as his own drink burnt an incandescent path to his stomach. 'The regulars call it dragon's breath.'

Merton barked a rueful laugh, rubbing his sternum, where the effects of the liquor could still be felt. 'Ain't that the bottom fact.'

'I'm sure you understand the need for complete secrecy,' stated Jonas.

'Umble cum stumble,' concurred Merton with a knowing wink.

'Good,' replied Jonas. 'I'm interested to know how much you are aware of the Ministry of Dark Affairs and how you came to intercept its aether mail.'

Merton nodded. 'I'm trusting I won't end up as dead meat over this,' he said, giving Jonas a searching look.

Jonas shook his head. 'Have no fear, Mr Wells. I have no intention of reporting your faux pas to the ministry. In fact, I'm hoping you will be able to help me out of a bind I find myself in.'

Merton looked relieved. 'Good enough,' he said. 'I'm not one for those cramp words, so I don't reckon on what a foe par is, but I'd be happy to save your bacon if you think I can.'

Jonas nodded in satisfaction. 'Carry on and tell me what you know of the ministry,' he prompted.

Merton nodded and took up his glass for another sip but, after giving it a considering look, placed it gingerly on the table.

'One day I happened to shake a flannin with a group of rusty-guts fellows. I was giving them a good batty fang, I can tell you. Three to one, it was. Quick on my feet, me, so they couldn't land the blows. Anyway, once it was all done and dusted, a sly cove came up and asked me if I wanted to make use of my skills. He reckoned he could put me in the way of doing that kind of thing for a living. Told me some things about a skilamalink government department and how I was just the type of young man they needed. He made me a bit all overish, to be honest, but I liked the idea of being a secret agent.

'Couldn't take him up on it though because my ma was poorly. I'm not one to ever beat the devil around the stump, so I stayed and took care of her until she was in God's acre. Never saw the cove again, but I did me some digging around. Learned all I could, kept my ear to the ground. Got a job as a bounty hunter. Once I had a bit of dosh, I got a fellow to make me a scanner. Started intercepting aether mail, trying to get an edge over the competition.

'I figured if I kept at it, one day that cove'd be back, and I'd get my chance over, but I won't sell you a dog or give you any fumble-famble. I just don't seem to make headway on it. It's one cold coffee after another. Somehow I get all balled up or too late to the party. After tonight, I'm tail down. Got a right case of the morbs. I'm about ready to hang up my fiddle, to be honest. The chances of me being an agent for the ministry are about as likely as catching a weasel asleep, as I see it.'

'Maybe not,' suggested Jonas thoughtfully. 'I have a plan, which I'm hoping you'll be willing to help me with. It would be a back-door kind of way into the ministry, but if we pull it off, you'll be an agent – an assassin, to be precise – for the Ministry of Dark Affairs.'

'Fizzing!' exclaimed Merton. 'This is some pumpkins. I won't ask no adds, but if you can get me in, I'll be a pig in clover.'

Jonas nodded, relieved that Merton Wells was so willing to be a part of his plan. He looked the young man over. He judged him to be only a few years younger than himself, but he had about him an air of immaturity, as though he was still as yet only half formed, that made him seem much younger, and Jonas felt a twinge of conscience. As desperate as he was to extricate himself from the ministry, he didn't like the feeling he was leading Merton Wells along the path to the sacrificial altar. He decided he would need to put some time into the young man to bring his skills up as well as train him in the use of the various pieces of technology he used.

'So how can I help you?' queried Merton. 'What's the plan?'

Quickly, Jonas informed Merton of the quandary he found himself in and how he hoped Merton would be able to help him.

'So you wish to absquatulate,' verified Merton once Jonas was done.

Jonas nodded. 'In a way. But I won't actually disappear. You would just take my place. No one should be any the wiser. The ministry very rarely makes physical contact with its agents. If, for some reason, you are contacted by the ministry in person, you bear a close enough resemblance to me that you won't rouse suspicion.'

'So I'll have to change my moniker to yours too then?'

Jonas shook his head. 'No. Jonas Emerson is not my name. At least, it's not the name I was born with. I've changed my name a few times over the years I've been with the ministry as needs have arisen. The ministry will be none the wiser if you keep your name for now. They only refer to us by a number anyway.'

'It's all a bit hugger mugger, ain't it?' said Merton thoughtfully.

Jonas nodded wearily. 'Unfortunately, yes,' he replied. 'Having second thoughts?'

Merton shook his head. 'No, this is bang up to the elephant. I won't be backing and filling. This is what I've always wanted. I missed my chance before. I'm not passing up on it again.'

'That's what I thought too once,' pointed out Jonas.

Merton merely shrugged. 'I wasn't born in the woods to be afraid of an owl, Mr Emerson,' he replied. 'You've handed me my dream on a plate. I'm in, boots and all.'

So saying, he reached out his hand, and Jonas took it, and the two men shook hands heartily.

'I think you should call me Jonas, don't you?' Jonas was saying when a commotion from the doorway interrupted them.

'Mutton shunters!' exclaimed Merton as a group of the local enforcers shouldered their way through the door. 'Quick – we better back slang it.'

Jonas nodded, and the two men leaped up as one, upending their table as they did so into the path of the approaching enforcers before making their way swiftly out the back door and into the night.

Racing back down the hill towards Grahamstown, they soon left the confusion of the raid behind them. Slowing down and catching their breath, they grinned at each other.

Merton slapped his thigh and laughed out loud. 'It's not often I have occasion to amputate the timber,' he declared.

Jonas laughed too. 'It certainly added an element of excitement to the evening,' he said. 'I'll be in touch soon. I need to go over the technology you'll be using and maybe do a bit of training with you.'

Merton nodded. 'I'm mad as hops to get started,' he said, 'although I may need to find other digs if I'm staying. Do you know of anyone who might be willing to keep a pig?'

Jonas scratched his head. He thought of Edgar and Morag, but not only did they already have quite a houseful with the children and Rabbie, but also, they were just newly married, and he felt they probably didn't want to have a complete stranger foisted on them at this stage of their lives.

'Leave it to me,' he told Merton. 'I'll see if I can get Millicent to let you stay on board with us.'

Even as the words left his mouth, he could feel his mood sinking. He wasn't going to be able avoid having a conversation with Millicent after all.

CHAPTER 23

Jonas, Merton, and Lady Elspeth stood just inside the door of the rooms Millicent had hired for her birthday party and took a moment to absorb the atmosphere. Millicent had spared no expense, and the venue was magnificently opulent. As Millicent had predicted, no one had refused the invitation, and the place was already beginning to feel overly warm from the press of bodies circulating. The noise of conversation was almost overwhelming.

Jonas could feel his spirits sinking at the prospect of an evening spent in this hot and noisy environment, but he could see Lady Elspeth was looking forward to it and, knowing it was important for their plans, resigned himself to it with only a twinge of regret over having to leave the peaceful quiet of the *Elizabeth Anne*.

Beside him, he could see Merton's incredulous expression as he looked about him and stifled a laugh. It was not hard to see this was his protégé's first foray into the social scene, and the various thoughts racing through his mind were showing themselves on his face.

'Let's find a quiet corner, shall we?' Jonas suggested to him.

Merton nodded. 'This is some rackety shindig. I've not seen the likes. It makes my thoughts go every which way, bottom fact.'

'Mine too,' admitted Jonas, 'but maybe we can find a spot for a quiet drink.'

'Well, you two can do that, but I'm going to mingle,' declared Lady Elspeth. 'Millicent said there'd be dancing later, so I'm off to fill in my dance card. Can I put you down for the supper dance, Jonas?'

Jonas nodded with weary resignation. 'Go ahead,' he said before he and Merton began to shoulder their way through the throng in search of a secluded spot in which to have their quiet drink.

Finding a table with an excellent view of the main room, the men sat down with their drinks and watched the crowd with some interest.

'This is pretty much butter upon bacon,' stated Merton as he looked on, astounded.

Jonas nodded and filled Merton in on the purpose of the evening.

Merton gave a low whistle. 'Seems an immoderate means to bring the big bugs together,' he said.

Jonas shrugged. 'Maybe, but it would be hard to get the information to the airship captains without alerting any spies they may be harbouring on board their ships.'

'Umble cum stumble,' said Merton, 'but how'd you know the waiters ain't whiddlers?'

Jonas felt a chill run through him. 'We don't,' he said, realising Merton had hit upon a flaw in their plan. Quickly, he weighed up the options. 'Where's Millicent?' he asked, looking about the main room as he formulated his plan.

'Over there with the cove smothering a parrot,' said Merton, indicating with a nod to where Millicent stood in conversation with Cornelius, who was downing a shot of neat absinthe.

'Come on then,' said Jonas. 'We need to alert the others to the possibility of some of the waiters being spies.'

Millicent watched as the two young men made their way through the crowd towards her. They seemed unlikely companions to her, but maybe their close physical resemblance brought with it a meeting of kindred souls.

She hadn't been enthralled with the idea of welcoming Merton aboard the *Elizabeth Anne* and had at first refused Jonas's request to allow Merton to live on board for the time being. When she questioned Jonas as to why he wanted Merton to stay with them, he had become almost shifty and hadn't offered her an explanation that had satisfied her. When pressed, Jonas had only replied that she needed to trust him.

'Have I ever done anything to bring harm to the *Elizabeth Anne* or the crew?' he had asked.

As Millicent knew from experience the answer to that, she felt she had no choice but to allow Jonas the benefit of the doubt and let him pursue his mysterious plans unchallenged.

When she shared her misgivings with Phineas, he had only given her a swift hug and told her not to worry.

'Don't fret over it, Millie,' he had said. 'Whatever he's up to, no harm will come to us by it.'

Not quite as reassured as Phineas felt she ought to be but not having anything concrete to go on, she let the subject drop.

As Jonas and Merton came alongside, she merely nodded to them. Cornelius, having downed his drink, excused himself to return to the bar, giving the two men a brief nod.

'Fancies himself the biggest toad in the puddle, don't he?' murmured Merton to no one in particular.

'If you only knew,' replied Jonas before turning his attention to Millicent and quickly filling her in on the danger of one of the waiters being a spy.

'What should we do?' asked Millicent, appalled.

'I'll go and alert Phineas and get the others together. We'll need to be watchful. Merton and I can mingle with the intent of keeping the waiters under surveillance. I'll get Kev and Edgar to help with that too. Maybe even Orson and Sherlock.'

Millicent nodded and turned to Merton. 'Thank you, Merton,' she said gratefully. 'It just never occurred to me.'

Merton shrugged. 'Glad to be of service, ma'am.'

Millicent looked worried. 'Should I carry on talking to the captains, do you think?'

Jonas nodded. 'Go ahead. Just be mindful of who's standing close by. In the meantime, I'll round up the others, and we'll patrol the rooms. If there is a spy, we'll flush him out.'

Millicent nodded and left to mingle with her guests. Jonas, with Merton in tow, made his way to the room Millicent had set aside for card games.

⌛

Phineas sat at the poker table feeling completely in his element and keeping a watchful eye on Orson, whom Millicent had allowed to play on the understanding he didn't try to fleece her guests.

Orson, well aware that he was reaching an age where his youth would no longer be any benefit to him, was not tempted to pursue his tricks as a card sharp and was playing honestly. Both he and Phineas were happily accruing a nice little pile of winnings.

Placing his cards on the table and enjoying the exclamations from the other players, Phineas noticed Jonas trying to catch his eye. Scooping his winnings up, he excused himself and went over to see what the younger man wanted. Frowning unhappily at Jonas's information and leaving the poker table with a longing glance, he joined Jonas and Merton to go and find Kev and Edgar.

As luck would have it, both young men were sitting together, chatting happily with Persephone and Morag, and it didn't take long before the men were circulating watchfully.

The evening progressed without incident, and Phineas was beginning to feel more reassured when he noticed Kev trying to catch his eye from across the room. Once he reached him, Kev nodded into the crowd, where one of the waiters could be seen hovering behind a group of captains in what could only be described as a shifty manner. Quickly, Phineas alerted the others, and they began to close in on the waiter, who was too intent on trying to eavesdrop on the conversation beside him to notice the encroaching men.

Deftly, Phineas and Jonas grabbed the waiter by the arms, and Kev took the tray he was holding from his hands.

'Stay quiet and come with us if you know what's good for you,' murmured Phineas as he and Jonas firmly propelled the man from the room, Kev, Merton, and Edgar following behind.

Once safely in one of the smaller parlours, Phineas sent Edgar to fetch Millicent, who soon arrived with Persephone. The waiter was sullen and not inclined to answer the questions Phineas threw at him but in no way acted like an innocent man mistakenly apprehended. Eventually, Phineas gave up trying to extract information out of him, reluctant to use force.

'So what do we do with him now?' asked Kev. 'He won't talk, and we can't let him go.'

Jonas and Merton exchanged glances.

'There's probably only one thing that can be done,' said Jonas.

Millicent shook her head. 'No, absolutely not. I don't like the thought of killing a man in cold blood.'

At this, the man paled visibly but still refused to talk.

'What else can we do?' queried Phineas. 'I hate the idea as much as you do, Millie, but I don't see we have any choice.'

'I've got it!' exclaimed Persephone. 'Wait here.' She rushed from the room and returned with Dr Wilton Barry. Quickly, she introduced Dr Barry to the others. 'Can you hypnotise this man into forgetting why he's here?' she asked Wilton.

Wilton Barry looked doubtful. 'I'm not sure, to be honest, but I'd be intrigued to try. Is this some kind of parlour trick?'

'Yes, exactly,' said Persephone brightly. 'I was telling the others how the hypnotherapy is working so well at the hospital, and we thought it would be amusing to see if it could make someone forget something.'

Wilton stroked his chin thoughtfully. 'It's unlikely I can make him forget completely, to be honest with you.'

'What can you do?' asked Phineas.

Wilton considered for a while. 'I could attempt to implant the suggestion that the evening becomes irrelevant and not worth thinking about further, perhaps.'

The others exchanged glances.

'If that's the best you can do, then please proceed,' said Millicent.

Wilton looked at them and then at the man in the chair, seeds of doubt beginning to germinate in his mind. 'I say, this is all above board, I hope,' he said.

The waiter winced as Phineas's fingers dug deep into his shoulder but offered no comment.

Persephone gave a fluttering giggle. 'Of course, it is,' she insisted.

Wilton gave her a searching look. Persephone felt her cheeks blushing a fiery red, and she dropped her gaze. Wilton's face fell into a disapproving frown. He opened his mouth to speak, but before he could, Millicent stepped forward.

'The truth is, Dr Barry, we're in a bit of a pickle. This man has come to my birthday party with the intention of hurting me and my friends.' She turned to regard the waiter, who stared back at her with ill-concealed contempt. Millicent turned back to Wilton. 'We find ourselves in a position of needing to be rid of this scoundrel before he can do any more harm but not wanting to rid him of his miserable existence. Persephone was hoping you would be able to help us with this, you see.'

Wilton nodded. 'Yes, I see your dilemma,' he said as he gave the waiter a considering look. 'I will be happy to hypnotise him for you, and I'll give you a trigger phrase to use to – hopefully – maximise the effects. I must caution you that it will only work if he's willing to allow me to use hypnosis on him.'

Everyone looked over to where the waiter sat, with Phineas's hand clamped firmly on his shoulder. Jonas leaned over and whispered in the man's ear. Slowly, the man nodded as he weighed up the options Jonas had laid before him.

'Clever man,' murmured Phineas grimly as Wilton Barry left to fetch his goggles. 'Wise choice.'

The man merely shrugged, realising if he wanted to live to fight another day, he needed to go along with the plan.

Once Wilton had returned and fitted his goggles over the waiter's eyes, he began to feed the man's subconscious with hypnotic suggestions, and the crew huddled together in a worried group.

'What are we going to do with him once Dr Barry's finished?' asked Millicent worriedly. 'I don't like the idea of just letting him back in with the others. What if he remembers why he's here?'

'Yes,' agreed Persephone. 'We don't really know how well Wilton's hypnotic suggestions will work or how long for.'

'Go get Mina Myra and Rosalind,' said Kev. 'I've got an idea.'

⧗

Wilton Barry removed the hypno-goggles from the waiter's eyes. 'Wide awake!' he declared, snapping his fingers, and the man blinked and looked about him.

'What's going on?' he asked, looking about him a little suspiciously. While he was under hypnosis, the others had left the room, and only Kev and Wilton were left behind.

At that moment, Millicent bustled in. 'Ah, there you are,' she declared happily, 'just the man I need.'

Bewildered, the waiter looked behind him. Seeing as how there was no one else around him, he raised a finger to point at his chest. 'Me?' he asked.

Millicent nodded. 'Yes, you,' she confirmed as Persephone came in with Mina Myra, Norman on her shoulder, and Rosalind.

Neither girl looked happy at being dragged from what was turning out to be the best night of their young lives.

'We need you to mind these two young ladies for the rest of the evening,' said Millicent as Mina Myra drew in a breath of outrage.

'Now look here,' said the waiter belligerently. 'I'm not no childminder.'

'You were hired to be of assistance to me at my birthday party,' declared Millicent tartly, ignoring the waiter's look of confusion, 'and if you wish to be paid at the end of the night, you will do as you are requested.'

'I was?' queried the man. 'That don't sound like me, to be honest with you, missus.'

'Nevertheless, you signed up for it. However, if you feel there has been a misunderstanding, I shall not force my money onto you, and you are free to go.'

A look of cunning calculation crossed the man's face as he considered Millicent's offer, and he slowly nodded.

Mina Myra's bottom lip was beginning to jut mutinously. 'I do not wish to be childminded!' she declared emphatically. 'This is not fair!'

Rosalind too was looking very upset about the turn of events and was staring at the waiter as if this was all his fault. The man was beginning to wilt under the hostility of her glare, and even though Kev felt he had no one to blame but himself, he was feeling a little sorry for him.

Millicent held up her hands. 'I'm sure Persephone explained to you the necessity of you remaining here in this room with this nice man,' she said.

'But we'll miss out on the dancing and the food!' Mina pointed out. 'Those are the best bits.'

'You can have food in here, lots of it,' said Kev, 'and I'm sure this man will love to hear all about how clever Norman is and all the wonderful new tricks you've been teaching him.'

Mina Myra looked the waiter over thoughtfully before turning her back on him. 'He doesn't look like he does, Kev, to be honest with you. He looks like a scoundrel, if you want my opinion. Besides, why doesn't Sherlock have to be babysat?'

'Ah . . . Sherlock's needed in the kitchen,' adlibbed Kev hastily. 'They've run out of people to wash the dishes, and he's got to wash all the pots.'

Mina Myra narrowed her eyes at the adults and Rosalind gave them a look so heavy with disgust, they all flinched.

'Tell you what,' offered Millicent soothingly. 'Stay here, and you can have anything you want.'

Mina Myra exchanged looks with Rosalind, who raised her eyebrows, and nodded. 'OK then,' said Mina Myra challengingly. 'We want a pony . . . no, a unicorn! And a gold collar with jewels in it for Norman and candy floss every day for breakfast and what else?' she asked, going into a little huddle with Rosalind.

Millicent watched sourly as the girls consulted over their wish list. 'That's enough,' she declared. 'You're just being ridiculous. If you won't stay here, I'll have to let this nice man go as we have no other work for him to do.'

'Well, that's not my problem, Millicent,' said Mina Myra. 'I can't be responsible for your mistakes.'

Millicent turned to glare at Kev, who merely shrugged and gave Millicent what he hoped was an encouraging smile. 'Well, what if I told you you were allowed to practice stabbing him with your swords?' asked Millicent, waving the man's objections away with a flap of her hand.

Mina Myra and Rosalind exchanged glances, clearly tempted, before Mina shook her head. 'No, sorry, Millicent. You can't fool me. No grown-up ever would let a little child do that. The answer is still no, I'm afraid.'

Millicent sighed. 'Very well. You've got the best of me. You can go back to the party.'

The girls whooped and ran out, leaving the adults regarding the waiter thoughtfully.

'There you have it,' stated Millicent regretfully. 'I'm afraid we'll have to terminate your employment. But don't worry. We will pay you what you would have been entitled to plus a bonus for the inconvenience.'

She pulled out a wad of money from her bosom and thrust it into the man's hands as she and Kev manhandled him out through the door and onto the street.

'Goodbye and thank you so much for *all your help* this evening,' gushed Millicent, repeating the words Wilton had given her as Kev firmly pushed the man out the door, shutting it firmly behind him.

'That went well,' said Millicent with satisfaction, 'although I'm not sure I like letting Mina Myra think she can get one over on me.'

Kev grinned. 'A small price to pay for such a good outcome,' he said, giving her a wink.

Millicent shook her head, not entirely convinced.

Back in the parlour, Wilton Barry was swinging his hypno-goggles by their strap and regarding Persephone thoughtfully. 'Why do I get the feeling there's more to this than meets the eye?' he asked her.

Persephone shrugged. 'If there's more to tell, I promise you, you'll be the first to hear of it.'

Wilton just gave her a look that told her he wasn't buying it but was too much of a gentleman to press her before leaving to go back to the party.

Millicent and Kev came back in, and they stood looking at each other, realising they'd had a close call.

'This is getting out of hand,' declared Millicent. 'We need to get organised and make a move on Silas Elmstone before he has us all tied in knots.'

Kev put an arm around Persephone's shoulders and pulled her close. 'Yeah,' he said soberly. 'Let's just hope we've not left it too late.'

Kev and Persephone meandered their way back to the docks hand in hand. The evening was cold and clear, and the night sky was thick with stars.

Persephone pulled the collar of her coat up and the brim of her hat down in an effort to keep the chilly air off her face. The only part of her showing was the tip of her nose, which was quickly turning pink in the cold night air. Kev looked at her fondly, thinking she looked very endearing like that, and lifted her hand in the same gesture he'd seen Phineas use and gave it a kiss.

Persephone laughed softly and tucked her hand under Kev's arm. 'Are you happy here, Kev?' she asked him.

'Yes, I am,' replied Kev. 'Why?'

'Oh, you know, with everything that's going on, I wondered if you had regrets about coming back. It can't have been what you were expecting.'

'Well, that's true, I suppose,' said Kev, 'but I came back for you. It hardly matters what's happening around us so long as we can be together.'

Persephone laid her head on Kev's shoulder. 'I'm so glad to have you here,' she told him softly. 'It makes such a difference to me not to be facing this alone.'

Kev stopped walking and turned to look at Persephone. Taking her face in his hands, he looked at her earnestly. 'Me too,' he said. 'I'm so grateful to be back here with you. It is scary, thinking about all that's going down here, but I can't imagine being anywhere else. I know we're going to be fine, Seph.'

Persephone nodded and lifted her face to Kev as he lowered his to kiss her softly on the lips.

'Your face is so cold.' Kev laughed when they separated.

Persephone laughed too. 'Maybe it's time for you to warm it up for me,' she suggested.

Kev looked at her, not quite catching on for a moment. Slowly, as Persephone began to blush under his gaze, the penny dropped, and he gave her a grin.

'What are we hanging around here for then?' he asked before grabbing her hand and running towards home.

Breathless and laughing, they reached the lifting platform. Getting in and sending it upwards, they stood entwined in each other's arms, exchanging kisses. Reaching the top, they stumbled aboard. Persephone took Kev's hand and, with a shy little smile, led him to her cabin.

Chapter 24

They came in ones and twos or occasionally small groups, moving stealthily through the bush, coming up the river in small boats or every now and then in small personal aircraft.

No one spoke much, just the odd nod of acknowledgement to colleagues, a few muttered words here and there. The mood was sombre, and everyone was on edge, not in the mood for idle conversation.

On one side of the natural clearing in the bush, the airship captains of Grahamstown clustered around Cornelius and Millicent, watching as Huia and the pirate captains congregated.

In spite of Cornelius's best efforts at negotiation and persuasion, the captains were uneasy at the thought of joining forces with their old enemies. Everyone knew what was at stake and what they needed to do, but the years of enmity were hard to put aside, and each faction viewed the other with a mistrust born out of the conflicts they had been involved in.

Events had moved swiftly after Millicent's party. The list of spies compiled by Nellie Sprocket and passed on by Cornelius had been distributed to the captains. Each spy had been apprehended and, for now, imprisoned. In many cases, the spies had been trusted crew members, and everyone was feeling the sting of their betrayal. Many had wanted to exact swift and immediate revenge, but Phineas had pushed for a slower approach, not wanting to alert Silas Elmstone too soon. After some argument, the captains had agreed, mainly because Millicent and Cornelius emphasised the need for a unified front.

Once everyone had arrived, Cornelius stepped forward and motioned for the captains to move forward. Reluctantly, they moved closer together. It had been agreed ahead of time that everyone would come unarmed, a fact that further added to everyone's unease.

'We all know why we're here,' Cornelius began. 'I know this is not comfortable for most of you, but we need to work together if we're to defeat Silas Elmstone.' Turning to the pirate cohort, he addressed them directly. 'I know Huia has persuaded you to keep a truce until we have dealt with him, and for that, we thank you.'

The Danish pirate Aksel Jensen stepped forward. He was an imposing sight, tall and muscular with piercing blue eyes and long blond hair twisted into braids on either side of his head. He prided himself on styling himself on his Viking ancestors, and his face and arms were covered in Nordic tattoos, while his bushy blond beard was forked and bound in the Viking manner. He looked about him, glaring at Cornelius and flexing his massive arms.

'I do not fear this Elmstone,' he declared. 'I say we fight him soon so we can go back to raiding.' He sneered at the Grahamstown captains and folded his arms over his chest.

'We would be wise to weigh our actions carefully,' warned Cornelius. 'Rushing headlong into battle against an enemy we have no intelligence on is a foolhardy venture.'

'I am not afraid to earn my place in Valhalla. You know to your cost I am strong to fight,' boasted Aksel, laughing as the airship captains bristled with indignation and not a little trepidation.

'Aue! Enough!' exclaimed Huia, stepping forward to stand beside Cornelius and Millicent. 'You act without thought,' she told Aksel. 'If this truce is to work, we must stop thinking of ourselves as being on different sides and work as one.'

The pirate captains muttered amongst themselves. It was clear that while most of them appeared in agreement with Huia, there was a faction, led by Aksel, who were not entirely convinced.

Aksel placed his hands on his hips and lifted his chin, trying to stare Huia down. Huia remained unperturbed. She had always known Aksel coveted her title as Ruler of the Skies, believing himself to be the true unofficial leader of their community. Although none of them bowed or listened to another, each pirate captain was aware of Huia's mana, and she knew this fact rankled in Aksel's mind.

One day she realised she would have to fight him – probably to the death – and although this didn't worry her, at this moment, his jealousy and troublemaking did. Left unchallenged, he could sabotage their hopes of defeating Silas. If that happened, they were all lost, regardless of which side of the law they stood on.

Stepping forward, she raised her arms, and instantly, the muttering amongst the pirate captains ceased, much to Aksel's chagrin. As his attempt to undermine Huia had failed at this point, he reluctantly took a step back, and Huia began to speak.

'Listen to me, each of you,' Huia declared. 'You have heard my words before, and you know in your hearts I speak the truth regarding this matter. Be assured, I do not speak them lightly. I know how this will change us. We will not be the same once this is over, and I understand this worries some of you. But we must embrace this or face defeat at the hands of an enemy who will surely destroy our way of life and rob us of our freedom.'

A murmuring of assent began to ripple through the men and women surrounding her, and Huia knew she was winning them over.

'You all remember the history between myself and my sister captain, Millicent Darlington,' Huia continued. 'You all know she has no cause to trust me or forgive the consequences of our meeting in the past.'

The pirate captains nodded amongst themselves, and the murmuring increased as they were swayed by the power of Huia's presence and the truth of her words. Huia looked around her, the exaltation of holding them in the palm of her hand sweeping through her.

'Let this be the symbol of our joining,' she declared.

Stepping forward, she held out her hand to Millicent, who stepped forward too without hesitation and clasped Huia's outstretched hand. As the two women held hands warmly, Huia leaned forward. At last, Millicent understood what she was doing, and touched, she too leaned forward, and the two women touched noses, standing forehead to forehead.

Millicent closed her eyes as she shared the breath of life with her former adversary, allowing the deep significance of the hongi and what Huia was doing to sweep over her. She knew Huia was right; they couldn't go back to the old ways after this.

Maybe Silas is doing us a favour, she thought as she and Huia stepped back and released each other's hands.

The atmosphere in the clearing had changed. Somehow the deep mistrust and apprehension had dissipated. It was almost as if each one were awakening from a dream, and they were able to look at one another through new eyes.

Huia and Millicent stood quietly regarding each other. Huia gave Millicent a small nod, and Millicent inclined her own in return.

'We have more in common than we realise,' Huia said.

Millicent nodded again. 'You may be right,' she replied, 'although that is not something I had expected you to acknowledge.'

Huia shrugged. 'I had not expected to say it,' she replied.

'I'm not sure how to react, to tell you the truth,' said Millicent.

'Nor I,' Huia replied. 'This is new land for all of us. We must rewrite the rules as we go.'

Millicent nodded, and the women turned to where their companions were standing, still somewhat apart, but a few were beginning to acknowledge one another with small respectful nods in one another's direction.

Cornelius stepped forward once more. 'We need to elect a war council,' he told the assembled captains. 'Let us proceed with the nominations.'

After a heated discussion, it was decided to elect three councillors from each faction, with Cornelius standing as the chairman and holding the deciding vote, should it be needed. Each faction then separated to opposite sides of the clearing to hold their own elections.

Once this had been achieved, Cornelius called them back together, and the six councillors were officially asked to represent their communities. From the airship captains of Grahamstown, Millicent, Jebediah Strangewayes, and Leander Bagley had been chosen. The pirate captains had elected Huia, Violet Flint, and, despite Huia's best efforts to persuade them otherwise, Aksel Jensen.

Millicent looked at her fellow councillors and hoped they would be able to agree on the course of action ahead of them. Like Huia, she had grave misgivings about Aksel. He seemed too hot-headed and stubborn for the delicate negotiations needed to reach agreements, and she felt too that he had an agenda of his own.

But for better or worse, they had to find a way to work together. As the two factions swore to abide by the decisions of their war council, she exchanged glances with Huia and saw she too was uncertain about the influence of Aksel on their plans.

CHAPTER 25

Millicent deftly brought the Hummingbird through the still night air to land on the deck of the *Elizabeth Anne*. She stilled the engine and sat for a moment before opening the cockpit cover and clambering out.

She sighed as she closed the cover. The first meeting of the war council had gone much as she had expected. She made her way to the galley to make a cup of tea. At this point, she wished fervently for something stronger and wondered if Phineas still had anything left in that bottle of whiskey of his.

She picked up the oil lamp left out for her by a thoughtful crew member, probably Lenore, and went below deck. Pushing the galley door open, she found Phineas sitting at the galley table, the bottle of whiskey and two glasses in front of him.

She sat down next to him gratefully as he poured them both a good stiff measure. 'Thanks, Phin,' she said before taking a sip.

Phineas took his own sip and sat back, regarding her in a thoughtful manner. 'How'd it go then, Millie?' he asked.

Millicent looked at him, her eyebrows raised. 'How do you think it went?' she challenged.

'That bad, eh?' ventured Phineas.

'It could have been worse, I suppose,' said Millicent wearily. 'At least no one drew swords. I daresay we could have reached agreement sooner if not for Aksel Jensen. That man seems hell-bent on causing as much difficulty as he can.'

Phineas nodded soberly. He had had experience of many men like Aksel over the years – ambitious, driven, and in many ways, self-deluded. They were dangerous, and he didn't envy Millicent or the others on the council having to manage him.

'It's not so much that he's able to sway the others to his point of view,' explained Millicent, 'but he challenges every. Single. Thing on the agenda. It's exhausting and frustrating, and it slows things down so much.'

'Have you managed to form a war plan?' asked Phineas.

Millicent nodded. 'Pretty much. No thanks to Aksel. We have a rough idea of what we need to do. We all go back to our captains and inform them of the next steps and preparations we need to make.'

Both of them sat drinking quietly as the import of what they were about to undertake settled over them. The future was hazy at this point, but they were aware of having set their feet upon a road that could end up with any number of outcomes, some of them not favourable.

Millicent was grateful for Phineas's calm presence as the anxious thoughts chased themselves through her mind and reached out a hand to give him a squeeze on the knee. He didn't look at her but merely grasped her hand in his and gave it a comforting squeeze in return.

They finished their whiskeys without further talk, and when Phineas got up to go above deck to smoke a pipe, Millicent accompanied him. They stood shoulder to shoulder, leaning against the rail and looking out at the looming ranges behind the town.

Millicent was struck with the realisation that the life they had made for themselves here in this town was hanging in the balance. She wondered what would happen to them if Silas Elmstone prevailed. She supposed if they survived, they would have to leave. At first, she felt the grief rise up, threatening to overwhelm her. She wasn't ready to leave Grahamstown, but then she remembered all she and Phineas had been through in the past and knew so long as she had him by her side, all would be well.

Phineas must have sensed something of the feelings surging through her as he reached out with his free arm and held her close to his side. 'I don't know how this will play out, Millie,' he told her, 'but you know we've been through a lot together and always come through. We'll get through this too. You'll see.'

⧗

The following evening, the airship captains congregated in the galley of Jebediah Strangewayes's ship, the *Invincible*, to hear what their war council had decided. Cornelius had decided to join Huia and her councillors, feeling it politic to do so.

Millicent was surprised to see Nellie Sprocket had joined them and wondered what new intelligence she had to share. It made her feel uneasy, wondering what Nellie felt was so important that she needed to be here in person.

Once everyone was seated, Jebediah opened the meeting and stood to share the council's decisions.

'We have agreed that we need to make some haste in preparing for war. It's obvious Silas Elmstone is targeting Grahamstown and our businesses for some reason, and if we don't act, he will destroy us or at least the freedom we have enjoyed to this point.

'The trouble we have is that we have very little knowledge of him and his plans. We don't know how far along his preparations are or how he intends to attack us. It's possible he intends to continue to act as he has to this point, using spies and subterfuge to stir trouble and disrupt our businesses, but it's also likely he's planning a physical attack. This could come in the form of attacks on our ships, or he may even be planning an attack on Grahamstown itself. We just don't know.

'The council have decided that for now, we begin to prepare for a battle. Amass some weapons and recruit more men. While we're doing this, we will try and gather information on just what he's up to. It won't help to go into a fight blind, as it were.'

'And just how do you propose we do that?' queried one of the captains.

Nellie spoke up. 'That's where I come in. The Network have been keeping a close eye on Elmstone for some time, mainly because of his ties to time slavers, which is why I have been able to collate the information to date. What we don't know is how prepared he is and what his next move will be. For that, I need to get closer.

'It's very difficult to get close to his stronghold. It's deep in the bush and surrounded by wetlands. Elmstone has a clear view of anyone approaching. Getting near enough to observe without being detected has always been a problem for us.

'Fortunately, we've come up with a way to get close without being noticed – or at least, that's what we hope. I plan to leave tomorrow night for the reconnaissance attempt. What I need is for one of your ships to drop me and my equipment off further up the Waihou River, closer to Elmstone's fortress.'

The captains murmured amongst themselves, unwilling to commit their ships to flying so close to their known enemy. Millicent mentally rolled her eyes; this felt more like a gathering of old ladies at a knitting bee than a council of war.

'I'll take you, Nellie,' she declared, staring down the other captains, many of whom had the grace to look a little ashamed – most but not all – and Millicent wondered how committed they were and if they would manage to unite against Elmstone.

Nellie inclined her head in gratitude, and the talk moved on to other matters. Jebediah quickly organised for the captains to take inventory of all available weapons and men and canvas the surrounding area for likely recruits, and the meeting wound up, the captains feeling in a more positive frame of mind now that actual steps were being taken to negate Silas's influence on their livelihoods.

⏳

The wind was building as the *Elizabeth Anne* sailed south, hugging the ranges. The clouds were also building, racing across the night sky, obscuring the moon.

It was a bad night to be out, and Millicent watched uneasily as Orson and Sherlock steered the airship, compensating for the wind gusts pushing against her. She wished fervently they were all back in Grahamstown, safely tethered to their berth on the docks, but Nellie had been adamant that her spying mission should take place tonight.

'We're running out of time,' she'd told Millicent earnestly. 'It's tonight or never.'

Reluctantly, Millicent had given in and issued the orders to sail. Nellie was on deck, readying her equipment with Kev's help.

It was a rough trip. The storm was gathering strength, and the winds buffeted the *Elizabeth Anne*, causing her to rock and shudder. Luckily, none on board suffered from airsickness apart from Merton, who had retired to his bunk looking a dreadful shade of pale, tinged with greenish undertones.

As Kev and Nellie put the finishing touches to the assembly of Nellie's equipment, the rain began to fall. As yet, it was still sporadic, and the falls were not overly heavy, but in the distance, they could hear the rumble of thunder. Millicent ordered Orson to sail the *Elizabeth Anne* into the shelter of one of the steep-sided valleys and sent Sherlock to ready the Hummingbird.

Kev and Nellie loaded the Hummingbird with the equipment, and Nellie clambered in beside Sherlock. The Hummingbird lifted off the deck and, rocking in the wind gusts, made off for the spot Nellie had chosen for her foray into the swampy wetlands, where Silas Elmstone had his fortress hideout.

After a while, the Hummingbird returned, and Kev climbed in. Millicent could only watch from the wheelhouse as the tiny craft disappeared into the worsening storm and hope for the best.

Sherlock brought the Hummingbird in to land. Kev lifted the cockpit cover, climbed out, and went over to where Nellie was already assembling the equipment. Nellie had chosen a spot opposite a shallow channel that meandered through the wetlands and emptied into the Waihou River. Her plan was to enter the wetlands through the channel and make her way to where it was thought Elmstone had his lair.

Kev handed Sherlock a length of cable, which he secured to the Hummingbird before lifting off again. Kev stood watching as the tiny craft, buffeted by the storm, crossed the Waihou River. Sherlock, opened the cockpit cover and swung the cable down towards the ground, trying to hook it around one of the mangroves at the river's edge.

It took several attempts before he managed to snag the cable around a branch that was sturdy enough to take the cable. Giving a few hefty tugs on the cable to ensure it was secure, he closed the cover and flew back to the others.

Cutting the engine, Sherlock climbed out and handed the other end of the cable to Kev, who secured it to a small scrubby tree. Twanging it experimentally, Kev hoped the cable was secure enough to take Nellie's weight. Thankfully, Nellie was slight and barely taller than Sherlock, so in spite of the precarious tethering, Kev felt it would hold – with any luck.

Kev went over to where Nellie was hunched over a tiny monitor under a canvas hastily stretched over another patch of scrub. The wind was blowing the rain in sideways, and she was trying to shield the monitor from the elements with her body. Sherlock was peering over her shoulder with interest as she carefully adjusted the dials and knobs.

Looking up as Kev approached, she gave him a brief nod. 'It's working, Kev,' she told him. 'You'll be able to see everything I see.

Take note of all the things I've told you. After tonight, we'll have a much better idea of what we're up against.'

Kev nodded grimly. Nellie stood up and went to where the rest of her equipment lay. She shook out a suit made of oilskin. It was accompanied by a heavy brass helmet that had strange-looking antennae attached. Nellie would wear this to swim up the channel and into the wetlands. Nellie beckoned to Kev, and he followed her as close to the river's edge as they could get before the land got too boggy.

Pointing out the channel, Nellie said, 'As far as we can tell, Elmstone's hideout is in there. We have a fair idea where from the spy birds we've sent over. It's now a matter of getting in and having a closer look. All going well, I should be back in a couple of hours.'

Kev nodded, and they turned to head back to the shelter. Overhead, the storm unleashed a deluge of rain and a crack of thunder. Nellie jumped, her nerves already heightened, and her foot slipped on a stone. Kev reached out to try and save her from falling, but he was too slow, and Nellie crashed heavily to the ground, falling back and hitting her head hard on the stone. Kev rushed forward.

'Nellie!' he exclaimed, horrified. 'Are you OK?'

Nellie sat up, dazed, and rubbed the back of her head. Kev helped her to her feet and supported her as she hobbled over to the shelter. Nellie sat down heavily, a blank look on her face. Concerned, Kev and Sherlock hovered over her.

Nellie waved them away. 'Stop fussing, you two,' she admonished. 'I'm fine.' She went to stand but sat down again with a groan.

Kev and Sherlock exchanged glances.

'Do you think you're OK to do this?' asked Kev worriedly.

'I'm not sure, Kev,' replied Nellie, rubbing the back of her head where it was beginning to throb. 'Give me a minute.' After a minute or two, she tried once more to stand before being overcome by dizziness and needing to sit once more.

'How long do we have?' asked Kev.

Nellie grimaced. 'I really need to get going,' she said worriedly. She tucked her head between her knees in an effort to clear the dizziness. Trying unsuccessfully to stand once more, she sat down unhappily. 'I'm not sure if I can do this, Kev,' she said worriedly.

Kev ran his hands through his hair and looked around him desperately as if the solution would fall down with the raindrops.

'I can go,' volunteered Sherlock quietly.

'Ah no, Sherlock,' said Kev. 'I don't think Millicent would be happy with that, do you?'

Sherlock shrugged. 'Millicent's not here, is she?' he observed. 'Besides, I can look after myself. Millicent forgets all us children managed to survive before she found us and offered us a home with her. We're tougher than we look, all of us.'

Kev and Nellie exchanged glances.

'Sherlock may be our only chance, Kev,' Nellie pointed out.

Kev sighed and nodded. 'OK. You're probably right, Nellie. Take Sherlock through what he needs to know, and let's hope I don't have to try and explain to Millicent why one of her beloved children isn't coming home.'

CHAPTER 26

S herlock made his way through the swampy waters of the channel, grateful to be leaving the river. The current had pulled at him the entire way across, and in spite of the harness he wore attached to the cable keeping him on track, it had been exhausting to fight it.

Completely covered in Nellie's oilskin suit, his hands covered in webbed gloves that helped to pull him through the water and his feet encased in flipper-like shoes to propel him from behind, he resembled a sleek lizard as he wriggled up the shallow channel.

The brass helmet was heavy, and he found it an effort to keep his head up, but he merely paused now and then to ease the aching muscles in his neck. As well as the transmitting antennae on the top, it had a breathing tube that snaked down from the top and into his mouth, so he needed to keep his head steady and the tube above water.

Nellie had given him detailed instructions, and he knew where he needed to head. Leaving the channel, he headed over land, sliding on his belly across the soft ground, keeping his profile low.

The dark and the storm helped conceal his presence, and he slid from swampy puddle to swampy puddle, weaving his way through the reeds. The weight of the helmet meant he couldn't really lift his head to look around, so it took him by surprise when he suddenly slithered into a deeper body of water.

The water was too deep for him to feel the bottom, and he sank beneath the surface, the weight of the helmet pulling him under. He pushed upwards with all his strength, kicking powerfully with his flipper shoes and clawing at the water with his webbed gloves.

The helmet broke the surface, and Sherlock gulped in a grateful breath through his breathing tube, his heart pounding in his chest. Using the flipper shoes, he managed to tread water, steadying himself in place by using his gloves.

As his heart rate steadied, he looked out through the glass visor of the helmet. In front of him, tall wooden palisades rose out of the swamp. A fortress. Silas Elmstone's hideout.

It had been built on land that had been raised above the level of the swamp and surrounded by a deep moat – into which Sherlock had fallen. The moat was wide and would not be easy to cross. Sherlock turned his head in every direction, allowing Nellie's transmitting antennae to send back the information.

High above him, sentries patrolled. They appeared oblivious of his presence, the storm masking his splash into the moat and the falling rain disrupting the surface of the water, so his continued movements were undetectable from above.

Cautiously, he swam around the moat, hoping Nellie was getting the images. He came to a spot where a drain of some sort emptied out into the moat from inside the fortress. It was not wide, but neither was Sherlock. Gingerly, he tried to see if the helmet could fit inside without getting wedged. It was a close fit, but the helmet scraped along the sides of the drain, which appeared to be relatively smooth.

Realising that if he kept the helmet on, the roof of the drain would tear off the antennae and breathing tube, he unclipped it and pushed it through the drain ahead of him. The water inside the drain smelled overwhelmingly bad, and Sherlock tried not to think too closely about what he might be crawling through. Thankfully, the drain wasn't a long one, and it wasn't long before he was lying just inside the entrance, looking into the fort.

The drain was fed by a shallow channel that took the overflow from a cesspool that lay just inside the wall. Carefully, Sherlock edged the helmet out of the drain and hoped the antennae hadn't been damaged by the trip through the drain and were sending pictures back to Nellie and Kev.

The compound was lit by flickering torch lights, some of which had been extinguished by the rain. The only human life out in the weather were the sentries atop the walls, but the inside of the fortress held row upon row of gleaming metal bodies. The automatons, as yet lifeless, stood rank upon rank, shoulder to shoulder. They were huge and menacing in the dim light. Their bodies were well armoured, and each arm ended in massive cutting blades.

Sherlock wondered if Nellie's and Kev's blood was running as cold as his at the sight of them. If this was the army Silas was amassing against them, they were in big trouble indeed.

On the other side of the compound, Sherlock caught sight of a lifting platform that led up to tall airship docks. A few ships were tethered to it, bumping into one another now and then in the force of the storm winds. Like the compound, no human life could be seen aboard, everyone sensibly taking shelter from the storm.

Retreating back through the drain backward, pulling the helmet with him, Sherlock slithered back into the moat and allowed the relatively cleaner water to wash the filth off. The stench, however, lingered in his nostrils, making him feel queasy.

Ducking his head under the water, he tried to clear the smell from his senses before donning the helmet once more and retracing his way across the moat and into the safety of the wetlands.

By the time he got back to the Waihou River, his neck and shoulders were aching with fatigue, and he decided to remove the helmet for the trip back across the river.

Clipping the length of rope from the cable back onto his harness, he launched himself into the river. Reaching the other bank, he clambered out to find Kev waiting for him. Gratefully, he reached out, and Kev grabbed his arms and hauled him out onto the bank, where he lay exhausted. Concerned, Kev took the helmet from his hands as he held it out and helped him to sit up.

'Did you get the pictures?' he asked.

Kev nodded. 'Clear as clear,' he replied.

Neither of them mentioned the automaton army as if by not mentioning it, they could make it go away. Kev helped Sherlock to his feet, and they made their way back to the shelter in the scrub. Nellie was waiting for them, her face sombre. Sherlock stripped off the oilskin suit, thankful to be rid of it.

Silently, they broke down their camp and repacked the equipment. Sherlock climbed behind the controls and lifted off with Nellie aboard, heading back to the *Elizabeth Anne*.

As Kev waited for Sherlock to return, he sat and stared into the night, thinking about all he and Nellie had seen on her monitor screen, and wondered just what the next step could possibly be. He wasn't sure they were in any way able to fight the kind of army they had just had a glimpse of, and he wondered if he had come back just in time to see this place as he knew it destroyed forever.

CHAPTER 27

Silas Elmstone sat at his desk, studying the map spread out in front of him. He traced the path of the Waihou River with a bony finger, and a feeling of quiet satisfaction spread through him. This was as close as he came to experiencing what other people might term happiness.

Silas was aware others viewed him as a cold man. In odd moments of introspection, he conceded they might have a point, but he preferred to think of himself as lacking in sentimentality. He had never felt his lack of emotion to be in any way a deficit of character and believed it was to his advantage to unencumbered by those ties to his fellow man that others seemed to find so necessary.

He was pale and nondescript to look at, not even interesting enough to be ugly, and this had often meant people in general tended to overlook and underestimate him. He had long since figured out how to use this prejudice against them, enjoying in a cool, detached manner their discomfort as they realised their mistake, usually just before he dispatched them into the presence of whichever god they believed in – not that he spent too much time thinking or worrying about how others saw him. He didn't believe them to be important enough in his schemes to warrant the expenditure of energy it would take, only considering other people if he could see they would serve his purpose or if, like the airship captains of Grahamstown, they thwarted his ambitions.

He had built himself a secure stronghold here, deep in the wetlands. Hidden away from the notice of most of the world, he had slowly amassed a huge fortune from dealing in human misery. He had started with one small airship and a stolen time machine, and from there, he had constructed an empire of time-slaving vessels.

Always patient when realising his goals and never tempted to act too soon or in reaction to events around him, he had waited years to extend his influence across the river, building his strength and resources until now. He was almost ready to strike.

He had been long planning to subdue the proud and independent pirate fleet that worked the far side of the Waihou River. Believing if he could defeat Huia, the others would fall into line, he had plotted tirelessly towards her downfall.

His plans had taken an unexpected turn, however, a little detour that had led his attention to the settlement of Grahamstown. Events and his reaction to them meant he had felt compelled to adjust his plans for the time being. The destruction of one of his airships along with its time-slaving crew as well as a very expensive time machine had caused him to direct his attention onto Grahamstown.

He didn't know which ship sailing out of there had destroyed his ship, and he didn't care. He intended to wage war on all of them. The death of his crew didn't distress him in the least. He felt no more loyalty to his men than they did to him, but the loss of his property affected him deeply.

At first, he had been content to merely disrupt their businesses. He planted spies where he could, turning their trusted crew members against them. But this didn't have the effect of easing his outrage in the way he imagined it would, and so he had decided to destroy them completely.

Not an airship still flying, not one person left alive, and Grahamstown in ashes were the only things he wanted now. At night, thinking of them all going about their normal lives with no knowledge that he lurked in the shadows, waiting to strike, and their horror when he did was the only thing that soothed him enough to sleep.

It had taken over a year to bring his plans to the point where he felt ready to move on Grahamstown, but now he felt he was in a position to strike. The construction of his automaton army was nearly complete. He was only waiting for the finishing touches, and then he would be ready to move.

The discovery of his tame scientist had been the breakthrough he needed. Lured away from his old life with the enticement of unlimited funds to research and build it, the man had been working hard to perfect a continuous energy source to power Silas's army.

Finally, all the long tedious evenings of enduring the man's company at dinner were about to pay off. He would be glad to be rid of him. The man talked enough to make a donkey lame, and only the idea of his invincible army had kept him from placing a bullet in his head to shut him up. There had been some evenings, even so, when his trigger finger had twitched uncontrollably and he had been forced to sit with his hands in his pockets.

Getting up from his desk, he left his den and made his way to the lower reaches of the fortress. His surroundings were spartan. Unlike many others, he wasn't the kind of man who enjoyed seeing the material evidence of his wealth. It was the money itself he loved, not the things it could buy.

Reaching a door, he pushed it open and made his way down the stone staircase within. This part of the fortress was below water level, and the stone walls constantly wept moisture, making it a dank and unhealthy environment in which to linger.

Reaching the lower level, he arrived in a tomb-like room. It was well lit by artificial means and, unlike the rest of this area, kept free of seeping water by pumps manned by hapless victims of Silas's main trade – time slaving.

Silas went over to where a dishevelled man sat hunched over his workbench, muttering to himself. Silas suspected the man was going a little mad, possibly from sitting here for long hours for months on end. He had certainly noticed that the man's stories at dinner were becoming ever more erratic and rambling.

He felt little interest in him or concern for his condition other than to notice the man's decline in a detached manner and to wonder how long before he sank irretrievably into madness – not that it mattered, really, as Silas intended to dispatch the unfortunate scientist once he had no further use for him. From the looks of him, he would actually be doing him a favour. He only hoped the man would hang in there until the power source was fully operational.

Silas knew his automaton were virtually indestructible, but he needed a way to keep them operational in the field. He had no intention of taking to the field of battle himself, so he required a way to power his army from a distance. That way, he could sit here in the relative safety of his lair and direct his troops from afar.

'Well done, Popkiss,' he gloated as the trembling figure placed a small round crystal in his hands.

Professor Popkiss's hands trembled, and his head jerked with intermittent tics. He was unrecognisable as the jovial and rotund gentleman of Lady Elspeth's acquaintance.

The long months of working in the deep reaches of Silas's fortress had indeed taken a toll, but it wasn't only the damp and lack of fresh air that had made such a dramatic change in the professor. The long, long months of waiting for his signalling device to beckon Walter home and the disappointed hopes when it hadn't worked out that way had combined with the unrelenting burden of abandoning his friend originally to finally tip the balance of the professor's mind. The letter from Walter had never reached the professor, and the nagging guilt over not being able to bring his friend home had begun to cloud his mind once more. Seeking a means of relieving the pressure, he had grabbed at the opportunity to invent the power source Silas commissioned.

Working for Silas hadn't proved to be the distraction the professor had hoped it would be. Not only was the environment overwhelmingly depressing inside Silas's fortress, but also, the man himself was distinctly creepy. The long months of enduring Silas's cold gaze and the unhealthy atmosphere underground took a heavy toll on the professor's well-being.

Slowly but surely, the professor's mind had been eroded away until there was very little left aside from the consuming focus of creating the power crystal. It was now the only thing holding the fragile threads of the professor's thoughts together.

Now he watched anxiously as Silas turned it over in his hands. When Silas held out an impatient hand, he turned and, picking a wooden box off the workbench, handed it over. Silas took the box from the professor. Here in his hands was the means of powering his entire army. Each automaton had a crystal heart which would only respond to the power crystal once it was connected into the box. When he fired it up, it would keep his army moving. No need for rewinding them anymore – so long as the control box was operational, the automatons could not be stopped. A tireless, relentless army of destruction, he was about to unleash on Grahamstown.

Ignoring the professor's presence entirely, Silas left the workroom and headed back to the surface. Reaching ground level once more, he slammed the door shut behind him and dropped a bar in place across it, effectively trapping the unfortunate professor and the slaves manning the pumps in the bowels of his fortress. He'd deal with them later.

Eagerly, he climbed up onto the catwalk that ran around the perimeter of his fortress walls. When he was at the point where he was standing in front of the rows of silent automatons, he stopped and turned to face them.

The rain was easing off, and a watery dawn was beginning to show above the dark outline of the ranges to his east. The automatons stood, water dripping from them and pooling at their feet.

Taking the power crystal, he placed it reverently in the snug cradle constructed to hold it, and the box began to vibrate with a strange, intense energy.

Below him, his automaton army stirred, their crystal hearts responding to the frequency of the mother crystal. They lifted their heads and turned lifeless faces towards their power source.

A cold smile tugged at the corner of Silas's mouth. At last, he was going to exact the revenge he had waited so long to bring down. There was no escaping for the residents of Grahamstown. Soon, he'd be able to turn his attention back to Huia and the pirate cohort, and his plans would be complete.

CHAPTER 28

Kev lay still, his arm around Persephone and her head resting on his shoulder. She was lying very still, but he knew she wasn't sleeping. Neither of them had slept much, too keyed up to be able to rest effectively. Kev suspected everyone aboard the *Elizabeth Anne* had spent a similarly sleepless night.

The grey light of dawn was beginning to seep around the edges of the curtains over the small round window, and Kev knew that soon, they would need to stir and face whatever the day would bring.

His stomach was a churning knot of nerves, as if a writhing nest of snakes had taken up residence there, the uncertainty of the day's outcome weighing heavily on his mind.

He knew they were all prepared as well as they could be, but it felt very precarious to Kev. After he and Nellie had returned to Grahamstown with the news of Silas's automaton army, the war preparations had been hastily brought forward.

Nellie had been worried, Kev knew, and she had convinced the war council to strike now before Silas had a chance to move on them. Kev wasn't convinced it was much of an edge – he had seen the automatons – but it was all they had.

Quietly, he stirred, and Persephone too sat up, and without speaking, they both readied themselves for the battle ahead. Once dressed, they joined the others in the galley.

No one spoke or ate much. Even Mina Myra was subdued, sitting solemnly, feeding Norman the breakfast she wasn't eating. Having given eating up as a bad job, the crew collected on the deck as Mina Myra unlocked the ship's arsenal and handed out weapons. Jonas and Merton had their own and were checking them over carefully when the ship's lifting platform graunched into action.

The crew exchanged glances and waited to see who was arriving. Edgar and Rabbie stepped aboard and greeted the crew soberly. Both men were well-armed. Rabbie's mechanical parts glowed in the early dawn light, and he looked fearsome, as intimidating, in his own way, as Silas's automatons.

Persephone approached him. 'Are you sure you can do this, Rabbie?' she asked, concerned.

Rabbie merely nodded grimly. 'Oh aye. I ken what I'm doing,' he declared.

Persephone nodded doubtfully, trying to put her doctor's instincts aside.

'I ha' as much at stake as ye,' Rabbie pointed out. 'If the town falls, we all fall wi' it, aye?'

Persephone nodded again and laid a supportive hand on his good arm. 'Thank you, Rabbie,' she said. 'If you're willing, I need a good man to help coordinate the first aid craft. I can't be in all places at once.'

Rabbie frowned.

'Please, Rabbie,' pleaded Persephone. 'It would mean a lot to me if you would do it. I need someone I can trust.'

Rabbie sighed and acquiesced. Persephone sent him a grateful smile, quietly pleased she'd managed to save Morag from the possibility of losing both a husband and a brother.

Phineas looked around at the crew as they all gathered on deck and realised this may be the last time they would all be together like this. Even if they won the day, there was no guarantee they would all escape unscathed. He badly wanted to say something stirring and inspiring, something to carry them along on a wave of courage, but the words wouldn't form in his mind.

Silently, he held out his hand to Millicent and pulled her close to his side. Together, they looked at the crew around them, who were so much more than that. Mina Myra and Rosalind crept forward and clung onto their legs as everyone moved in to be closer to one another.

'This is it,' Phineas said eventually. 'Whatever happens today, it's been a privilege to have flown these skies with you all. Kia kaha. Be strong, all of you.'

⧗

Kev stood shoulder to shoulder with Phineas and Edgar on board the *Invincible* and watched as the *Elizabeth Anne* peeled away from the fleet of airships sailing from Grahamstown and headed closer to the ranges. Because of her size, she had been designated as the hospital ship.

Around the airships, a flock of smaller craft swooped and buzzed, support craft for their larger sisters and a means of ferrying the wounded and supplies back and forth.

From out of the steep-sided valleys between the mountains poured the pirate fleet, sailing to join them. A strange, piercing shriek could be heard as they approached.

Puzzled, Kev looked at Phineas, who laughed and explained, 'That's Aksel's howler you can hear. He's not at full speed yet, so you're not getting the full effect.'

Kev nodded and shuddered. Even at low speed, the howler emitted an eerie, screeching wail that made the hairs on his arms stand up.

Phineas pointed out the howler in the gaping mouth of the dragon carved into the prow of Aksel's longship-styled airship, the *Valkyrie*. Aksel himself was standing at the prow, and seeing them looking, he waved his battle axe in the air in exultation.

'Good to see one of us is looking forward to this, at least,' muttered Phineas.

⧗

Jonas and Merton stood checking over their weapons yet again, more as a means of distraction than because they required it. They looked up at the *Valkyrie*'s approach.

'So much for the element of surprise,' commented Jonas wryly. Turning to Merton, he said, 'I know I've said this before, but you don't need to be here, you know. This isn't your fight.'

Merton shrugged. 'It's become my fight, Mr Emerson, bottom fact, the night I took you up on your offer. This is a bad box you find yourselves in, and you and me are hand in glove now. What hurts you hurts me. This Elmstone sounds a right bad egg. Maybe I'm off my chump not to just saw the timber, but you're a man to ride the river with, I reckon, and I plan to see this out to the end. It's above my bend to say if we'll be able to whip our weight in wild cats, but I aim to try.'

Jonas nodded. 'It will be good to have you by my side,' he said sincerely.

Merton looked pleased. 'Thank you, Mr Emerson. I appreciate the chance you've given me, bottom fact.'

'Perhaps you could stop calling me Mr Emerson,' suggested Jonas. 'Surely, we've known each other for long enough to make it acceptable.'

Merton shook his head. 'I fear that wouldn't be right, Mr Emerson,' he said, looking slightly scandalised at the very idea of such informality.

Jonas shrugged and let the matter drop. He had come to like Merton over the weeks they had been training together. The two young men had begun to develop a strong rapport as Jonas instructed Merton on the various pieces of technology given to him by the Ministry of Dark Affairs, and this had been strengthened by the hours of physical training together.

Jonas was gratified to notice that the negativity that had hung over Merton when he had first met him had lifted as he became more and more confident, and he was feeling much more assured of Merton's ability to fulfil the role he was preparing to take over. He no longer felt as though he was pushing Merton along a path he wasn't equipped to handle.

He didn't think his new friend would ever call him by his Christian name, and it felt odd to be referred to in such a formal manner by someone more or less his own age, but that didn't negate the deepening friendship between them. He was feeling much more relaxed and peaceful as he could see the end to his troubles and allowed himself to look forward to his future with Lady Elspeth. He was grateful for the opportunity Merton was giving him and resolved, once this fight was over, not to waste a moment of it.

A cry went up from the bow of the ship, and the two men leaned out over the railing to see Elmstone's time-slaving fleet sailing towards them. Jonas was pleased to note that the slavers were well outnumbered by their combined forces. Maybe there was hope to believe in a victory after all.

As the slavers approached, they began to fire their cannons. None of the airships were nimble enough to evade the flying cannonballs. The only thing to be done was to continue to sail full steam ahead and hope for the best.

The first round fell short, the balls falling harmlessly into the wetlands below, but the gap was closing. The skill of the pilots became evident as the mighty ships began to weave through the air, relentlessly surging forward towards their foes.

Jonas could see the pirate slavers hastily attempting to reload their cannons and take aim once more. Up ahead of the *Invincible*, Cornelius's airships were launching an assault of their own. The delicate wings used to harvest aether had been dismantled, and on the decks, huge catapults had been built. Jonas watched with interest as Cornelius's men loaded jars and a mishmash of other small containers full of aether into the slings. Even Kev's teapots, their spouts stuffed with rags, had been utilised.

The catapults were released, and the tiny missiles flew through the air towards the enemy ships. The volatile aether within exploded on contact, and numerous small fires blossomed where they made a direct hit on the slavers' ships.

The catapults were quicker to reload than the cannons, and just as the slavers managed to send off another volley, the second wave of aether bombs peppered them with exploding fire.

Cornelius's men had managed to synchronise their attacks so that each ship released their missiles seconds after the other, which meant that a continuous rain of aether bombs fell on the slavers' ships. The aether did no real lasting damage as it evaporated as soon as it ignited, but it was distracting and left nasty burns where it made direct contact with human flesh.

The gap between the two fleets was closing rapidly, and Aksel's longship, agile and swift – its howler screaming – swooped in to deliver the first wave of men onto the decks of the enemy ships.

Aksel himself lead the first wave, and the screaming of his ship's howler and the war cries of his boarding party chilled and intimidated the unfortunate men in their path, who cowered under the assault. Their careers as slavers made them ill-equipped to face an armed enemy, and they gave very little resistance to the ferocious Viking crew.

From the deck of the *Taniwha*, Huia's men lifted off in their bat wings and swooped in to join Aksel's boarding parties. The men manning the cannons were soon overpowered, and the threat of being blasted from the sky disappeared.

The slaver fleet rallied as one of the captains, a seasoned mercenary, gathered the men to him. Bellowing threats at the men, he managed to direct them back into the battle. Goaded into the attack by their commander, the slaver crews joined in combat with the boarding parties.

The huge ships danced and wove around one another, each captain trying to manoeuvre their airship into a position for their men to board an opposing ship.

As the hand-to-hand combat waged, the smaller aircraft began to swoop and dive between their bigger sisters and fire off their own ammunition. The air was filling with the haze from the gunpowder and aether fires, and visibility was dropping. A few of the smaller craft collided in mid-air, sending them and their occupants spinning to the earth below.

As the air battle continued to rage, the *Invincible* separated from the main fleet and flew for Silas's fortress. The men on board gathered on the decks and waited tensely for the ship to carry them to the point where they would be dropped directly into the compound.

Kev stood surrounded by his friends, beyond mere nervousness now. He felt almost light-headed as his blood pounded in his ears. He couldn't help but wonder if he had travelled so far through time and space only to end his days in the muddy reaches of Silas's swampy stronghold.

He thought of his mother, who would not know what had happened to him, and then thought that maybe that was for the best. Better for her to imagine him happily living out his life with Persephone, producing grandchildren she would never meet, than to know he had fallen in a battle so far removed from her reality.

Whatever happened, he hoped he would be brave and fight his best. He didn't think he was a cowardly man, but he'd never been tested like this before either. He knew he'd come a long way from the young man he'd been when first kidnapped from his old life. He could only hope he had come far enough to be able to hold his head up at day's end – if he survived.

CHAPTER 29

The *Invincible* hovered above Silas's stronghold, flying in as low as Jebediah dared to bring her. Quickly, his men threw the rope ladders over the sides, and the men massed on the deck began the precarious descent into the compound.

There were very few of Silas's men manning the catwalk around the perimeter, and most of the men made it down safely, only a few sustaining injuries from the half-hearted attempt to deflect their attack. This was so odd that once the men reached the ground, they all milled around uncertainly, not sure quite what was expected.

Having reached the ground himself, Kev stood with Phineas and Edgar and looked around him. The compound was eerily silent. Silas couldn't have sent all his men out on the airships, but there was no one to meet them and no sight of the fearsome automaton army Sherlock had seen.

'This doesn't feel right,' said Phineas, looking about warily.

Kev felt it too, as if they were being watched by a silent and invisible foe. The hairs on the back of his neck lifted. Jonas and Merton joined them, the atmosphere affecting them too.

'I feel all overish about this,' offered Merton uneasily.

The men descending from the airship were soon standing around uncomfortably. With them having prepared mentally for a battle, this strange emptiness was unsettling.

Phineas was disturbed. This was a bad situation – he could feel it – but he couldn't see a clear way ahead. Just as he was deciding to separate the men into groups to search the compound, the walls around the edge of the compound splintered and fell forward.

From all sides, an army of automaton soldiers pushed their way through the flimsy partitions erected to conceal them and advanced on the men. *A trap!* Phineas looked around for an exit, but they were completely surrounded.

Silas hadn't been as ill-prepared as they assumed. He had managed to conceal his army until they were all inside his compound. *Fish in a barrel* were the words that flashed through Phineas's mind.

He looked up at the *Invincible* above and signalled to Jebediah to get help. He hoped the man understood. Without backup, they were unlikely to survive. The *Invincible* lifted up into the sky and turned back to where the other ships were still locked in the air battle. As he watched it leave, Phineas hoped and prayed Jebediah and he were on the same wavelength.

Turning back, he drew his blaster from its holster. Priming it, he took aim at one of the automatons advancing towards him and fired. The blast blew an enormous chunk out of the robot's side, but still, it advanced.

All around him, the men were firing their guns and blasters, and while the damage to the automatons was extensive, it didn't stop their advance. They seemed invincible. Phineas was beginning to worry they wouldn't be able to hold out until Jebediah returned with reinforcements.

'Split up!' he commanded. 'Keep moving! Don't let them get too close!'

At his words, the company of men separated into smaller groups, dodging and weaving away from the less agile automatons.

The combat flowed around the compound like water in the bathtub of a very enthusiastic bather. The men leaped and rolled between the automatons, avoiding the sharp weapons at the end of each arm and trying as best as they could to shoot enough rounds into them to stop them. No matter how often the men managed to get a direct hit, the automatons kept coming. Some of them were trailing limbs from twisted strands of wire and cable, but still, they fought on. The men were beginning to tire and, one by one, as the fatigue bit hard, fell victim to the relentless onslaught of the automaton force.

Jonas and Merton had begun the battle with Phineas and the others, but slowly, as the fight went on, they found themselves separated from them. They fought well together, their hours of training creating a strong intuition and anticipation of each other's movements. The adrenaline rush of the battle enhanced this to the point where it was as if they were one man.

Even so, they were no match for Silas's automatons, and Jonas could see the battle wasn't going well for them. The automatons were taller and appeared almost indestructible, and he wondered how long they would be able to hold out against such powerful foes.

As the fight went on and men began to fall victim to the automaton onslaught, Jonas began to wonder if any of them would get out alive. This was unlike any battle he'd been in before, and he was unsure of how to take action to turn the tide.

Looking around him, he noticed he had lost track of Merton. Ducking beneath the stabbing arm of an automaton, he rolled between its legs. Remaining low, he searched around for his companion.

He caught sight of him not too far away. He was being pushed back under the flailing arms of a robot. He was managing to parry the blows, but Jonas could see the amputated limb of another automaton lying on the ground just behind Merton's feet.

Sensing that the inevitable was about to happen, Jonas yelled out a warning, but Merton, unable to hear above the noise of the battle, caught his foot on the fallen limb and fell onto his back, helpless for a moment of time. A moment was all the automaton needed, and it raised its arm to finish off its fallen adversary. Desperately, Merton lifted his sword to parry the blow.

All Jonas could see at that moment were all his hopes of leaving the ministry and living the rest of his life with Elspeth being dashed into the ground along with Merton's brains. Not stopping to think or weigh it up, he launched himself through the air towards Merton in a heroic attempt to save the young man's life.

He skidded on his side through the melee, and the force of his momentum knocked Merton aside. Merton rolled over and over, coming to rest face down the dirt of the compound grounds.

Merton lifted his head, his mouth full of foul-tasting dirt, and looked for his sword, only to discover it still clutched in his hand. In a flash, he was one his feet, momentarily thinking Jonas would be proud of him. Looking for Jonas, he was in time to see the automaton that had had him pinned down lift its arm and drive its blade deep into Jonas's abdomen.

As the automaton pulled its blade from his body, Jonas looked disbelievingly up at its lifeless face. His hands clutched at his stomach as the blood welled through his fingers, and he realised he was badly wounded.

Knowing the battle couldn't finish in time for help to reach him, he thought briefly of Elspeth, sorry he couldn't have given her what she wanted, before the darkness gathering in the corners of his mind flooded in, and he was aware of nothing more.

⌛

Kev was fighting back to back with Edgar. His blaster had long since run out of rounds and been flung aside in favour of his sword. Both men were fighting for survival, each parry keeping them alive for a few seconds more as they hoped for rescue from above.

The dead and wounded lay all about them, and they had lost track of the whereabouts of their companions. Kev fought with a desperation borne out of a strong will to live. He was exhausted, and he could feel a faint trembling begin in his limbs that heralded the end of his physical resources. He had no idea what had happened to Phineas and the others and truly had little energy to spare to wonder if they were alive or dead. It was taking all his effort to keep focusing on the fight for his own life.

The battle brought him up against a small knot of men led by Phineas. Kev felt reassured to see he was still alive, but he could see the older man was fast coming to the limits of his strength.

Catching his eye, Phineas nodded to a corner of the compound where a stone staircase ran upwards towards a tower in the corner of the fortress. Kev nodded back. If they could fight their way over, they could defend themselves from the staircase or even barricade themselves into the tower until help arrived. Alerting Edgar, Kev began to fight his way towards the staircase.

Inch by bloody inch, the small group of men pushed their way through the heaving mass of men and automatons towards the staircase. Once there, they were able to take turns on the higher steps to get a small break from the fight. The staircase led up to a stout door that was firmly barred from the inside, not a ready means of escape, but Phineas sent men up to see if they could get through somehow.

Kev sat on one of the higher steps for his turn to rest. His chest heaved, and he wondered if he'd have strength in his wrists to lift his sword once more when it was time to go back to the fight at the bottom of the stairs.

The automatons were tireless, and the men, of course, were not, and Kev wondered how long they would be able to keep going before they were overrun. He didn't know much about robots, especially not the ones that inhabited this world, but it seemed to him as though these ones were being driven by a force other than mechanical.

The next group of men sent by Phineas arrived to take their turn on the step, and reluctantly, Kev rose and, hefting his sword, went to join the battle once more.

As he reached the lower reaches of the staircase, he could see the fight wasn't going well. He spied Merton fighting his way through towards them and reached down a hand to help pull him onto the relative sanctuary of the stairs. The young man looked pale and shocked.

'Where's Jonas?' shouted Kev above the noise of the battle.

Merton only shook his head, and Kev felt his heart sink into his stomach as grief pricked at his eyeballs. Unable to spare the time to feel the full extent of Jonas's loss, Kev turned his mind back to the fight, which was not going well.

Slowly but relentlessly, the automatons were beginning to push through, and men were being flung aside like helpless toys as the robots began to climb the stairs. The men were being pushed farther and farther up, and soon, they would be caught between the door and the automatons. Kev realised that even if they managed to break through the door, they could still end up trapped, helpless as the automatons picked them off one by one.

CHAPTER 30

Nellie Sprocket was anxious. She'd been on edge from the moment she'd seen the fuzzy pictures of Silas's automaton army sent back by Sherlock on the viewer.

She'd been keeping track of Silas's doings for a long time and believed she had come to know the man quite well. He didn't strike her as the kind of man to leave the fate of his machinations in the hands of a bunch of clockwork dolls. There had to be something more to them than met the eye. The fact that, as yet, she didn't know what bothered her. It ate away at the edges of her mind and kept her restlessly pacing, unable to settle to any task.

She looked around her at the preparations being made aboard the *Elizabeth Anne*. Persephone was organising for the smaller craft to be loaded with first aid supplies, ready for dispatching into the field, and she had put the others to work rolling bandages and taking inventory of all the medical resources.

From the decks of the *Elizabeth Anne*, they could see the air battle raging. It was hard to see the details through the clouds of smoke, but it looked as though the slavers were being soundly beaten – not without casualties as the *Dauntless* and the *Skywarden* had fallen from the skies, along with their crews.

They had seen the *Invincible* head for Silas's fortress and knew the battle for the compound would be underway.

Nellie started. It felt as though someone or something had slapped her hard on the back of the head, and she was suddenly painfully aware of her surroundings. In this heightened state of being, she knew what she needed to do.

Quickly, she went to find Millicent and beg the use of one of the small aircraft. Thankfully, Millicent was happy to release one to her, and she quickly took to the skies.

Skirting the air battle, which was in its final throes, she headed into the wetlands towards Silas's fortress. She flew the little aircraft close to where it rose out of the wetlands, surrounded by its moat.

Clambering out and pulling out her water suit, she quickly pulled it on and, adjusting the helmet firmly onto her head, slipped into the muddy channel leading to the moat and disappeared beneath the water. Reaching the moat, she swam quickly around to where Sherlock had discovered the drain and pulled herself through it hand over hand. Once at the far end, she removed her helmet and took stock of her surroundings.

Out in the compound, the battle was raging. At first, she couldn't make any sense of what she was seeing. There were too many bodies moving in what seemed totally unrelated ways. Slowly, she began to figure out what was happening, and she could see a group of men fighting on some stone stairs. Looking up farther, she could see that the stairs led to a tower built into the corner of the fortress. At the very top of the tower, she could see a room with windows on all sides, and sitting in a throne-like chair in the window facing the compound was Silas Elmstone. Somehow she was going to have to get in that room because she knew that was where the answer lay.

Looking back to the battle to try and figure out a way across the compound without getting hurt – or worse, killed – she caught sight of Merton fighting for his life. Nellie watched in horror as Jonas saved Merton at his own expense. Gathering her emotions, she scurried out of the drain and followed Merton as he fought his way over to the stairs.

⌛

Back at the aircraft abandoned by Nellie, a small furry shape emerged from underneath the seat and perched itself on the edge of the cockpit. Norman sat for a while, blinking and scratching as his mechanical eyes focused on his surroundings, analysing and storing the information he received through them.

Kev's harness had done a wonderful job of keeping the mischievous monkey well under control. It had been so tight fitting and well secured that Norman had been unable to break free from it. He had spent many hours twisting and turning, hissing angrily as he tried in vain to reach the padlock behind him. After weeks of this, he had fallen into what the crew mistakenly thought was a state of passivity.

As wonderful as Kev's harness had been, it had had one fatal flaw. Kev had stitched it together along one shoulder. The stitching was remarkably firm, and the thread unusually strong, but even so, Norman had managed to unpick the seam with his sharp little teeth.

What the crew had thought of as his acceptance of the harness was in fact Norman working quietly away at the thread by swivelling his head as far as his metal frame would allow and worrying away at the stitch closest to his mouth until he had worn it through.

Once he had loosened the seam enough to get his fingers into it as well, it was only a matter of time until he had wormed his way free of the harness's constraints.

As luck would have it, today was the day he managed to escape his captivity. At first, he had scampered about the ship looking for Mina Myra until the lure of an open cockpit proved irresistible, and he had stowed away aboard the aircraft Nellie had been given by Millicent. After giving himself a bit of a brush-up and a satisfying scratch on the back, he turned his head back and forth until he detected the way Nellie had gone.

Finding himself at the edge of the moat, he looked for a way to cross. He didn't like water. His clockwork innards were well insulated from the damp, but it tended to stiffen his articulated joints, which meant he needed oiling – a process he detested, not liking how the oil made his fur clump and the hours of grooming he needed to do afterwards.

He ran around the perimeter of the moat, looking for a way across. Not finding one, he hesitated for a moment before leaping into the water and swimming across to the fortress, scolding loudly.

On reaching the high wall of the fortress, he clambered his way upwards until he was perched on the top. He shook his fur dry and began to run along the top of the wall.

His instincts were leading him towards a room at the top of a tall tower. Once he reached it, he climbed up onto the roof and began to scrabble at the clay tiles until he managed to dislodge one. After that, it was quick work for him to wriggle his way into the roof space and from there to a vent that overlooked the room within.

A man sat with his back to the room, looking out of the wide window before him, but this didn't really register with Norman, who wasn't programmed to be attracted to humans. What he was programmed for and what his whirring clockwork brain was seeking sat on the table behind the man. Perched in a wooden box, nestling securely in its cradle, sat a glowing crystal.

As Norman's eyes rested on it, all the circuits of his brain began to light up, and he was drawn to it like a moth to a flame. Hopping onto the table, he sat in front of the box and gently ran his hands over the crystal. Reaching the conclusion that it was a suitable size, he plucked it from its cradle and, forcing the joints of his jaw as wide as they could stretch, swallowed it whole.

⧖

In his chair before the window, Silas was absorbed in the battle before him, to the exclusion of all else. He was vaguely aware of the sounds outside his door that told him the men outside were trying to break through, but having absolute trust in the sturdiness of its construction, he gave them little heed.

He had been surprised on hearing the news of the fleet setting sail from Grahamstown to confront him but not overly concerned. He had had enough warning to devise a plan of sorts before they had arrived. He had sent his slaver fleet to what he assumed would be its destruction and prepared his ambush in the compound.

He was a little annoyed by this as it would mean he would need to regroup before making his final move on Grahamstown, but he had never had any doubt that he would eventually win the day.

The inevitable demise of his slaver fleet only gave him a momentary pang of regret. Men could always be bought. He would replace his pirate crews, set sail for Grahamstown, and burn it to the ground – once this nuisance attack was dealt with.

Suddenly, as he watched, his automatons abruptly fell silent, halted mid-move as if someone had flicked a switch. Giving a cry of disbelieving rage, he heaved himself from his chair and turned to face the table behind him.

The master control box sat empty on the table, devoid of the glowing power crystal. How was that possible? Unable to believe or accept what his eyes were telling him, he searched for the thief.

But none could be found. There weren't many places for a person to hide, and even though he couldn't fathom how anyone could have got into the room, he looked in those few spots, already knowing he wouldn't find anyone there. All he found were a few screws and a grill lying on the floor under what must have been a faulty vent.

On the other side of the door, Phineas, Kev, and Nellie stood disbelievingly as the battle below them ended in complete silence.

The automatons had malfunctioned spectacularly, frozen in their last move. Not one fell to break the silence, and slowly, the men put down their weapons. At first, no one moved, but slowly, their minds returned from survival mode, and their senses returned. One by one, they began to look for survivors amongst the fallen.

Phineas turned his attention back to the door. He ordered men to find something to batter it down. He wanted the man within. Nellie reached into her pocket and drew out her toolkit, but the delicate tools she used to mend clockworks were no match for the sturdiness of the door.

As a group of men clambered up the stairs, lugging a wooden bench between them, a shattering of glass sprayed out into the compound. Silas wasn't waiting to be cornered. Having broken a window, he pulled himself out and onto the roof.

'Quick!' yelled Kev. 'Give me a leg up!'

Without hesitating, Phineas boosted Kev up and over the overhang of the tower roof. Climbing to his feet, Kev found himself face to face with Silas Elmstone.

Kev wasn't a violent man by nature, but seeing the man who was the cause of all the trouble and destruction, not to mention the death of a friend, something shifted in him, and a red mist came down over his mind.

Afterwards, Kev couldn't remember exactly what had happened on the roof. It was as though he was no longer in control as a rage like nothing he had ever felt before took a hold of him, and he launched himself at Silas. He came to himself with Phineas, who had clambered onto the roof after him, pulling him off a barely conscious Elmstone, whose face was beaten and bloody.

Together, Phineas and Kev manhandled Silas off the roof and back into the room. Nellie was inside, inspecting a wooden box.

'I think this must be some kind of master control system,' she said as the men dragged a limp Silas between them to the door.

Phineas nodded. 'Lucky for us, it malfunctioned,' he said grimly.

Nellie shook her head, looking thoughtful. 'Yes, I guess so,' she replied. 'I'd like to know what happened to the missing part. Maybe Silas can tell us once he's in more of a state to do so.'

As soon as the automatons had stopped moving, Merton Wells had grabbed hold of Edgar by the arm and began pulling him back down the stairs and into the tumble of bodies littering the compound.

The men made their way to where Jonas had fallen. Pulling aside the dead bodies that lay on top of him, the men lifted him in their arms – the old friend and the new.

Merton was openly weeping. 'He saved my life, Mr Whitby,' he choked. 'I'd be the one pushing up daisies if not for him.'

Edgar's eyes were damp too as he laid his cheek close to Jonas's face. He didn't expect to feel anything, but a faint breath brushed his cheek. He felt for a pulse, and under his fingers, he felt a tiny flicker. He looked at the blood staining Jonas's clothes and knew that even though he was hanging on, there was little guarantee his friend would make it.

Overhead, the sound of the *Invincible* returning alerted those on the ground that help had arrived. Along with the *Invincible* came a small fleet of smaller craft carrying the first-aiders. Edgar lifted his fallen friend in his arms and staggered back through the fallen bodies, Merton going ahead to clear the way.

The men reached the stairs where most of their army had gathered to watch as Phineas and Kev dragged a slowly reviving Silas down to ground level and pushed him to his knees in front of them.

Merton pushed his way to the front of the crowd of men around Silas. 'So this is the arsworm responsible, is it?' he queried.

When Phineas nodded, he drew his sword and, in one swift movement, oblivious to the murmurs and gasps around him, cut off Silas's head.

'That's for Jonas,' he declared as he did so.

Nellie made her way back through the wetlands to where her aircraft sat waiting for her, her water suit slung over one shoulder and the master control box tucked under one arm. As much as she would have liked being able to question Silas about it, she wasn't at all sorry to see him dispatched so quickly.

She would take the control box home and dismantle it to see what she could find out about how it worked. She had ordered the men to dismantle the automatons and had been intrigued to discover each one contained a crystal heart – all dead, of course – but it made her wonder if and how the control had been able to animate them. A master control could explain why they seemed indestructible.

Approaching her craft, she noticed a small furry shape sitting on the ground in front of it. Getting closer, she realised it was Norman. He was sitting hunched over and immobile, and Nellie bent over to pick him up. He looked at her with eyes that reflected a certain amount of misery, and she felt through his fur that his joints appeared quite stiff.

She tried moving one of his arms, and she heard a faint but definite squeak coming from his joints. As his fur felt a bit damp, she guessed he must have fallen into the water. There was certainly enough of it around.

'You're lucky you're so well made, my little friend,' she told him with a chuckle. 'This is nothing a bit of oil can't remedy.'

CHAPTER 31

Millicent watched as the initial wave of first responders came in to land aboard the *Elizabeth Anne* and pondered the conversation she had just had with Lady Elspeth.

She had come upon that young lady rolling bandages, and something about her had stirred a half-forgotten memory. The more she watched, the more certain she became. Knowing how difficult things had been between Lady Elspeth and Jonas, she hoped and prayed she was wrong. They didn't need another complication.

Coming alongside and picking up a length of cloth and rolling it, she glanced sideways at Lady Elspeth before saying as casually as she could, 'So how far along are you?'

Lady Elspeth started and blushed. 'Not long,' she stammered, embarrassed. 'How did you guess? Persephone hasn't even picked up on it.'

'Persephone is a surgeon,' Millicent pointed out. 'I doubt early pregnancy is her field of expertise. I only noticed because I once had a very dear friend who found herself in your condition, and you have the same look about you as she did.'

'I didn't plan it,' Lady Elspeth sighed. 'But I'm not unhappy about it. It's just that the timing is a bit off, you know?'

Millicent nodded and offered a quick comforting hug. 'I know,' she replied. 'These things seldom happen when we're ready for them.'

Now as she waited to receive the first of the wounded, she hoped that maybe this new little soul would be the means of healing the rift between its parents.

The first craft landed, and Edgar and Merton clambered out. Gently, they eased an injured man from the aircraft, and Millicent watched as Edgar carried the young man over in his arms. She rushed forward to help, calling for Persephone as she did so. As she reached Edgar, she suddenly realised who he was carrying.

'Oh no! Oh no!' she cried as Edgar's knees buckled and Merton rushed to support him.

Millicent helped support Jonas as Persephone hurried over. She too exclaimed at the sight of Jonas, so very pale and unresponsive. She could see something of the wound he had sustained, and her heart sank. Jonas was in a very bad way. Quickly, she helped Edgar and Merton get Jonas over to where she had set up an open-air medical centre. Looking for Rabbie, she motioned him over.

'Hurry,' she instructed him. 'Go at once to Grahamstown Hospital and fetch Dr Barry. Tell him I need him and his hypno-goggles.'

Rabbie nodded and turned on his heel.

Persephone watched as he took to the air and turned for Grahamstown. Turning to Millicent, she said, 'Send Lenore to Lady Elspeth. Get her to break the news. She'll want to be here, but it's best if she doesn't come at the moment. This isn't going to be pretty.'

Millicent hurried off to deliver the news to Lenore. Persephone turned her attention to Jonas and quickly began to prepare him for surgery. She looked at Merton and Edgar. They both looked the worst for the battle, sporting grazes and cuts to various parts of their body. Merton had what looked like the beginning of a black eye, and both men were dirty and exhausted.

'Do you think you can help me with Jonas?' she asked them gently. 'I need you to cut his clothes away while I scrub up.'

Both men nodded and carefully began to do as Persephone instructed.

Lady Elspeth sat by Jonas's bedside, holding his hand where it lay on the bed cover. He was still very pale, and no one was sure if he was going to pull through.

Persephone hadn't been optimistic when she had come to let her know he had survived the surgery. Even if he lived, Persephone was sure he wouldn't be able to walk again as the automaton blade had severed his spinal cord.

As yet, Lady Elspeth found she couldn't cry. All her emotions sat cold and heavy in the pit of her stomach, an unbearable weight she longed to shed through tears – if only she could.

She bitterly regretted making such an issue over Jonas's unwillingness to marry her. At this moment, she only wanted him to live. Should he survive, she would be happy to live with him on his terms forever.

The thought that he may never live to see or hold his unborn child overwhelmed her, and the tears began to flow, hot and stinging, but they brought little relief.

From the deck of the *Taniwha*, Huia stood beside Cobb Milburn as they, along with her crew, watched the blaze in the sky that turned the waters of the Waihou River a fiery red.

The mighty pirate Aksel Jensen had fallen in battle, and now his ship, the *Valkyrie* – the chooser of the slain – was taking him to Valhalla.

Huia didn't look at Cobb or make any comment. If Aksel had had his way, it would have been she her men would have been farewelling.

She thought back to the moment in the battle with the slavers when she had fallen to the deck. She had fully expected to feel her opponent's blade slice through her and had steeled herself to accept it.

The man had indeed raised his sword to dispatch her when a look of surprise had blossomed on his face. It was almost comical, had she been in the mood to appreciate it. Slowly, he pitched forward and fell on his face to the deck, pinning her legs under him. From his back, a battle axe protruded.

Casually, Aksel strode up and wrenched his axe from the man's back. Seeing her lying there, struggling to free her legs, a look of speculative cunning crossed his face, and he raised his axe.

Huia couldn't tell if he had really meant to strike her or not because at that moment, a knife bit deep into his bicep. The shock of it stopped him, and he appeared to come to his senses.

He pulled the knife from his arm with a laugh and tossed it back at Cobb, who had come to his captain's aid. Still laughing, Aksel had turned his back on them and strode back into the fight, and Cobb had extended his hand to help Huia to her feet.

Once the battle was over and it was discovered that Aksel was amongst the dead, she had accepted the remnants of his crew into her own and had agreed to giving him a Viking funeral. Now watching as the *Valkyrie* burned, she reflected on the fact that this day had rid her of two enemies.

⏳

Nellie sat at the galley table, Norman before her, Mina Myra and Rosalind watching intently as she carefully oiled and eased his stiff joints.

Norman was not in the least grateful for these ministrations and fixed her with a baleful gaze that, had he been bigger than a bread box, might have filled her with trepidation. As it was, she was able to endure his laden stare with equanimity.

Once Nellie had finished, Norman began the distasteful task of ridding his fur of the oily residue. Abruptly, he stopped his licking, and a furtive, inward look came over his face.

'Ooh!' exclaimed Mina Myra excitedly. 'He's going to poop! Quick,' she instructed Rosalind, 'go get Sherlock.'

Rosalind skipped off to fetch Sherlock as Nellie and Mina Myra watched Norman, who was rubbing his belly in a speculative way. By the time Sherlock and Rosalind had arrived back, Norman was ready and, with a funny little scrunching movement, expelled a glowing crystal onto the galley table.

'What is that?' asked Sherlock with interest.

Mina Myra shrugged and shook her head. 'I don't know. I don't think anyone on board has a thing like that. Do you think he might have found it when he fell in the water, Nellie?'

Nellie picked up the glowing crystal with interest, and it slowly dawned on her just where Norman had picked it up. 'Better than that, sweetie,' she said with satisfaction. 'I do believe your little pet may just have saved the day.'

Phineas strode around Silas's compound as the extraction of the wounded and taking care of the dead was taken care of. Most of the crews wished to take their fallen comrades away from this place and bury them in their own fashion, so the identification and returning of the fallen was being handled by Jebediah and his crew.

'Over here!' Kev called, waving to him from across the compound.

Phineas crossed over to where Kev was standing in front of a door. Seeing it locked by a sturdy bar, Phineas lifted it, and the men made their way down the staircase they found within.

At the bottom, they found another door that led them into a large room that looked to them to be some kind of laboratory. Looking around, Phineas decided this room would make a good holding cell for the captured time slavers until they figured out what to do with them.

A rustling in the corner alerted the men to the fact they weren't alone. Instinctively, they both reached for their swords.

'Please, sirs, don't hurt us,' a voice from the corner pleaded, and out of the shadows, a group of gaunt figures emerged.

Dressed in ragged clothing and so filthy, it was impossible to tell if they were men or women, they supported a shambling, raving figure amongst them. Kev drew in an outraged breath. Here before him was evidence of his fate had he not been rescued by the crew of the *Elizabeth Anne*. Phineas's face was set in grim lines as he too surveyed the pitiful figures before him.

'Have no fear,' he reassured them as he and Kev began to guide them gently back to the world above. 'You're safe now.'

CHAPTER 32

Persephone knelt down before Lady Elspeth where she had fallen asleep in the chair in the corner of the room. Gently, she shook her awake. 'He's awake,' she whispered as Lady Elspeth slowly became aware of her surroundings.

Lady Elspeth sat up, her heart beginning to thud in her chest. 'How is he?' she asked with a softly trembling voice.

Persephone smiled sadly. 'He's conscious, which is something. He's very weak. He's been asking for you.'

Lady Elspeth nodded and turned her head and looked across the room to where Jonas lay. He managed to turn his head on the pillow to look at her, but she could see it was an effort for him to do so.

She stood up and went over to the bed. Persephone quietly moved Lady Elspeth's chair over to the bedside and tactfully left the room. Lady Elspeth took Jonas's hand in hers, and he smiled at her weakly.

'Elspeth,' he whispered with effort, 'I didn't think I'd see you again.'

'Shhh,' admonished Lady Elspeth. 'Don't talk.'

Jonas shook his head. 'No, I must tell you things,' he insisted. 'Please.'

Lady Elspeth, tears standing in her eyes, nodded. 'All right, my dear. If it's important to you.'

Jonas closed his eyes, gathering his strength. Opening them, he looked deep into the eyes of the only woman who had managed to capture his interest and make him love her.

Although his body felt very weak, his mind was clear and sharp. It was as if all the issues clouding his thoughts had fallen away, and he saw his life like a road stretching out before him.

He saw with his mind's eye how the road behind him had been very difficult and rocky, shrouded in dark icy clouds until the day he met Lady Elspeth, and how the rays of sunlight, like the fingers of God, had pierced the clouds, illuminating the road around them.

He knew his life was ebbing away – he could feel it in his body – and he wanted desperately to tell Lady Elspeth what a difference her love had made to his life while he could.

'I want you to know how much I love you,' he began. 'You have always been and always will be the love of my life. I want you to believe this.'

'Oh, I do, I do,' insisted Lady Elspeth through her tears, 'and I'm so sorry for making your life miserable. I don't care if you don't want to get married. I just want you. I don't care about a silly ring.'

Jonas tried to quiet her with a little pat on her hand. He was beginning to tire, and he needed to finish while he could. 'Listen, Elspeth,' he said, 'I do want to marry you. I'm asking you now. Will you please marry me?'

Lady Elspeth blinked away her tears. Pulling out her handkerchief, she dabbed at her eyes and blew her nose. 'Did you just ask me to marry you?' she queried.

Jonas nodded. 'I did, my darling. What do you say? Will you marry me . . . please?'

'I don't want you to marry me because you feel sorry for me,' said Lady Elspeth.

Jonas almost laughed, but he had no strength. 'I think the boot is rightly on the other foot, to be honest,' he pointed out. 'I'm the one on my deathbed. The pity is all on your side.'

'Hush!' exclaimed Lady Elspeth. 'Don't talk like that. Of course, I'll marry you. I love you, and I'd be so happy to be your wife for however long we have together.'

Jonas smiled and closed his eyes. As he drifted back into unconsciousness, his fiancée lowered her head to the bed and cried her heart out.

Without wanting to be tactless, Persephone quietly hastened the wedding preparations along as Jonas continued to hover between life and death. Some days, he seemed a little better, but she felt helpless as the days he didn't do so well became more frequent. Wilton Barry had been a regular visitor, treating Jonas with hypnosis. Persephone felt it couldn't do any harm, and who was she to say it wouldn't do some good? Jonas's body needed all the help it could to heal.

The wedding guests were limited to the crew of the *Elizabeth Anne*, on Persephone's instructions. There would be time for more extensive celebrations if Jonas survived. Millicent had insisted on decorating Jonas's sickroom as best they could and persuaded Lady Elspeth to purchase herself a pretty dress to wear.

'Your husband will want to see you looking lovely on your wedding day,' she pointed out. 'It's supposed to be a happy day, after all.'

They chose a day when Jonas seemed a little better and propped him up a little on pillows. Persephone wouldn't allow them to lift him too high because of his wound. Once the brief service was over, Persephone made sure he was as comfortable as possible, and everyone left the newlyweds alone.

Carefully stretching out and lying beside him, Lady Elspeth held Jonas's hand while he drifted in and out of sleep, worn out by the day's events. The rest of the day passed with Lady Elspeth barely moving, trying not to disturb Jonas or cause him discomfort. In spite of the shadow of death that hovered over them, she felt peaceful, content to lie here beside her husband and not thinking too far into the future.

Eventually, as the day began to wane, Lady Elspeth sensed a shift in Jonas's breathing. It seemed to her as though he had moved from sleep into unconsciousness, and she could feel him drifting away from her. She brought his hand up to her breast and held it against her heart, wishing her love for him had the power to pull him back from the brink. He awoke briefly and gave her hand a little squeeze but didn't speak.

Lady Elspeth laid her head next to his and, with her lips close to his ear, whispered softly, 'You're going to be a father.'

Jonas closed his eyes, a smile on his lips, and quietly passed away.

Epilogue

Kev got out from the shiny new steam carriage and turned to look back down the road he had driven up, surveying the settlement of Grahamstown, where it spread out below him. Here and there, cottage roofs peeked through the trees, and farther down, looming over the firth, the mighty airships swayed in their moorings. Looking out over a scene at once so familiar and yet also completely foreign, he was overwhelmed with gratitude for having found his place in time.

Behind him, Persephone climbed out of the steam carriage and came to stand beside him. He wrapped an arm around her shoulders and drew her close to his side. He thought about his mum and wished he could let her know how well he was doing and how happy he was. He wanted to thank her for releasing him to follow his heart. He hoped that somehow she would know these things and that it would give her comfort. Persephone laid her head on Kev's shoulder, and together, they watched as a procession of other steam carriages chuffed up the hill towards them.

It had been a little over a year since the battle with Silas Elmstone and his automaton forces, and they were about to celebrate a milestone. Grahamstown itself remained blissfully unaware of the narrow escape it had had from complete destruction at Silas's hand. Life appeared to go on as usual, but for those involved, it had changed, just as Huia had predicted it would.

Most of the pirate cohort had left the district, not comfortable raiding the men and women they had fought beside against a common enemy. Huia remained but tended to raid farther south, away from Grahamstown. Kev had heard she had a new enemy in the form of a red-headed Irish pirate by the name of Kathleen O'Hara. He had heard reports that the two women had had many a bitter clash, and Kev suspected Kathleen kept Huia's life interesting, to say the least.

Cornelius had given up his outlaw way of life and moved into Grahamstown, where he was now the mayor - spending his time battling government bureaucracy. He continued to be a friend of the airship captains, and under his influence, a new culture of tolerance towards their less legal businesses had taken hold. It was a golden age for adventurers in Grahamstown.

The gleaming steam carriages hissed to a halt on the road beside Kev and Persephone. Millicent and Phineas emerged, followed by Mina Myra and Rosalind. They were joined by Orson, Sherlock, Edgar, Morag, Rabbie, and the children. They all stood together, not saying much but happy to be together.

Eventually, the last steam carriage made its way up the hill, and Lady Elspeth climbed out, her little daughter in her arms. From the depths of the carriage, Professor Popkiss emerged, assisted by his nurse.

Lady Elspeth had bought a picturesque little cottage where she lived quietly with her daughter and Professor Popkiss, content to use her energies in raising her child and looking after her old friend. The professor was much changed and not expected to recover from his ordeal in the bowels of Silas's fortress. After his rescue, Lady Elspeth had hired a nurse and taken him under her wing. Her gentle friendship had gone a long way to easing the pain in his mind, and on his better days, he had been able to unburden himself over the guilt he had felt over Walter.

Once they had been able to untangle the professor's convoluted meanderings on this subject, Kev realised the origins of the mysterious box he had discovered in the bush on his return and had related this to Lady Elspeth along with his experiences inside the portal, and it had dawned on them that Kev owed his safe return to the professor. They tried to explain this to him but were unsure of how much of what they were saying he really understood. It did seem as if his recovery was a little quicker after that. He was still inclined to ramble and often became confused between reality and the world of fantasy in his own mind, but under Lady Elspeth's care, he appeared happy.

Lady Elspeth approached the others, and they exchanged heartfelt greetings. The professor blinked owlishly at them as if he couldn't quite figure out who they were but appeared content to follow them as they gathered up their things and made their way through the gates of the cemetery that sat on the slopes of the hillside overlooking the town. It was a peaceful spot, far removed from the bustle of the town below, and the early spring day was warm and still.

From the road behind them, they heard the tinking of many metal items, and as they turned to watch, Nellie Sprocket, riding astride Flora, came up the road. Her cows came to a halt beside the steam carriages, and Nellie sprang down and came to join them. Nellie, like Cornelius, had remained a friend and often visited when her wanderings brought her into Grahamstown. She had made a special trip to be with them today, knowing it was a significant one for them all.

As one, they moved through the gates and made their way to where Jonas lay beneath his new marble headstone, shrouded in a covering of white linen. Phineas led them in a prayer, and Lady Elspeth stepped forward to draw off the cover. One by one, they each stepped forward and gently laid a small stone on the headstone before spreading out their blankets beside him and sitting in quietude, each lost in their own thoughts.

Softly, they began to talk and catch up, every now and then one of them glancing over to the headstone as if including Jonas in their conversation. As the time passed, they slowly began to laugh and share stories, reminiscing about the old days, the good times, the funny times they had shared with Jonas. The tears flowed, but so did the laughter, and a gentle healing took place in each heart as they each remembered the quiet young man who had been such a large part of their lives.

As the afternoon faded and the evening shadows began to stretch out towards them, they saw a figure approaching through the setting sunlight. He wore a pair of dark round-lensed glasses, and for a moment, it was if Jonas had come back to life before them.

It was Merton Wells. Silently, he came through the graveyard towards them, and after resting a hand on Jonas's headstone, he sat down with them. They sat together, watching as the sun set over the firth below them. No one spoke. They didn't need to.

GLOSSARY

harakeke — New Zealand native flax
heru - a comb
hongi — a traditional Maori greeting where two people press noses
    and foreheads simultaneously
kahikatea — New Zealand native tree
kia kaha — be strong
korowai — a traditional woven cloak featuring tassels
mana - authority, prescence, prestige, respect
manaia — a mythical creature in Maori culture, widely accepted as
    a tribal guardian
moko kauae — traditional chin tattoo worn by Maori women
Ponga — New Zealand native tree fern
Pounamu — New Zealand greenstone, jade
ruru — New Zealand native owl
taniwha — supernatural creatures in Maori legendary tradition
taonga — a treasure, an object or resource that is highly prized
wahine toa — a strong woman

Slang Terms

above one's bend — out of one's power
absquatulate — to disappear
acknowledge the corn — admit the truth
all overish — uncomfortable

amputate the timber — run off

arsworm — a small man

ask no adds — ask no favour

back slang it — go out the back door

backing and filling — changing one's mind

bad box — a bad situation

bag of nails — confusion

balled up — confused

bang up to the elephant — perfect, complete

batty fang — to thrash thoroughly

beat the devil around the stump — to evade one's responsibilities

beat the Dutch — beat all

bend the elbow — to have a drink (alcoholic)

big bugs — important people

biggest toad in the puddle — the most important person

born in the woods to be afraid of an owl — not being afraid because
    of prior experience

bottom fact — undisputed fact

bricky, bricks — brave, fearless

butter upon bacon — extravagance

case of the morbs — temporary down mood

catch a weasel asleep — unlikely to happen

chirping merry — drunk

cold coffee — misfortune

cramp words — difficult words

crowbar hotel — jailhouse

fizzog — face

foozler — bungler

fumble famble — lame excuse

God's acre — cemetery

grab the wrong pig by the tail — get the wrong man

hang up the fiddle — to give up

hugger mugger — underhand, sneaky

keep a pig — to have a lodger

mad as hops — excited

make a stuffed bird laugh — preposterous
man to ride the river with — someone to trust
mind the grease — excuse me
moniker — name
mutton shunters — police
off one's chump — out of one's mind, crazy
rusty guts — rough, blunt
saw the timber — be off
sell a dog — mislead, lie
shake a flannin — have a fight
shoot into the brown — to fail
skilamalink — secret, shady, doubtful
sly cove — a shifty felloe
sly grog — illegal bar
smother a parrot — to shoot neat absinthe
some pumpkins — a big deal
tail down — lose heart
umble cum stumble — fully understood
whiddler — a spy
whip one's weight in wild cats — to win the day

CPSIA information can be obtained
at www.ICGtesting.com
Printed in the USA
BVHW071029020519
547199BV00004B/41/P